THE LIGHTNING CATCHER

ANNE CAMERON

GREENWILLOW BOOKS
An Imprint of HarperCollins*Publishers*

The Lightning Catcher
Copyright © 2013 by Anne Cameron

Black-and-white illustrations by Victoria Jamieson

The text of this book is set in 12-point Times New Roman.
Book design by Paul Zakris

Library of Congress Cataloging-in-Publication Data

Cameron, Anne.
The lightning catcher / by Anne Cameron.
pages cm.
"Greenwillow Books."
Summary: When eleven-year-old Angus McFangus learns that he is a storm prophet, someone who can predict and control catastrophic weather, he must stop the villainous Scabious Dankhart from unleashing an unending storm and achieving world domination.
ISBN 978-0-06-211276-7 (trade ed.)
[1. Weather—Fiction. 2. Adventure and adventurers—Fiction.] I. Title.
PZ7.C1428Li 2013 [Fic]—dc23 2012042848

13 14 15 16 17 LP/RRDH 10 9 8 7 6 5 4 3 2 1
First Edition

GREENWILLOW BOOKS

To Paul, who always believed this book would happen.
And to Mum, for expert help and advice.

RAINING NEWTS AND FROGS

If you have ever tried to find the Isle of Imbur on a map of the world, then you'll know by now that it simply doesn't exist. You will not find it tacked on to the end of Italy, or nestling under the armpit of the Antipodes, or even skulking off the coast of Mexico, disguising itself as a humpback whale. And even if you spread your map across the entire kitchen table and study it through a magnifying glass, you will find nothing in the empty spaces of the map but a few melted chocolate stains and some dead flies.

Yet it is precisely in one of these empty spaces that the Isle of Imbur lurks, quietly minding its own business, growing its own potatoes, fooling the rest of the world into believing that it is nothing more than an accidental smudge. And that is exactly the way the islanders wish to keep it.

One islander in particular had gone to extraordinary lengths to conceal its existence from the rest of the world. Her name was Principal Delphinia Dark-Angel. She was a practical, businesslike woman at heart, with closely cropped white hair and a stubbly, neatly trimmed mole on her left cheek that resembled one of the Galapagos Islands. She wore a long, yellow weatherproof coat, buttoned all the way up to her chin, and she did not like surprises.

Unfortunately, a rather large one had been delivered to her office at precisely ten past six that morning, along with a pot of hot tea. The principal shot a furtive glance at this surprise, which was sitting in the middle of her desk and took the form of a photograph. The photograph showed showers of newts and frogs raining down on the Houses of Parliament in London. They tumbled from the skies in a blur of webbed feet.

Principal Dark-Angel picked up the photo and turned it over with a sigh. She read the note on the back for the tenth time that morning, hoping that she might have misread it on the previous nine occasions.

Raining Newts and Frogs

Dear Principal,

A weather warning has just been issued for Buckingham Palace, Westminster Cathedral, and the Glow Worm Café on Hyde Park Corner. The risk of heavy amphibious showers falling in all three locations is extremely high and will remain so for the next few hours. Anyone venturing outside is being advised to watch where they're putting their feet and to wear hats, boots, and safety goggles.

Luckily, climatologists are blaming this sudden invasion of flying amphibians on global warming. They're predicting the problem could become far more serious in the future, eventually leading to heavy showers of bison, followed by prolonged downpours of sheep.

Please advise immediately.

Yours sincerely,
Trevelyan Tempest

Principal Dark-Angel put the photograph down and turned away from her desk with a frown. It was not that she was particularly shocked by showers of frogs. On the Isle of Imbur, last Tuesday at lunchtime, a small shower of tadpoles had been rapidly followed by a torrential downpour of newts, and so it had continued, raining newts and frogs, until no one on the isle dared leave home without an umbrella.

What really troubled the principal was the reason the showers had started in the first place, why they appeared to be getting worse, and why, according to Trevelyan Tempest—one of her most trusted colleagues—they were now falling in places where they simply shouldn't exist. If her suspicions were correct, it had absolutely nothing whatsoever to do with strange atmospheric disturbances or global warming, as London's top meteorologists had proclaimed. It did, however, have quite a lot to do with an eleven-year-old boy called Angus McFangus.

Her thoughts were interrupted by a brisk knock at the door.

"Fresh pot of tea, Principal?" A plump woman with soft brown curls entered, carrying a tray. "I've already strained it for tadpoles."

"Thank you, Mrs. Stobbs." Principal Dark-Angel sank gratefully into the chair behind her desk. "And could you please tell Felix Gudgeon that I need him to deliver an urgent message as soon as possible?" she added, setting a small sheet of blue writing paper on her desk and scribbling down the words that would change the life of one boy forever.

THE WINDMILL

If you met Angus McFangus in person, you would not find any extraordinary mysteries stuffed up his left nostril, or nestling under his armpits, or even skulking under his eyebrows, disguised as bat-shaped birthmarks. And even if you studied his face closely through a magnifying glass, you would find nothing exceptional upon it, except a few stray smudges of raspberry jam. Nor would you discover the slightest trace of the great secret that had been lurking about his person since the day he was born.

Angus himself had known nothing of this secret until a few weeks before, when he'd suddenly started having nightmares. A huge dragon with claws and a thick armor of fiery scales had begun forcing its way into his dreams, causing him to wake up abruptly in a cold and clammy sweat. He had no idea why this glittering, combustible creature kept bothering him, almost every night. And he couldn't seem to shake it off, no matter how many hot milky drinks he sipped before bedtime.

He knew nothing about the Isle of Imbur, of course, or how that extremely secretive island was about to affect his life. At the moment, he was free of nightmares, fast asleep, snoring gently in one of the bedrooms at his uncle's old windmill in Devon. His pale gray eyes closed fast against the morning sun, his short brown hair flattened across the tops of his small bear-shaped ears. Even the scattering of freckles across his nose had a sleepy sort of look about them as he snored.

This slumber was about to be shattered, however, by a series of loud bangs and explosions, the first of which would wake Angus with a start and cause Mrs. Mavis Fish-Hook, in the nearby village of Budleigh Otterstone, to drop a teapot on top of her husband's head.

BOOOOOOOOOOOOMMMMM . . .

Angus sat bolt upright in bed, his eyes instantly open.

The floorboards in his room shook as if something large and heavy had just collided with the side of the Windmill and then settled again. He held his breath, listening for any nasty cracks, snaps, or thumps that might follow. Then he jumped swiftly out of bed and stumbled around his bedroom, quickly pulling on a T-shirt and jeans before—

"ARRRGGGGHHHHHHH!" A strangled yell suddenly came up from the kitchen below; it was followed by an ominous *smash!*

Angus flung his bedroom door open and raced down the spiral staircase. Loud noises first thing in the morning always meant that Uncle Max was in big trouble.

Uncle Max was a brilliant inventor who built highly volatile machines that often went up in smoke, shattering the peace of the countryside. And so far that summer, the peace had been shattered twenty-seven times already—twenty-eight if you counted this very latest explosion.

"Uncle Max?" Angus called urgently, skidding to a halt outside the kitchen. "Is everything all right?"

There was no answer. Angus opened the door cautiously, sticking his head all the way inside the room and—*THUD!* He was instantly knocked off his feet by something resembling a large copper-colored washing machine. It scuttled quickly past him, across the hallway, and into the room beyond, trailing several pots and pans behind it, as well as the plug from the kitchen sink.

Angus picked himself up quickly and darted into the steam-filled room. "Uncle Max?"

"Ah, good morning, good morning, dear nephew!" came his uncle's cheerful-sounding voice in reply, and Angus found him under the kitchen table.

Uncle Max had large amounts of bushy white hair sprouting in great tufts from both his eyebrows, the ends of his nostrils, and the insides of his ears. This morning his face was also shining like a boiled lobster; the arms had been ripped violently from his coveralls and were trailing on the floor behind him like a pair of soggy blue pythons.

"Er . . . is everything all right?" Angus repeated, kneeling on the floor beside him. "Do you want me to call out the fire brigade again?"

"Everything is quite under control, my dear Angus." Uncle Max beamed. "Just a few minor hiccups with my latest invention."

Angus glanced nervously over his shoulder. What Uncle Max referred to as "a few minor hiccups" often resulted in dangerous explosions, sudden fires, and broken bones. Just last summer, an arctic ice smasher had broken Angus's arm in two places, and he'd spent weeks in a cast. And this summer was already proving to be much more perilous.

"What was that thing that knocked me over, anyway?" he asked warily as the sound of splintering furniture drifted across the hallway.

"That was the automatic steam-powered blizzard catcher," Uncle Max said, smoothing out his singed eyebrows. "And it's one of my more brilliant inventions, even if I do say so myself."

Angus frowned. "But . . . why's it gone running off?"

"The blizzard catcher has been programmed to forage for its own fuel," Uncle Max explained with the air of a proud dog owner talking about his favorite wolfhound. "Unfortunately, it's already consumed a large quantity of hot tea this morning, not to mention my best pair of slippers, and it now appears to be letting off some excess steam. I would appreciate it if you didn't mention this to your mother," he continued, showing signs of real concern for the first time. "After what happened with the arctic ice smasher last summer . . . well, she may never speak to me again if she hears that another one of my inventions is causing trouble."

Angus grinned. "I promise I won't tell her anything."

Luckily for Uncle Max, Angus's mum and dad, Alabone and Evangeline McFangus, both worked in London and only visited him at the Windmill during the school holidays and on the occasional weekend. He had never been entirely sure what his parents did for a living, except that they worked for some big government department, and their jobs involved large amounts of boring paperwork. Although once, in the middle of a very wintry January, his mum had arrived at the Windmill with severely sunburned kneecaps. Her shoes had also left a mysterious trail of golden sand behind her wherever she went, and when Angus had pointed this out she'd tried to convince him—rather shiftily—that the exotic-looking grains had merely come from the sandbox in the local park.

They'd also given him some extremely odd Christmas presents over the years, including a pair of reindeer antlers from Lapland and some hairy camel's-milk chocolates. All of which had made Angus wonder, more than once, if there was something his mum and dad weren't telling him.

The arrival of his eleventh birthday present, on the fifth of August, had done nothing to dispel his suspicions. Posted in Iceland, and wrapped up tightly in sheep's wool and straw, it had turned out to be a large chunk of black volcanic rock. Angus longed to quiz his mum and dad in person about which volcano this impressive rock had come from. But it had been more than three weeks since their last letter, and Angus had started to worry.

They'd never gone this long before without visiting or phoning to check that Uncle Max was feeding him enough brussels sprouts. They'd never forgotten to ring him on his birthday, either, and he still felt a sting of disappointment whenever he thought about the fact that this year, the phone had remained silent.

An ominous clatter of pots and pans interrupted his thoughts at that precise moment, and he spun around to see the blizzard catcher scuttling back into the kitchen. Large jets of hot steam were now belching out of its pipes, as if dozens of kettles were all coming to a boil at once.

Angus backed away from it speedily, before it could poach him like an egg.

"Bother!" Uncle Max exclaimed, grinning and not looking in the least bit bothered. "I think the time may have come to ask the Budleigh Otterstone fire brigade for their assistance after all, if you wouldn't mind telephoning them, my dear nephew."

"Oh . . . right, yeah," Angus said, trying to sneak past the blizzard catcher without attracting its attention.

"It might also be a good idea to mention that it's something of an emergency," his uncle added, his excited face just visible through the thick clouds of steam. "Judging by the smells it's now making, I'd say the blizzard catcher has been guzzling down cold tomato soup, chocolate liqueurs, and wooden matches and is in imminent danger of exploding."

Angus abandoned all attempts at creeping quietly and flung himself across the kitchen, hoping to reach the telephone in the hallway before his uncle's invention went into total meltdown. He'd barely managed to grasp the doorknob, however, when—

BOOOOOOOOOOOOOOMMMMM . . .

Somewhere in the village of Budleigh Otterstone, Mr. Wilfred Pyke tripped and fell into a wheelbarrow full of manure. Angus was blasted off his feet and thrown clean across the kitchen, where he landed with a thump, feeling like he'd just been flattened by a herd of buffalo. He sat shakily on the floor, with large purple blobs dancing before his eyes, and for a split second, he even caught a brief glimpse of the fire dragon that kept nudging its way into his dreams.

He shook the lingering image from his head and stared around the devastated room. Cold tomato soup dripped from the kitchen walls like an eruption of volcanic lava. The pantry door had been ripped violently off its hinges.

"Now *that* is what I call a highly successful morning," Uncle Max declared, crawling out from under the wreckage of the smoldering table, his hair now a shocking shade of orange.

Angus spent the rest of the day knee-deep in tomato soup, helping Uncle Max scoop great bucketloads of the stuff off the kitchen walls. It also took ages to pry the melted blizzard catcher off the floor, to which it had attached itself like a limpet, and he didn't get to bed until well past eleven o'clock that night.

He was awakened by the doorbell ringing downstairs. Angus blinked groggily at the luminous alarm clock on his bedside table and frowned—it was ten past five in the morning.

The sound of muffled voices came drifting up the stairs. Angus heard a door opening directly beneath his bedroom, and then the conversation faded. He hesitated, wondering if Uncle Max was in trouble with the Budleigh Otterstone fire brigade for causing yet another explosion and if he might be in need of some help. There was only one way to find out.

He crept quietly out of bed, crawled across the floor on his hands and knees, and lifted the edge of the rug that covered the bare boards beneath. Several years ago, one of Uncle Max's other inventions (a self-inflating portable bathtub) had exploded in the middle of the living room, creating a small hole in the ceiling directly below Angus's bedroom. So far, Angus had only used this spy hole twice—once to discover what his mum and dad had bought him for his birthday, and another time to see the

end of a scary film about flesh-eating zombies that Uncle Max had refused to let him watch . . . although afterward, in the long dark hours of the night, Angus wasn't sure this had been such a good idea.

He eased the rug back again now, being careful not to make any noise, and pressed his eye to the hole. Uncle Max was standing directly beneath him dressed in a pair of red flannel pajamas and a purple-spotted bathrobe, both of which clashed horribly with his soup-stained hair. And hovering in the doorway, wearing a long, weatherproof yellow coat and black rubber boots, was the most astonishing person Angus had ever seen in his life.

2

THE FERRY WITH NO NAME

The stranger was the same height as Uncle Max, his straggly beard a stony, marbled gray; he was also completely bald and appeared to be wearing a single silver earring—shaped like a snowflake.

"Come in, Felix, come in!" Uncle Max boomed, in a manner that made Angus think the two men had known each other for years. "If I'd known you were going to be in this neck of the woods, I would have made one of my famous fish-and-raspberry-jelly stews for supper."

"I'm still recovering from that disgusting muck you made me eat the last time I was here," the stranger growled in a deep, gravelly voice. "What was it again—snail-and-seaweed pie?"

"I'll have you know my snail-and-seaweed pie has won first prize at the Budleigh Otterstone village fair for the last two years," Uncle Max said, his eyes twinkling with pride.

The stranger snorted loudly. "First prize for what, though?"

He then positioned himself by the fireplace, forcing Angus to shift all his weight onto his left shoulder and wriggle himself around on the floor until he could see both men properly again.

"So, to what do we owe this unexpected pleasure, old friend?" Uncle Max asked jovially.

"I'm not here to enjoy myself," the man barked. "I've come to deliver an important message from Principal Dark-Angel, in person."

He took a crumpled piece of blue paper from one of the pockets in his yellow coat and handed it to Uncle Max.

"Ah." Uncle Max frowned. "If this concerns the delivery of the automatic steam-powered blizzard catcher, I think I ought to warn you that there have been one or two unexpected complications—"

"It's got nothing to do with any of your crackpot inventions," the stranger interrupted rudely. "This concerns the boy, Angus."

Angus felt his left foot twitch suddenly at the mention of his own name.

"Angus?" Uncle Max sounded equally surprised. "Why, my dear Felix, I don't quite understand—"

"Then you'd best hurry up and read that letter. I haven't got time to sit around this drafty windmill, explaining myself to you. The boy's in danger, and I've come to take him away."

Angus gulped. What could he possibly be in any danger from—other than one of his uncle's inventions? And he cast a nervous glance over his shoulder, just in case the blizzard catcher was on the prowl again. But there was nothing sinister lurking in the shadows of his room, and he pressed his eye back to the spy hole.

Uncle Max unfolded the letter. Instead of reading this mysterious message, however, he thrust it straight into the glowing coals of the fire, promptly setting it alight. Angus quickly stifled a gasp. But Uncle Max waited patiently until the flames had burned themselves out before calmly rescuing the only scrap of paper to have survived the inferno. He read it carefully. It was several moments before he spoke again.

"It would seem, Felix, that the situation is far more serious than I realized," he said, sounding slightly shell-shocked. "I've seen the news reports, naturally, but . . . you agree with Principal Dark-Angel that Angus must go tonight?"

The stranger nodded solemnly. "The principal feels the boy's no longer safe at the Windmill. I've got a taxi outside waiting to take us both to the ferry port. And I've brought a couple of these with me, just in case we run into any trouble on the way." He took a small glass ball from his pocket and held it up to the light, where it glittered and sparkled impressively.

"Storm globes?" Uncle Max said, surprised, still clutching the charred letter tightly in his hand. "But surely such measures won't be necessary. . . ."

"Necessary or not, I feel happier knowing they're in my pocket. And the boy's to be told nothing, mind, until Principal Dark-Angel's had a chance to speak to him herself."

"But you cannot simply bundle Angus onto a ferry without a single word of explanation," Uncle Max protested, running a hand through his bushy orange hair. "He knows nothing about storm globes, or the real reason we're being bombarded with these ridiculous showers of frogs. Alabone and Evangeline have been most careful to keep the truth from him."

"You mean the boy still thinks his parents work for some boring government department?" the man asked, sounding mildly surprised.

Uncle Max nodded. "And I'm not convinced he'd believe the truth, even if we explained it to him."

"I wouldn't be so sure of that." The stranger grunted. "The boy's bound to start asking questions sooner or later. He won't have heard from his parents in weeks now, and he'll be wanting to know why—unless he's got snail-and-seaweed pie for brains. He's old enough to know the truth, I say."

Angus swallowed hard, his pulse beginning to race. The truth about what? Why had his parents been lying to him? And how did the stranger even know that there'd been no word from his mum and dad in weeks?

"You'd best go and wake him up." The man glanced impatiently at his watch. "The two of us have a ferry to catch. It's the only sailing this week, so it'll be packed to the portholes. But Principal Dark-Angel wants the boy brought to her tonight, and that's final."

"Oh, very well." Uncle Max sighed. "But I absolutely insist that you join me in a cup of tea first, and I won't take no for an answer. I want to hear everything you can tell me about this alarming situation. . . ."

They were still talking as they disappeared into the hall a moment later, closing the door behind them.

Angus sat back on his heels, his mind racing. He sprang to his feet a second later, struck by a sudden thought. Uncle Max and the stranger were planning to wake him up as soon as they'd finished their tea, which meant he now had only a few minutes to grab anything he wanted to take with him on this mysterious journey.

He found a large canvas bag lurking at the bottom of his wardrobe, which he quickly began to stuff with as many socks, underpants, T-shirts, and sweaters as he could find. As an afterthought, he also grabbed the last letter from his mum. He tucked it safely inside a spare pair of jeans and shoved the whole hastily packed bag under his bed. He glanced anxiously at the hole in the floor, hoping that he'd covered it up again properly, then jumped back under his covers and waited. And just a few seconds later . . .

"And the boy's in here, you say," a deep voice growled in the hallway outside his room.

The door burst open suddenly. A dark shape came striding in and flicked on the overhead light. Angus sat bolt upright in bed . . . and gulped. Close up, the stranger looked even more unfriendly than he'd appeared through the hole in the ceiling. His black eyes gleamed darkly, staring down at Angus with an extremely disappointed look on his face, as if he'd been expecting to find someone taller or far more intelligent looking.

"You've got five minutes to get yourself packed and dressed, boy, or you'll be leaving this windmill in your pajamas," he growled.

Before Angus could respond to this extraordinary statement, however, Uncle Max also entered the room, looking thoroughly out of sorts.

"My dear Felix, Angus will not be going anywhere until

you've introduced yourself properly. I absolutely insist—"

"We've already wasted enough time drinking tea." The man folded his arms stubbornly. "I haven't got time for introductions."

"Then I must make them for you." Uncle Max sighed wearily. There were dark circles under his eyes, which somehow made his hair look even more orange. "Angus, I would like you to meet a very old friend of mine, Felix Gudgeon."

"Er, h-how do you do, Mr. Gudgeon?" Angus said, smiling as politely as he could.

Gudgeon did not smile back.

"Felix has just arrived with some rather unexpected news," Uncle Max continued, hovering awkwardly at the foot of Angus's bed. "It seems your parents are quite unable to visit, so you must go to them instead. Gudgeon will see to it that you come to no harm along the way," he explained, not quite meeting his nephew's eye. "It's far too dangerous for you to stay here any longer—"

"Dangerous?" Angus gulped. What was so dangerous about the Windmill all of a sudden? Nobody had ever worried about him being here before, not even when the arctic ice smasher broke his arm. "But . . . Uncle Max, what's going on?"

"You'll find out what's going on when I decide to tell you, boy," Gudgeon snapped, his snowflake earring flashing dangerously. "But until then, I won't be answering any questions, so don't waste your breath asking any. Understand?"

Angus didn't understand anything; he nodded quickly, however, swallowing down at least a dozen questions that had just gotten stuck in his throat like fish bones.

By the time they reached the ferry port, twenty minutes later, Gudgeon had already made it crystal clear that he'd rather hold a conversation with a bucket of slugs than chat with Angus about any subject, including the weather. And as Gudgeon paid the driver, Angus clambered out of the taxi and stood shivering on the chilly pier, trying to work out what was going on.

He stared around the bustling port, searching for any clues that might give him the slightest hint about their destination. The large ferry looming up in the darkness ahead didn't even have a name.

To make matters more confusing, Gudgeon had insisted that Angus put on a long gray coat before they left the Windmill. It was made of thick, soft wool, with a deep velvet-lined hood that fell so far over his face Angus could barely see where he was going. He wondered if they were heading somewhere cold, perhaps, like Iceland or Norway?

"Right, boy, follow me." Gudgeon appeared by his side, clutching two ferry tickets. "And keep that hood pulled down low. That face of yours could get us into serious trouble if anyone gets a good look at it."

Angus frowned. What was wrong with his face? It had never gotten him into trouble before, at least not that he could remember.

He trotted nervously along behind Gudgeon, the strong smell of engine oil and gutted fish making his eyes water. They'd barely gone more than a dozen steps, however, when Gudgeon came to a halt.

"Hold your horses, boy," he growled. "There's trouble coming our way."

Angus turned, half expecting to find an escaped rhinoceros charging through the early morning toward them, and peered anxiously into the gloom. Halfway along the pier, an angry fish seller had just kicked over an entire bucket of wriggling eels. Then he saw them. Beyond the eels, two figures emerged, heavy coats with upturned collars making them look like sinister shadows.

"I've been expecting those two mongrels to show up somewhere," Gudgeon informed him, a note of satisfaction in his gruff voice.

"But . . . who are they?" Angus asked, watching as the two shadowy figures cut swiftly across the street toward them.

"Nobody you need to worry about, boy. And by the time I've finished with the great useless pair, they'll be wishing they'd picked another ferry port to go prowling about in!"

Gudgeon took a small glass ball from his pocket, clutching it tightly in his weathered hand. Angus recognized the glittering storm globe instantly. It was the same one he'd seen through the spy hole in his bedroom floor, and he felt his pulse quicken.

"Keep that hood pulled down low," Gudgeon warned again. "And stick close to me. This isn't going to be pretty."

Suddenly the ferry's whistle blew, making Angus jump,

and all along the pier passengers began to dash toward it. At the exact same moment, Gudgeon raised his hand high above his head . . . and smashed the storm globe hard on the ground, where it shattered into a hundred tiny pieces.

Angus leaped back as a thin curl of gray mist rose instantly from the broken sphere. The mist snaked its way upward, gathering swiftly into a small, fluffy-looking cloud, which hovered twenty feet above Gudgeon's bald head. The cloud grew thicker and darker until it looked as if it was about to burst, and then . . . Angus almost jumped out of his skin as a small rumble of thunder echoed around the quayside. He stared up at the cloud in disbelief—not even his uncle had ever made it thunder before.

"That should keep those two mongrels busy for a bit!" Gudgeon growled, grabbing Angus by the elbow and marching him hastily toward the ferry.

Ten seconds later, the cloud finally burst, releasing a spectacular, monsoonlike deluge. Huge, angry drops of rain bounced off the ground with a deafening noise, like a bag of marbles being dropped from a great height.

People scattered in all directions, running headlong into one another as they slipped and skidded, desperate to escape the vicious storm. And the two shadowy figures disappeared from view, swallowed up in a wet and dizzy blur.

Angus stared over his shoulder, wondering if he was in the middle of an extraordinary dream. Nobody could create their own weather. Nobody could whip up a thunderstorm just because they felt like it. It was totally impossible. . . .

"Stop gawping, boy, and get on that boat!" Gudgeon barked in his ear, forcing him up the gangway between the last of the stragglers.

Angus was jostled along the ferry's deck, his feet sliding hopelessly on the wet wooden boards, and he groped around for something to hold on to. Somebody shoved him from behind, and he lurched sideways.

"Watch it, boy!" Gudgeon yelled, making a wild grab for his arm, but it was already too late.

Angus tripped on the hem of his own coat and fell headfirst, his skull making extremely painful contact with a solid-looking post—

CRACK!

And suddenly everything went dark.

3

DARK-ANGEL

"And the boy's been unconscious since you left, you say?"

"Haven't heard a peep out of him, Principal. He's been twitching like a rabbit, tossing and turning, mumbling some nonsense about dragons."

"Dragons?"

Voices drifted toward Angus like a whispered story on a cool evening breeze. He'd been having the most amazing dream: he'd been riding a dragon over monstrous gray waves, swaying groggily as the fiery creature soared and plummeted with a violent pitching motion. He was now lying perfectly still, however, and his head was aching like he'd just been hit with a baseball bat, several times.

"Well, Doctor Fleagal isn't overly concerned." Somewhere close by, the voices started talking again. They sounded impatient. "He says Angus will wake up in his own time, but this really is most inconvenient, Gudgeon. I had hoped to talk to the boy as soon as he arrived. . . ."

Gudgeon? Angus had a sudden vision of a gruff-looking stranger dressed in a yellow coat and black rubber boots, and the glorious dream faded in a flash.

He opened one eye warily and blinked. He was lying on an old sofa with the long coat thrown over him like a blanket. Gudgeon towered above him with a face like thunder. Standing next to him was a woman with short white hair, pale skin, and a bristly mole on her left cheek. She was dressed in a yellow coat identical to the one Gudgeon was wearing. It was buttoned all the way up to her chin.

"Looks like the boy's waking up now, Principal," Gudgeon grunted, noticing that Angus had his eyes open. "And about time too."

The woman turned toward him, smiling faintly. "Ah, Angus, you've had us all quite worried. I'm afraid you've been unconscious for some time."

Angus sat up slowly, feeling a hard lump on his forehead. It was the size of an egg and throbbed painfully.

"What happened?" he asked as the room swayed dizzily before him. "Where am I?"

"I will answer all of your questions in a moment, but first Doctor Fleagal has prepared a special tonic to help you feel better," the woman said, handing him a tall glass. "You must drink it all while I have a quick word with Gudgeon." And with one last look, Gudgeon followed her out of the room, closing the door behind them.

Angus took a sip of the tonic. It tasted like black cherries and cinnamon, and he drank the rest of it down greedily. The last thing he remembered was being frog-marched onto the ferry by Gudgeon, but they could have been at sea for hours, or days even, while he'd been unconscious and dreaming of dragons. So where was he now?

Angus stared around the room, looking for clues, but it didn't give much away. It was sparsely decorated, with a single desk sitting in the center. The stone walls were covered with dozens of weather charts and maps of the world. He stood slowly, testing out his legs, a nervous buzzing in his ears. Staring back at him from the other side of the solitary desk was a long row of pickling jars, and inside each jar—Angus blinked and edged closer for a better look—inside each jar there appeared to be collections of newts, frogs, toads, or tadpoles, all suspended in a briny-looking liquid, with wide eyes bulging.

"Please allow me to introduce myself properly, Angus." The woman's voice came suddenly from behind him, making him jump. She had returned to the room alone. "I am Principal Lightning Catcher Dark-Angel." She shook his hand firmly as she reached the desk.

"H-how do you do, Principal."

"How are you feeling now? A little better, I hope?"

Angus nodded. Thanks to the tonic, the throbbing pain in his forehead was slowly beginning to ease.

"Good. I trust your uncle Maximilian is also well?" she said, sitting down behind her desk and signaling that he should take the chair opposite.

"You . . . you know my uncle?" Angus asked, almost missing his seat in surprise.

"Certainly. Maximilian has produced many magnificent machines for us over the years. In fact, we were

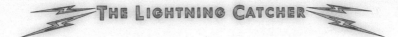
expecting him to deliver his latest invention this week, the automatic steam-powered blizzard catcher, I believe it's called. Perhaps you have seen him working on it during your stay at the Windmill?"

"Er . . ." Angus thought of the temperamental machine that had knocked him off his feet and that was now sitting in his uncle's workshop, a twisted blob of melted copper and pipes. He wondered how he could answer without getting Uncle Max into trouble. He was saved from having to explain anything, however, by the principal's next question—which took him completely by surprise.

"Forgive me for asking something so personal, Angus, when we've only just met. I'm sure you have many questions of your own, but there is a small matter that I wish to clear up first, if I may." She gave him a faint smile, which looked rather forced and unnatural. "Have your parents sent you any letters through the mail lately?"

Angus twitched in his chair, the cogs turning slowly inside his befuddled brain. There had been the letter from his mum . . . and he remembered that he'd stuffed it into the jeans he'd packed before leaving the Windmill. His bag was now lying on the floor, next to the principal's desk. Angus looked away from it swiftly. There had been nothing remotely unusual or interesting about the letter. Plus it had been addressed to him, not Principal Dark-Angel. Who had yet to explain why he'd been dragged from his bed in the middle of the night. Or what his mum and dad had to do with any of it.

"They—they haven't sent me anything in ages," he lied, swallowing guiltily.

"And you are quite sure of that?" The principal's gaze settled upon him like an extremely bright searchlight, making the hair on the back of his neck tingle. "They haven't sent you any messages or maps of any kind? Perhaps you have accidentally opened an envelope meant for your uncle? Think carefully, Angus. It is most important that you remember."

Angus concentrated hard on the principal's left earlobe, then shook his head, hoping that his face wouldn't give him away.

"I see." Principal Dark-Angel deflated like a punctured balloon. "That is a great pity. I've been expecting something important from your parents, but it seems to have gotten lost in the mail. It had occurred to me that they

may have sent it to the Windmill by mistake. But please, forget I even mentioned it," she said, waving the matter aside. "We have far more important things to discuss now that you have arrived here safely."

Angus got the distinct impression that there was nothing the principal wished to discuss more. He shifted uneasily in his chair.

"Arrived where, exactly?" he asked. "Are my mum and dad here? Can I see them now?"

"We will come to the matter of your parents shortly, Angus. But to answer your other question, you have been brought to the Isle of Imbur." She opened a large map and spread it across her entire desk.

The map showed an island in the middle of the Atlantic Ocean. It was shaped like a kidney bean, with a sandy shoreline and a long range of snow-capped mountains to the west.

Angus frowned. The only thing in the middle of the Atlantic on his uncle's maps back at the Windmill was some dead flies. He'd definitely never heard of any island called Imbur before.

"Imbur is extremely unusual," the principal continued.

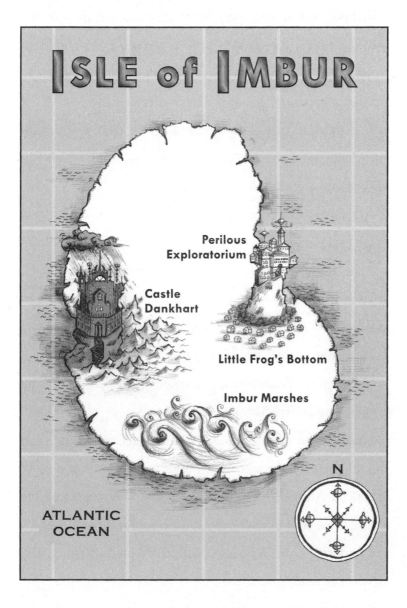

ISLE of IMBUR

Perilous Exploratorium

Castle Dankhart

Little Frog's Bottom

Imbur Marshes

ATLANTIC OCEAN

N

"You will not find it marked on any normal map of the world. Indeed, few people have even heard of it, and that is exactly the way we wish to keep it. For almost three hundred and fifty years, we have allowed the rest of the world to believe that our precious little island sank into the ocean after a terrible storm, and was lost forever. But as you can clearly see, that is not so."

Angus swallowed. An island that was supposed to have sunk into the sea—no wonder he'd never heard of it before!

"The history of our island is long and complicated, but I will try and explain it to you as best I can." Principal Dark-Angel paused for a moment as if gathering her thoughts. "I am sure that you must have heard of the Great Fire of London?"

"Er." Angus floundered, wondering what the Great Fire of London had to do with anything.

"It occurred in the year 1666, of course, and swept right across the city, destroying thousands of homes and other grand buildings in its path. You have also been told, no doubt, that this fire was started accidentally in a bakery on Pudding Lane, by a man called Thomas Farynor. But this is not true."

Angus gulped and stared at the principal.

"The Great Fire of London was in fact started by a group of men, among them Edgar Perilous and Philip Starling. They lived in a time of amazing scientific revolution, Angus, a time when fascinating new ideas about the world were being put forward by remarkable men such as Galileo. Starling and Perilous joined a group of scientists who had begun to experiment with the explosive forces of lightning, to see if it could be controlled and harnessed. They called themselves lightning catchers, and they constructed many lightning towers across the city of London in order to carry out daring experiments. As you can see from the picture behind me, these towers were an impressive sight, and the people of London were fearful of their power."

She pointed to a picture on the far wall of her office. Up until that moment, Angus hadn't even noticed it; it was painted in dark, earthy colors and showed a London of olden days, with a great muddy river snaking its way through the middle, its skyline dominated by dozens of towers shaped like pyramids. Each tower had a large lightning rod poking straight up into the clouds and a treacherous set of steps and ladders running through the heart of its open, skeletal frame. Angus felt dizzy just looking at it.

"These experiments quickly got out of control," the principal continued. "Philip Starling himself wrote a diary of his near-fatal dealings with this vicious force of nature. He was in favor of taking down the lightning towers and ending all experimentation. Unfortunately, before he could convince the rest of the lightning catchers, there was a terrible storm. One of the lightning towers was struck and caught fire. The fire quickly swept its way across London, killing many people and destroying a large portion of the city."

"But why doesn't everyone know about Edgar Perilous, Philip Starling, and the lightning catchers?" Angus asked, amazed.

"Because the Great Fire brought London to its knees, Angus, and the truth would have finished it off completely. It was far safer to convince everyone that the fire had been started quite innocently, in a bakery on Pudding Lane. The rest, as they say, is history. All evidence of the lightning towers was destroyed in the fire itself, and their existence has been conveniently forgotten over the years."

Angus thought of the history books he'd read at school, all of which had gone into lengthy detail about the unfortunate baker on Pudding Lane, and felt his head spin.

"Having convinced everyone that the fire was an accident, London's leaders were keen to remove any remaining lightning catchers from the capital to prevent another catastrophe. Philip Starling, Edgar Perilous, and their followers, therefore, were secretly offered refuge on Imbur, a remote island that few had ever heard of. The story that it had sunk into the ocean after a terrible storm was spread far and wide, enabling us to settle here and continue our important research in peace. For Starling and Perilous were determined that some good should rise from the devastation of the Great Fire. This secrecy is necessary to protect the work we still carry out at Perilous—"

"Perilous?" Angus interrupted, unable to stop himself.

"The Perilous Exploratorium for Violent Weather and Vicious Storms, to give it its full name," the principal told him proudly. "Indeed, the magnificent Exploratorium you are now sitting in, Angus, was built by the first lightning catchers to settle on Imbur. Our research has moved on a great deal since those early days, of course. During the past few centuries we have investigated the innermost workings of tornadoes, thunderstorms, monsoons, and droughts. We have plunged ourselves into the depths of

the chilliest blizzards; we have discovered exactly what makes a hurricane tick. And as a result, we are now responsible for dealing with some of the world's most extreme and unusual weather.

"Indeed, for many years now, teams of highly experienced lightning catchers have been dispatched across the globe, in the utmost secrecy, to snuff out violent electrical storms, or to trap mighty tornadoes and send them packing. We do not always succeed, Angus. On the contrary, a great many storms are beyond our expertise. Nor do we wish to change the weather simply for the sake of changing it. But we shall continue with our quest to protect mankind from the ravages of the weather at its most cruel and extreme. And we are proud of our efforts."

Angus swallowed hard, feeling thunderstruck—or as he now realized, it would be more accurate to say *lightning*struck.

"We are also responsible for dealing with some of the more . . . unusual meteorological situations that arise," the principal continued. "For instance, I'm sure you have noticed the odd showers we have been experiencing lately." She nodded toward the photographs lying flat on her desk. One showed Canterbury Cathedral being rained upon by a shower of warty toads, and in the other, the Eiffel Tower had been engulfed by a blizzard of newts. "Our biggest concern at the moment is to discover where these wretched showers are coming from, and how to make them stop before we all find ourselves knee-deep in sardines."

"So you're—you're weather forecasters?" Angus asked, uncertain.

"Some may call us that, yes. But perhaps this will help explain things a little more clearly."

From a drawer in her desk, the principal took out a small, round metal box and placed it in front of him. She flipped open the lid with a touch of her finger, and Angus suddenly found himself staring at an almond-shaped eyeball, resting on a velvet cushion. The eyeball was made of fine translucent glass. Inside the iris, impossibly deep swirls of blue, gray, and fathomless green seemed to melt and merge together, creating the most breathtaking patterns he'd ever seen.

"You are looking, Angus, into the eye of an ancient storm that caused a great deal of damage to our island many,

many years ago," Principal Dark-Angel explained. "It was discovered by those lightning catchers who first came to Imbur and founded our great and noble Exploratorium."

"But . . ." Angus faltered, gazing at the fascinating object. "I thought that the eye of the storm was a calm spot in the middle of a hurricane?"

"It was previously thought to be the benign center of a storm, yes, but as you can see, it is much more than that. Indeed, we have only just begun to understand its true power and force. But understand it we will. And one day we will have the power to control it."

The liquid eye gazed languidly at Angus, but before he could lean forward and get a closer look at it, Principal Dark-Angel had snapped the lid shut again and put the metal box back in the drawer of her desk.

"Is that what my mum and dad do?" Angus asked. "Do they capture the eyes of ancient storms and stuff?"

"Alabone and Evangeline McFangus are two of the finest lightning catchers we have here at Perilous. You should be very proud of them both."

Angus had a sudden vision of his mum grappling with an angry tornado and of his dad catching bucketloads of tadpoles as they fell over the Great Wall of China. "But I don't understand. Why have they been pretending to work for the government all this time?"

"Since the Great Fire of London, all lightning catchers have been bound by a strict oath of secrecy," the principal explained. "Your parents could not have told you about Perilous, even if they wished to. Besides, do you really think you would have believed the truth if you'd heard it? A top secret organization that controls the weather. It sounds most implausible, wouldn't you agree?"

Angus agreed completely. He was sitting right in front of Principal Dark-Angel with the evidence all around him, he'd actually seen Gudgeon produce spectacular down-pours of rain just by smashing a small glass ball on the ground, and he still wasn't sure he believed any of it. He knew the principal was right. If his parents had told him about the Isle of Imbur and the lightning catchers, he would have been utterly convinced they were telling him fairy tales.

"Can I see them now?" he asked again, his head begin-ning to throb once more.

"Ah, I'm afraid that will not be possible." Principal

Dark-Angel frowned. "Your parents have been sent on an important assignment, Angus. Their work has taken them over the mountains to the other side of the island, where they are currently assisting Scabious Dankhart with a most difficult project, and I understand they are to stay with him until it is finished."

"So . . . is that why I haven't heard from them in weeks now?"

The principal nodded. "It's highly unlikely that they have any spare time for writing letters. I do not expect to hear from them myself until their assignment is completed. I am sorry if you have been concerned for their welfare."

"Could I just phone them?"Angus asked hopefully.

"Telephones, computers, and most other electronic and communication devices are all but useless here on Imbur," the principal informed him matter-of-factly. "Due to the nature of our experimentation and the strong interference it creates, we have been forced to adopt other methods of contacting one another."

"But . . . will they be coming back soon?" Angus asked.

"I understand it may be several weeks or even months

before they return." The principal shifted uncomfortably in her seat. "Fortunately, in the meantime, we have many things here at Perilous that will greatly interest someone who has helped his uncle build hailstone hurlers and blizzard catchers."

Before she could say any more, there was a knock at the door and Angus turned around to see a boy only a few years older than him enter the room nervously. He was dressed in a yellow coat and looked wet through.

"Yes, what is it, Croxley?"

"Excuse me, Principal Dark-Angel, but Rogwood would like to see you straightaway, in the courtyard."

"Can't it wait?"

"I'm afraid not, Principal. There's been another . . . episode," the boy said, hovering anxiously.

"Oh, very well." Principal Dark-Angel sighed, dragging herself to her feet. "Tell Rogwood that I will join him outside directly. Angus, if you will please excuse me for a few moments . . ." And she followed the boy swiftly out of her office, grabbing a yellow rain hat from the back of the door as she went.

Angus stared at the jars of frogs and toads, his brain

suddenly overloaded with the most amazing information he'd ever heard. Principal Dark-Angel, Gudgeon, and both his parents were all part of a secret organization that could do incredible things to the weather. Even his uncle Max was in it up to his eyebrows, if the blizzard catcher was anything to go by. And now he himself was on an island that supposedly didn't exist. He tapped one of the jars with his finger and grinned. It had definitely been worth getting dragged out of bed in the middle of the night for this!

He passed the next few minutes staring at the floating amphibians. As he did so, something even more interesting caught his eye. Sitting on the far side of the principal's desk was a book. It was bound in soft brown leather with elaborate gold lettering on the front cover, which read:

The Perilous Exploratorium for Violent Weather and Vicious Storms
A HOLOGRAPHIC HISTORY
BY
OSWALD BLOTT
STORYTELLER

Angus glanced guiltily over his shoulder. Then he picked up the holographic history for a closer inspection.

The pages were spotted with mold and crinkled invitingly as he turned to the beginning of chapter one, but there was nothing on the page except a large, glossy-looking square. Angus tilted the page toward the light and discovered a strange man skulking in the corner of this odd square. He was dressed in bottle-green tights, a brightly colored tunic, and some extremely fancy pantaloons, which stopped just short of his skinny knees. He also had a long, pointy beard and a single gold earring and was scratching his nose, scowling. Angus realized that he must be looking at Oswald Blott, the holographic story-teller named on the front of the book.

"Many years ago," the man boomed in a deep, theatrical voice, making Angus jump, "the Isle of Imbur was a quiet backwater full of dull, smelly peasants who spent their entire time growing turnips and quaffing beer in the local taverns."

Angus snapped the book shut, breathing heavily. He waited several seconds to see if this noisy racket had attracted the attention of anyone outside Principal

Dark-Angel's office. Then he cautiously opened the book again at the same page, curious to hear what else it had to say for itself.

"It was very fortunate for everyone, therefore," Oswald Blott continued, "when a small group of men, led by Philip Starling and Edgar Perilous, arrived on the island one dark and stormy night, and decided to stay."

He paused here to hold up a portrait of the two great men, both of whom had red faces full of whiskers and very superior expressions.

"Indeed, it was the great Edgar Perilous himself who created the wondrous legend of an isle that had sunk into the treacherous seas, thus preventing any more turnip lovers from turning up on its shores. . . ."

Angus flicked eagerly through the pages. He thumbed quickly past several interesting-sounding chapters, including one entitled "Birth of the Lightning Catchers," and another that had something to do with a blizzard of jet-black snowflakes. He stopped abruptly at chapter five, however, and stared at the title, "The Rise of the Dankhart Family." Dankhart was the name of the person his parents were working with on the other side of the island.

Angus settled the book on the desk in front of him, and the holographic storyteller began to speak again.

"Like a plague of scurvy dogs, the Dankharts drifted to the shores of Imbur Island many years ago and, sadly, decided to stay. Worthless mongrels and cheats, the Dankharts were driven by their greedy desire for riches and power, and set about collecting both in disgusting amounts—not caring who they trampled on to get what they wanted!"

Oswald Blott paused here to mop his sweaty brow with a spotted handkerchief. Angus waited impatiently for him to continue, hoping that the storyteller was talking about different Dankharts than the ones his mum and dad were currently staying with.

But before he could find out any more, the door opened behind him. Angus snapped the book shut and shoved it hastily back over to the far side of Principal Dark-Angel's desk, hoping she wouldn't notice it had been moved.

"I'm afraid I will have to cut our little chat short, Angus," the principal said as she crossed the room toward him.

Angus was surprised to see that she was carrying a

bucket. She heaved it up onto her desk, sloshing quite a bit of water and several tadpoles over the side.

"A serious matter has just arisen that requires my full attention. But before you go, I understand from Gudgeon that he was forced to release a storm globe upon your departure from the ferry port this morning. I'm sure you must be wondering why."

Angus stared at Principal Dark-Angel. The truth was, he'd hardly given any thought to the sinister figures who had been following them.

"There are those on this island, Angus, who would go to any lengths to steal our most precious and powerful weather secrets," she explained. "But you need not worry about such despicable thieves at Perilous. You will be perfectly safe here."

She made a move back toward the door and then paused, waiting for Angus to follow.

"Edmund Croxley is waiting outside my office. He will make sure you learn your way around. Rooms have also been arranged for your stay with us. I trust you will find them comfortable. But if there is anything else you need, you have only to ask."

"Thanks very much, Principal," Angus said, suddenly remembering his manners.

"There is one last thing before you go." The principal hesitated as they reached the door. "For the time being, at least, I would prefer it if nobody else knew of your presence here. You will go by the name of Angus Doomsbury," she said. "If everyone finds out that we have an extra McFangus staying at Perilous, they'll all be inviting their families over, and we simply haven't got the facilities here to deal with it. This is an Exploratorium, not a vacation resort. I'm sure you understand."

Angus wasn't sure he understood any of it very clearly. But Principal Dark-Angel had already turned back toward her desk and the waiting bucket of tadpoles. And he left her office with more to think about than the time Uncle Max had crashed a portable frigidarium into the Windmill, showering it in hundreds of lethal icicles.

4

PERILOUS

Angus was met outside the principal's office by Edmund Croxley. Tall, gangly, and exceedingly pale, he was now wearing gray pants and a matching sweater, upon which an impressive FOG AFICIONADO badge was pinned. He also seemed to know the Exploratorium like the back of his hand, and without a single word of introduction, he strode off in front of Angus with an air of supreme self-confidence.

"The first thing you ought to know about Perilous, Angus, is that it's an extremely dangerous place," Edmund announced happily as they walked down a chilly, dark hallway. Angus hurriedly pulled his coat on over his sweater to keep himself warm. "Never venture into any room unless you're sure what's behind the door, and always check under your bed for storm globes before you go to sleep at night."

"But . . . why would I need to check my bed for storm globes?" Angus asked, puzzled.

"Because not everyone at Perilous can be trusted to behave like an adult," Edmund said with a superior tone. "I had one hidden under my hot-water bottle once, and it went up like a rocket just as I was dropping off to sleep. It had to be chased out of my room with a pair of emergency weather bellows, and my curtains have never been the same since."

He led Angus up several flights of enormous stone stairs until they reached an octagonal hall. The hall was like the entrance to a grand museum, with polished marble floors and cool white pillars that stretched all the way up to a golden domed ceiling high above. It also appeared to be empty, apart from eight solid-looking doors set deep into the impressive walls.

"You are now standing at the very heart of Perilous," Edmund announced importantly, his badge gleaming.

"What goes on behind these doors has been a closely guarded secret for almost three hundred and fifty years now. This, Angus, is where the lightning catchers work. You name it, the lightning catchers have studied it, bottled it, picked it apart, and sent it packing."

Angus had a sudden image of a very angry blizzard being squashed inside a large wooden crate and sent back to Greenland or Siberia or wherever it had come from.

"I've still got two more years before I qualify, of course," Edmund said, staring down his nose at Angus. "But as soon as I get my bolts, I daresay the other lightning catchers will be strapping me into a hurricane suit and sending me out to do some crucial research into wind."

Angus quickly stifled a grin. He was beginning to understand why someone had hidden a storm globe under Edmund's hot-water bottle. "What do you mean, when you get your bolts?" he asked as soon as he could control his face again.

"Every lightning catcher is awarded a number of lightning bolts when he or she completes training at Perilous, depending on how well they do in their final examinations," Edmund explained. "One bolt enables you to work in the forecasting department or to try your hand at some research into the twisting patterns of tornadoes and that sort of thing. Two bolts gets you a position up on the roof, measuring sunshine hours, hurricane howls, and the flakiness of snow. And only those with three bolts or more are allowed to work with experiments, inventions, and with lightning itself. I am, of course, expecting the full three bolts."

Angus tried to imagine what sort of exams a lightning catcher might have to sit through before earning the right to work with lightning. He had a feeling it involved something a lot more dangerous than answering a load of questions on a sheet of paper.

"Normally you wouldn't be allowed up here, of course," Edmund continued, "but seeing as how you missed the tour this afternoon with everyone else . . ."

"Er . . . everyone else?" Angus asked, puzzled again.

"All new trainees, or lightning cubs, are given a tour of the Octagon when they first arrive at Perilous," Edmund explained impatiently, "but as you turned up much later than all the others . . ."

Angus stared at Edmund and blinked.

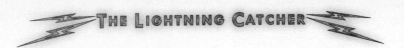

"Are you all right?" Edmund asked, frowning down at him. "You look a bit pale all of a sudden."

"Sorry, but did you just say that—that I'm going to train to be a lightning catcher?" Angus asked, hardly daring to believe that he'd heard this correctly.

"Naturally. Principal Dark-Angel herself asked me to give you a guided tour of the Octagon; she thought it might be wise to make sure you knew your way around. Look, you aren't about to be sick, are you?" Edmund asked, eyeing him warily. "Only we had a boy this afternoon who got an upset stomach all over the experimental division. It caused quite a mess, I can tell you. Bits of partially digested carrot splattered everywhere."

Angus felt his own stomach do several excited somersaults, followed by some extremely queasy swoops, but decided to keep this information to himself.

"I feel fine, thanks," he said.

"Well, if you're certain, then. . . ." Edmund kept a healthy distance from him all the same. "I think we'll start our tour in the experimental division. We should be safe enough in there at this time of the evening."

Angus followed Edmund through the first of the eight

doors, his head spinning. He was going to be a trainee lightning catcher! He was going to learn how to tame blizzards, talk to typhoons, and catch frogs in jars as they fell from the skies, and his heart began to thud against the walls of his chest with excitement at the thought of it. From the second that he'd heard all about Philip Starling, Edgar Perilous, and the rest of the early lightning catchers, he'd been imagining himself standing at the top of London's tallest lightning tower, wild and ferocious storms crashing about the skies all around him. And now he was actually going to follow in their brilliant, amazing, and highly dangerous footsteps.

He wondered for an instant why Principal Dark-Angel hadn't bothered mentioning this startling fact to him in her office. But the question vanished from his mind once he saw what lay on the other side of the door.

Unlike the Octagon, with its marbled floors and domed ceilings, the experimental division was in a very sorry state of repair, with deep gouges in the walls, large cracks that ran the full length of the floor, and water leaking from an exposed copper pipe beneath their feet. It wasn't hard to see why no one had bothered to fix any of these problems, for the experimental division was exactly like Uncle Max's workshop, only on a much bigger scale.

Angus was hit immediately by the familiar smell of scorched oil and steam, and he grinned. Everywhere he looked there were strange machines and fascinating inventions; some were old and rusted, while others were quietly stewing with menace. Several of Uncle Max's finest inventions, including his hailstone hurler, had been polished and placed under bright spotlights like the prize exhibits at a museum, and he wondered why he had never noticed before just how many of his uncle's inventions were weather related. He also realized, with another rush of excitement, that Uncle Max must be a fully qualified lightning catcher himself—with at least three lightning bolts to his name.

"I would advise you not to touch anything while we're in the experimental division, Angus," Edmund warned over his shoulder as they made their way into the long room. "It might also be a good idea to keep any breathing you have to do to an absolute minimum, just to be on the safe side. You never know what might be lurking in the air, toxic miasmas, poisonous fogs, infectious odors. . . .

The whole Exploratorium had to be evacuated only last week after a foul stink extractor allowed dangerous levels of sweaty-sock concentrate to escape back into the air."

Angus took a deep gulp of air before they went any deeper into the room, hoping that he hadn't just swallowed an infectious odor himself.

At the far end of the experimental division, a group of men and women were busy working on what looked like an enormous vacuum cleaner. It had a long suction pipe at the front and a gigantic collection bag, which resembled the body of a massive spider, behind it.

"What is that thing?"Angus asked nervously as they drew closer to it.

"Ah, now, that is one of our most sophisticated storm vacuums," Edmund declared as though he himself had invented it. "I have it on very good authority that it can suck up several small blizzards and a medium-sized gale before the bag has to be emptied. But the storm vacuum is just one of the many ingenious inventions created by our excellent team in the experimental division, as you will learn in the course of your studies."

Angus felt a small thrill of nerves shiver through him

at the mention of studies and grinned quietly to himself.

"My own personal favorite is the cloud-busting rocket launcher," Edmund continued, pointing to a large machine to their left, which had a giant harpoon attached to the front of it.

"What does it do?" Angus asked eagerly.

"Well, I don't wish to get too technical on your first day here, Angus, but the rocket launcher dissolves clouds. It simply melts them away with a bit of help from some silver iodide crystals and the basic laws of attraction. Only last year, in fact, it was used to disperse a very nasty storm that was threatening to spoil a sample-gathering operation by our rough weather research team. If all else fails, however, a storm snare must be used."

"A storm snare?" Angus asked.

Edmund Croxley pointed to a cabinet filled with antique-looking instruments, each shaped like a trumpet. "Storm snares can temporarily trap cloudbursts, thunderstorms, and almost any other type of weather you can think of. They're extremely rare and highly unstable, however. Hardly anyone knows how to use them, due to the great risk of death involved. Principal Lightning Catcher

Dark-Angel is the only person at Perilous who owns one."

Angus was tempted to ask more about the deadly snares, but just then, there was a very threatening *thump* from the far end of the room, and Edmund came to an abrupt halt, causing Angus to walk straight into him.

"Ah." Edmund turned pale as a second even louder *THUMP* followed the first and the storm vacuum burst noisily to life, causing several people to run for cover behind a pile of crates. "It seems the experimental team might be having a spot of bother with their suction valves. Perhaps, under the circumstances, we should just, um—"

Angus didn't wait for Edmund to finish his sentence. Years of living with his uncle at the Windmill had already taught him exactly what the thick clouds of black smoke now spewing out of the storm vacuum meant. He turned swiftly and tried to run toward the safety of the Octagon, but for some strange reason his legs appeared to be going backward.

"It's the storm vacuum!" Edmund yelled above the loud sucking noise that was beginning to fill the room. "Try to hold on to something, and whatever you do, don't let go!" He hooked his own fingers around the harpoon of the rocket launcher and closed his eyes tightly.

Angus quickly grabbed hold of a machine that appeared to be some sort of clobbering device for cracking hailstones—just as his feet were pulled out from beneath him and his body was dragged backward by the enormous sucking power of the vacuum. He hung on, his knuckles turning white with the effort.

"Bother!" Edmund shouted as something silver shot past Angus at high speed and disappeared into the vacuum. "There goes my fog aficionado badge!"

It wasn't the only thing to disappear, either. Every loose nut and bolt in the room was now flying toward the greedy vacuum like a shower of metallic rain. Angus ducked, trying to shield his head, as several wrenches went sailing past, along with a vicious-looking collection of jagged saws. He was almost knocked senseless by a heavy metal sundial, managing to swerve out of its path just in the nick of time.

The sundial proved to be too much for the vacuum, however. There was a horrible crunching sound as it disappeared into the spiderlike body, and then, all of a sudden, the vacuum ground to a halt. Angus fell to the floor in a heap—

"Ooof!"

And the room was quiet once again.

"Well, I think perhaps we'd better try a different department to begin with, after all." Edmund picked himself up off the floor and hastily straightened his sweater. "I'm sure you get the gist of things in here, and that's the important thing." And he bundled Angus swiftly back into the Octagon before the storm vacuum could start sucking again.

Hard on their heels was a man who had clearly been much closer to the vicious machine when it had gone wrong. Tall and beefy, with a stiff mane of blond hair that had been sucked back into a point, he was busy repositioning a greasy-looking monocle over his right eye. His left eye looked oddly round, as if his eyelid had been dragged back into the socket by the sheer force of the vacuum.

"What are you two looking at?" the man snapped, glaring at them both. "And what are you doing sneaking about the experimental division at this time of night?"

Edmund Croxley bristled. "I'll have you know that we are here by special permission of Principal Dark-Angel herself, and my name is Edmund Croxley, if you'd care to check that with her."

"And what about you, boy?" the man said, turning his attention swiftly to Angus. "What's your name?"

"Er . . . D-Doomsbury, sir," Angus said, remembering only just in time that he was not allowed to reveal his real name to anyone.

"Doomsbury, eh?" The man eyed him suspiciously. "Any relation to those money-grabbing Doomsburys who own the secondhand rubber boot store in town?"

"I—I don't think so, sir," Angus said truthfully.

The man glared at him for a few seconds longer before apparently losing all interest in them both. He then disappeared down the stairs without a backward glance.

"Who was that?" Angus asked, untangling himself from his coat.

"I'm afraid that was our new librarian, Mr. Knurling," Edmund explained. "He started today, as a matter of fact. Unfriendly sort of fellow, though. Doesn't seem to like lightning cubs terribly much, or books either, for that matter."

"What happened to the old librarian?" Angus asked, curious.

"He sold a rare book on ancient Egyptian wind socks to

a rich collector and retired to a beach house on the other side of the island. Now, if you'll follow me, Angus," he added, marching purposefully toward another of the doors in the Octagon, "I think we'll try the research department next."

The research department resembled an overstuffed archive and consisted of shelf after dusty shelf of old weather records and parchments, some of which dated all the way back to the days of Edgar Perilous and Philip Starling. Angus followed Edmund through the maze of crumbling records, resisting the urge to sneeze, and was eventually allowed to drag one of the weighty tomes off the shelves and study it for himself. He discovered that on November 3, 1887, the weather on Imbur had been behaving in a most peculiar manner, with a light scattering of pea-green hailstones falling just before lunchtime.

The next stop on their guided tour was the forecasting department. Angus almost fell headlong into a large vat of cold rice pudding as soon as they entered the room.

"Ah, yes, I should have warned you about the vats," Edmund apologized, "but it can't be helped, I'm afraid.

Rice pudding is a highly reliable substance for measuring humidity."

There were also mechanical pinecones of every shape and size, long strings of seaweed hanging from the ceiling, and a collection of small hedgehogs, bedded down in boxes of comfy-looking straw, all of which, Edmund explained, could tell when it was about to rain. There were submarine-type periscopes for observing unusual weather fronts and a weather cannon, situated on the roof directly above, which delivered an instant forecast to the islanders, every hour, on the hour, with an explosion of different-colored sparks.

At ten o'clock precisely, Angus felt the whole department shake as the rooftop weather cannon dispensed its latest forecast. He also caught a brief glimpse of some impressive purple and lilac sparks through a skylight above their heads—which, according to Edmund, meant they were in for a night of thick fog and chilly sea breezes.

The next door led them directly from the Octagon to a narrow set of steel steps, at the top of which was a round trapdoor leading up to the roof. But at Perilous there were none of the usual chimneys, bird's nests, or ancient television antennas that cling to the top of most people's houses. The entire area had been transformed instead into a large, flat, open-air weather station and was positively littered with wind socks, thermometers, and giant copper funnels for collecting rainwater or anything else that fell from the skies. Angus spotted a whole row of glass jars filled to the brim with frogs and tadpoles.

"If we left the weather to its own devices, it would soon be misbehaving itself all over the place," Edmund explained pompously, "which is why the roof is manned twenty-four hours a day, three hundred and sixty-five days of the year, including Christmas. In the summer months, it doesn't get dark on Imbur until well past eleven o'clock, of course, due to its northerly position, which can be exceedingly useful when you're on the lookout for any tricky twilight toads."

Angus stared, his mouth hanging open as they walked past a four-person weather balloon that was tethered to a post by a thick rope. The basket underneath the balloon was obviously being restocked with generous quantities of food and a baffling array of weather instruments. He also caught a tantalizing glimpse of a comfortable-looking bed inside, a small cast iron stove, and a claw-footed bathtub.

The roof was also the best place from which to see the rest of the island, Angus realized as they reached the safety railings at the edge, and he was met by the most incredible sight he'd ever seen in his life. Up until that moment, he'd been picturing Perilous as some sort of old-fashioned college. But now, as he peered over the railings, he could clearly see that the Exploratorium was an enormous stone building that looked like a cross between an ancient monastery and a grand palace. It sat on top of its own tall tooth of rock, which stuck up oddly from the fields and meadows surrounding it like a solitary skyscraper.

Angus gazed out across the mysterious island, his head swimming with the wonder of it all. To the west, he could see deep forests and snow-capped mountains gleaming in the late twilight. Directly below them—a very, very long way down—was a small town, which, according to Edmund Croxley, was called Little Frog's Bottom.

To the east, a large bank of fog was drifting across the sea, threatening to engulf Perilous.

"You'll be learning how to correctly identify all seventeen different types of fog, of course," Edmund said as they made their way back toward the trapdoor a few minutes later.

"There're seventeen different types of fog?" Angus asked, amazed.

"That's all we've identified so far. There could be others lurking about in the Imbur marshes, I suppose, but there's no need to panic, Angus. You'll be starting off with some simple ones first, such as freezing fogs, spooky fogs, and knee-high fogs," Edmund said, counting them off on his fingers. "Once you've gotten to grips with the basics of droplet densities, you'll be moving straight on to wispy fogs, wet-dog fogs, and amusing fogs—"

"Amusing fogs?" Angus interrupted.

"An amusing fog reaches right to the back of your throat and tickles your tonsils, making you cough and laugh at the same time. But it's nothing compared to the magnificent splendors of the great invisible fog itself."

"But if it's invisible, how do you even know you've seen it?" Angus asked, surprised.

"Well, I don't wish to boast, but when it comes to fog, I am something of an expert," Edmund declared, puffing his chest out proudly, and Angus couldn't help noticing

a tear in his sweater where his fog aficionado badge had been pinned—before the storm vacuum swallowed it. "Someone with my experience can spot an invisible fog with his eyes shut. If you young lightning cubs run into difficulties, however, you can always turn to the *McFangus Fog Guide* for some useful tips and hints."

Angus almost tripped over the weather cannon in surprise. "The what guide, sorry?"

"The *McFangus Fog Guide* teaches you how to identify the different types of fog and their individual characteristics. For instance, according to the McFangus guide, the fog that is approaching Perilous at this moment is a wispy fog. It has a slight smell of peppermint about it and has a tendency to make your eyebrows curl into extremely tight ringlets."

Angus glanced sideways at Edmund, whose eyebrows were indeed beginning to show the first signs of curling, and he grinned. He couldn't believe that fog could do such amazing things. Or that his mum and dad had written a whole fog guide without even telling him.

"Well, I think that's quite enough for one day," Edmund declared, glancing at his watch five minutes later as they stood once again in the Octagon. "I've still got an assignment to finish on the weather patterns of the Himalayan mountains. I just have to collect a map or two from the research department while we're here, then I'll show you to your room."

"But what about the other four departments?" Angus asked, glancing at the doors they had yet to venture through and feeling slightly disappointed.

"Oh, I wouldn't waste your time worrying about any of those," Edmund said dismissively. "There's nothing but the sanatorium through here—" He opened the first of the doors, and Angus caught a quick peek of a stark white interior and a whiff of disinfectant before Edmund closed the door again.

"Then there's the supplies department. They look after rubber boots, weatherproof gear, that sort of thing."

He flung open the second door, and Angus could just see a long hallway lined with crates, boxes, and some very orderly looking shelves.

"There's the Inner Sanctum of Perplexing Mysteries and Secrets, of course, but nothing very interesting ever happens in there."

The door to the Inner Sanctum had three extra locks on it, Angus noticed with interest. Edmund did not attempt to open it.

"And then there's the Lightnarium, strictly out of bounds to everyone except the lightning catchers themselves, and I would strongly advise you to stay well clear of it, Angus, unless you want to find yourself on the next ferry back to the mainland. Principal Dark-Angel sent two trainees packing just for sticking their heads around that door. Yes, you might get the odd burn or mangled leg from working in the experimental division," Edmund added importantly, "but what lies behind the door to the Lightnarium is deadly. Even I'm not allowed in there without a fully qualified lightning catcher by my side."

"But . . . what do the lightning catchers do in there?"

"Well, among other things, Angus, they produce enough power from their experiments to light the entire Exploratorium." Edmund pointed to a number of narrow fissures running through the walls and ceiling, which up until that moment Angus had been far too preoccupied to notice. Shaped like jagged bolts of lightning, the fissures sparked and flickered with lights that infused the entire Octagon with a warm yellow glow. "I think you'll find that light fissures are far more effective than normal lamps and candles," said Edmund.

And with that, he disappeared into the research department to collect his maps, and the Octagon went quiet. Angus marveled at the glowing bolts and rippled veins of light for a long moment. Then he took a step closer to the Lightnarium and frowned. Unlike all the other doors in the marbled hall, this particular one had been decorated with a figure in fine gold leaf. The figure had obviously faded over the years until it was now barely visible, but as Angus inspected it closely, he realized, with a start, that it looked strangely familiar.

The figure was shaped like a fire dragon, and every curl of flame, every fiery scale on its body, was exactly like the dragon he'd dreamed about.

He took a step closer to the door, curious, wondering how something that had appeared inside his head could have anything to do with Perilous or the lightning catchers— which, up until two hours ago, he'd never even heard of.

He stared at the golden dragon, touching the faded image carefully with his fingers, almost expecting it to feel hot. Then he moved closer and pressed his ear to the door. From somewhere deep within the Lightnarium, he could hear a strange sort of rumbling noise, like a herd of elephants stampeding down a hill, or a runaway steamroller squashing a row of bicycles. He could also hear the sounds of running footsteps and of people shouting urgently to one another. Something dangerous was about to happen, he suddenly felt sure of it, he could feel the force of it getting ready to burst through the door and squash him flat—

Angus gasped and backed away from the door, putting as much distance between himself and the Lightnarium as possible. He decided to wait for Edmund on the farthest side of the marbled hall.

Five minutes later, to his immense relief, Angus found himself being led away from the Octagon, down a steep spiral staircase and then along a curved hallway.

"The girls' rooms are through there," Edmund announced, pointing to a door that separated them from the other end of the hallway. "And are strictly out-of-bounds to all boys, of course. But this is your room." They stopped outside another door.

"Thanks for showing me around," Angus said.

"Happy to oblige, Angus, happy to oblige. Just remember my advice about checking your bed for storm globes, and you can't go far wrong. Now I really must finish that essay. . . ."

Edmund turned and strode quickly along the curved hallway and disappeared round a bend.

Angus opened the door to his new room and went inside, yawning. The room was small and cozy, with a dome-shaped ceiling just like the one in the Octagon, only on a much smaller scale. There was a heavy wooden bed in the corner, a fire burning brightly in a small fireplace, and a thick rug covering the stone floor. Several light fissures crackled and sparked overhead.

He kicked off his soggy shoes and flopped down on his bed, suddenly feeling weary. There was a hot plate of delicious stew and dumplings on his bedside table. He ate the stew hungrily, then sank back into his soft pillows and barely had time to wonder about the Lightnarium, his parents, or what was going to happen to him in the morning before exhaustion finally overtook him. And he fell into a deep, dream-free sleep.

5

THE WEATHER TUNNEL

The next morning, Angus was woken up suddenly by a clanging bell. He sat bolt upright in his bed, confused, wondering for a brief moment where he was. He stumbled out of bed, feeling dazed.

Daylight was streaming in through a small window. He pressed his nose against the glass. In the distance he could see snow-covered mountains. A slow grin spread across his face as he remembered that he was now a trainee lightning catcher.

He stared around the room, nerves tingling. A large pile of clothes had been left on a chair in front of the fire. Placed on top of these clothes was a note written on ivory paper. Angus rubbed the sleep out of his eyes, unfolded the note, and tried to focus on the words.

Please put on __all__ of the clothes provided and report to the lightning catcher at the end of your hallway as soon as the second bell has been rung. You should also sign the declaration attached to this note.

Angus set the instructions to one side and studied the clothes nervously. There was a pair of pants and a matching sweater in dark gray wool, with a white shirt and yellow tie, all of which looked fairly ordinary. He dressed himself quickly, then hesitated. The rest of the clothes in the pile were anything but ordinary. But the note had been quite clear. Therefore, with some difficulty, he pulled on a shiny weatherproof coat, which fell well below his knees like a vast yellow poncho. There was also a thick pair of black rubber boots; a waterproof hat (which covered his ears and half his face); a pair of gloves; a knitted scarf that was smothered in woolly lightning bolts (also in yellow); and a pair of fluffy blue earmuffs.

Angus picked up the instructions again and found the declaration he was supposed to sign. He unfolded the sheet of paper and read:

I, the undersigned, hereby understand that catching lightning bolts and giant hailstones without proper supervision is likely to result in my own extremely painful death, and I therefore agree never to attempt it.

Angus swallowed hard. If he hadn't already felt the full sucking force of the storm vacuum on his guided tour of the Octagon the night before, he would have been convinced that the declaration was somebody's idea of a joke. But there was something dangerous in the very air at Perilous. What was it Edmund Croxley had warned him about—toxic miasmas, poisonous fogs, and infectious odors? A sudden vision of the mysterious fire dragon on the door to the Lightnarium also flashed into his thoughts, but he quickly shook it off again. He didn't have time to think about any of it now. The second bell could ring at any second, and he wanted to be ready for it. He read the rest of the declaration, feeling distinctly clammy.

▲　▲　▲

I also understand that there is a big possibility that I will get my eyebrows singed, fingers squashed, ankles smashed, or elbows crushed during my time as a lightning cub, and that this will be nobody's fault but my own. If I had listened to the safety instructions issued by the lightning catchers in the first place, it never would have happened.

So let that be a lesson to me.

Finally, I agree never to divulge any of the weather secrets I will be learning to anyone outside of the Exploratorium, even if they offer to do my homework for the next seven years.

Angus found a pen on a small desk in the corner of his room; he wondered for a moment if he ought to sign the declaration with his real name or the one he'd been forced to adopt by Principal Dark-Angel. And in the end, he scribbled down something so illegible it looked like he was now called Angus Von Dungbeetle.

He stuffed the declaration into one of his voluminous pockets and was just about to venture out into the hall, to see if anyone else was waiting for the second bell to ring, when his fingers touched a small square box at the bottom of his pocket.

The box looked exactly like the kind that came from a jeweler's shop. He lifted the lid cautiously and peered inside it—half expecting to find some dangerous weather instrument he would be expected to use later. Instead it contained the most amazing watch he'd ever seen in his life.

A note had been stuck to the inside of the box. It read:

Your weather watch is a highly valuable piece of equipment. You are permitted to remove it in the shower building and during your monsoon training only. If you are caught without it at any other time, you will find yourself on boot-cleaning duty for the rest of the year. You have been warned.

Angus grinned. Uncle Max had made him a screaming alarm clock for Christmas once, but the weather watch was even more magnificent. It had a built-in thermometer, compass, and barometer, as well as an ordinary clock for telling the time. At that precise moment, tiny silvery clouds were scudding across this shiny face, partially obscuring a dazzling golden sun. Angus stared at the clouds in awe. Then he fiddled with the hour hand, watching carefully as the sun began to set and a luminous moon appeared in an inky black sky, followed by countless twinkling stars. He had just enough time to make out the minute constellations of Orion and the Plough before several shooting stars shot suddenly across the horizon, leaving a trail of sparkling dust.

"WOW!" he gasped, watching the brilliant spectacle before setting the watch back to the correct time again.

He turned it over then, and was surprised to find that his real name, Angus McFangus, had been engraved in sweeping, curly letters on the back. He slipped it onto his wrist quickly, hoping that no one else would ever see his name there and start asking questions for which he had absolutely no answers.

Two minutes later, the second bell rang. Angus opened his door and poked his head into the hallway, just in time to see half a dozen other lightning cubs emerging from their own rooms. The door that led to the girls' end of the hall was also open. He was extremely relieved to see that he wasn't the only one wearing a shiny yellow poncho. A girl with long hair the color of horse chestnuts was struggling to keep her own coat off the ground, and a short round boy with spectacles had been given a pair of extra-large earmuffs—which looked like they'd been made for an Indian elephant.

"Gather round quickly, everyone, we haven't got all morning!" came a loud voice, and Angus saw a tall man waiting for them at the foot of the spiral staircase. Dressed in his own yellow coat and rubber boots, he had a bushy mustache and a single eyebrow. Where the other eyebrow should have been, there was nothing but a shiny pink scar.

"First things first," he announced, smiling genially at them all. "I will collect your signed declaration forms, please."

There was a sudden scuffle of feet as everyone tried to hand him a form at once. Angus, at the back of the throng, noticed five impressive lightning bolts pinned to the front of the man's coat.

"Lightning Catcher Oliver Mint's the name," the man announced, stuffing the declarations into his pocket, "and

I'm here to get you started on your first day at Perilous. So, if you'll follow me . . ."

He led them away from the Octagon without any further explanation, then down into a series of long stone tunnels and passageways that crisscrossed Perilous like the rippling veins of a massive stone heart. Some of these tunnels were peppered with locked, rusting doors and dark, mysterious alcoves, while others were completely bare except for a few flickering light fissures, which crackled overhead. None had any windows, and Angus couldn't help shivering as they plunged deeper and deeper into the dark, twisting labyrinth.

They finally came to an abrupt halt outside a huge, round, steel-framed door set in the middle of a wall, with what looked like a steering wheel attached to the front of it.

"First thing tomorrow morning," Catcher Mint said as they gathered in front of him, "you will each be assigned to a lightning catcher and begin your training in one of the departments that you visited yesterday."

Angus crossed his fingers, hoping he didn't get assigned to the Lightnarium. Beside him, the boy in the extra-large earmuffs looked faintly sick.

"Before you begin your training, however, it is crucial that we test your weatherproof clothing for any faults, leaks, or hidden punctures. In a moment, I will be guiding you through the weather tunnel to do just that." He pointed to the round door behind him. "The tunnel is more commonly used to simulate the difficult and often dangerous weather conditions a lightning catcher may face, while coming to grips with wet sandstorms in the Sahara, for instance, or tackling ice fogs in the frozen north. Normally, you wouldn't be allowed inside it until you're a sixth-year lightning cub, but as we have been given special permission to use it by Principal Dark-Angel herself. . . ."

Angus gulped. Edmund Croxley had said something very similar on his guided tour of the Octagon—just seconds before a storm vacuum had tried to suck the hair off his head.

"Now if you'll all wait here, I will just make sure the weather tunnelers are ready for us."

Catcher Mint opened the round door with a twist and a tug, and before any of the lightning cubs could see what was lurking behind it, he'd pulled himself through and closed the door again with a loud *clunk*.

For a few moments, nobody spoke. Then, slowly, trainees all around began tightening their woolly scarves,
pulling up their socks inside their boots, and speaking
to one another with quiet apprehension. Angus tried
to calm the butterflies in his own stomach by glancing
around at his fellow lightning cubs for the first time.
There were nine others in all. And Angus couldn't help
wondering if any of them had been brought to the Isle of
Imbur by a bad-tempered lightning catcher in the middle
of the night.

"Hello," a voice suddenly said beside him, making him
jump.

Angus turned around to find the boy in the large earmuffs smiling at him warily. His face was round and
friendly, his deep green eyes hidden behind a pair of small
glasses. His hair was jet black and had obviously been cut
quite recently, with the aid of a mixing bowl and a pair of
blunt scissors. Angus liked him instantly.

"You weren't on the tour yesterday with everyone else,
were you?" the boy said.

"Um, no, I . . . got here a bit late," Angus explained,
hoping the boy wouldn't ask him why.

The boy turned faintly pink and grinned. "I'm Dougal Dewsnap."

"Angus . . . Doomsbury," Angus said, wondering if he'd ever get used to his new name.

"It's a bit different here, isn't it?" said Dougal. "My dad sent me because he says I need some gumption. I wanted to go to school on the mainland, but he wouldn't let me." Dougal grinned sheepishly. "What about you? Why are here?"

Angus hesitated. "Um, dealing with the weather sort of runs in our family," he eventually said.

Dougal nodded as if he understood this completely. "Which part of the island do you come from, anyway?"

"Actually, I live with my uncle in Devon."

"Really? You mean you're a mainlander?" Dougal looked deeply impressed.

Angus shrugged. "I . . . yeah, I suppose I am."

"Wow! I've read all about the mainland, of course, but I've never actually been off the island before. Dad says he'll take me on a holiday when I'm old enough, but I've been pestering him about Stonehenge and the Tower of London for ages now." Dougal grinned. "Nigel Ridgely says he comes from Yorkshire," he added, pointing to a pale, freckle-faced boy to their left. "Georgina Fox was born in Birmingham. But Millicent Nichols and Violet Quinn come from Little Frog's Bottom." He indicated a gaggle of girls who were standing together. "Do you know anyone else here yet?"

"Only Edmund Croxley and Principal Dark-Angel—"

"Well, I wouldn't go around bragging about it, Doomsbury." A voice interrupted them from behind.

Angus spun round to see two of the tallest lightning cubs, who had been standing on the far side of the group, turning toward them; both had the same thuggish features, thick eyebrows, and hairy, gorilla-like arms, and up close, it was obvious that they were twins.

"Just because dribbling old Dark-Angel invited you up to her office for a little chat, that doesn't make you special," the first twin spat, stopping only inches from Angus. "She probably thought you'd been sent to sweep her floor or something, so I wouldn't go getting all big-headed about it."

"I wasn't," Angus said, taking a step back. "How did you know I'd been up to her office anyway?"

"Our dad's one of the senior lightning catchers here, so

we hear about everything important that happens," the second twin sneered, dark eyes gleaming. "Everything that's worth knowing about, anyway, which is why no one's ever mentioned your name before, Dewsnap."

Dougal bristled. "Yeah, well, at least no one's going around calling me pea brain behind my back."

"Stop trying to be funny, Dewsnap, it doesn't suit you," the first twin said. "And just to teach you a lesson, you can clean my boots when we get to the end of the weather tunnel. I'd rather not get my hands dirty."

"In your dreams!" Dougal said, crossing his arms defiantly. "I'm not touching anything that's had your stinking feet inside it. Clean your own boots."

"You'll do what I say, Dewsnap." The first twin made a sudden lunge and shoved Dougal hard with one hand. Dougal stumbled backward and fell, his glasses skittering across the floor.

"Hey, pick those up, you idiot!" He scrambled back onto his feet again.

"I'm not touching anything that's been on your head." The twin mimicked Dougal's voice cruelly. "Pick them up yourself, Four Eyes, so you can see my boots properly when you're cleaning them. I'm serious, Dewsnap, you'd better do it—or else."

Both twins sniggered again, and Angus felt his temper boiling over. He scooped up the glasses before they got trodden on and handed them back to Dougal.

"Or else what?" he said, pulling himself up to his full height, wishing he was at least six inches taller. "You heard what Dougal said. He's going nowhere near your rotten boots."

A sudden hush descended. The other lightning cubs backed away, sensing trouble. The twins glared down at Angus with mean piggy eyes.

"Stay out of this, Doomsbury, it's got nothing to do with you."

"Maybe." Angus shrugged. "But I might just have another little chat with Principal Dark-Angel about it anyway. Plus I bet she'd be really interested to hear what you said about her being old and dribbling. She told me to pop up to her office any time I fancy a cup of tea," he bluffed, feeling reckless. "And I'm feeling really thirsty right now, as a matter of fact. . . ."

A flicker of doubt crossed the twin's ugly face. "Have it your own way then, Doomsbury. But I'd watch my

back from now if I were you," he said, threatening Angus with a hairy-knuckled finger. "Next time it'll be you sprawled across the floor, and your little friend Dewsnap might not be around to rescue you."

"Like we're scared!" Dougal glowered as both twins turned and stomped off, looking uglier than ever.

"Who are those two idiots?" Angus asked as soon as they were out of earshot.

"Pixie and Percival Vellum."

There was nothing remotely pixielike about either of them, Angus thought, staring over at the twins. Up until that moment he hadn't even realized that one of them was a girl.

"Not exactly friendly, are they?"

"They've been like that with everyone," Dougal said, inspecting his glasses carefully and giving them a gentle wipe on his sweater. "Just because their dad works in the Lightnarium, they think they own the place. Pity they haven't got a brain cell between them. A pair of chimps would make better trainee lightning catchers, if you ask me."

Angus grinned. "Are your glasses okay?"

"They're not even twisted. Thanks," Dougal added, turning pink with embarrassment.

A moment later, the round door opened behind them, and Catcher Mint began ushering them, one at a time, into the mouth of the weather tunnel.

Inside, the tunnel was vast, with a hard stone floor and a high arched ceiling that was covered, Angus noticed as he climbed nervously through the entrance, in a network of copper pipes and large wooden paddles. One of the paddles began to spin in a clockwise direction and a light breeze started to ruffle his earmuffs. In the distance, he could also see a long row of freshly laundered sheets, towels, and stripy thermal underwear flapping on a washing line.

"The first section of the tunnel is devoted to wind," Catcher Mint explained as soon as he'd sealed the door tightly behind them, "and is normally used for tornado training, hurricane suit testing, and the odd kite-flying competition. Today you will experience strong gale-force winds, measuring up to nine on the Beaufort wind scale, which will test the strength of the stitching on all your clothing. So make sure your coats are buttoned up tightly unless you want to find yourselves airborne."

The paddles above their heads began to gather momentum immediately, and before they'd made it even halfway across the tunnel, they were walking into a very stiff breeze. After another two minutes, the wind had somehow reached near gale force and it was almost impossible to stand upright. Angus battled his way into the fierce gusts, his head bent, his shoulders hunched. Several other lightning cubs were in much bigger trouble. Georgina Fox's coat had been blown inside out like a parachute, and she was now tumbling in the wrong direction. Dougal's earmuffs, already far too big for his head, were acting like a pair of fluffy wings and threatening to lift him off the ground completely.

Angus inched his way forward, one laborious step at a time. But finally, after what felt like several hours, he clambered through a round door at the other end of the tunnel and found himself standing in a small chamber, facing yet another door.

"Everybody make it?" the lightning catcher asked as the last of the windblown group finally appeared in the chamber. "Good, on to the next section, then. Follow me."

"How many sections do you reckon there are?" Dougal asked, looking worried.

The next section of the weather tunnel reminded Angus of a large greenhouse, and a blast of stifling heat hit him as soon as he stepped through the door, along with the heady smell of fresh compost. The tunnel was stuffed from floor to ceiling with large tropical palm trees, ferns, and exotic-looking flowers that were dripping pollen all over the floor. It was like being transported to the middle of a rain forest. A second later, torrential rain began falling from the ceiling.

"Keep moving, everybody!" Catcher Mint shouted happily above the deluge. "It's just a drop or two of water, nothing to worry about."

Within seconds, however, small warm rivers were running down the insides of Angus's rubber boots. The floor became a swirling torrent that tugged at his feet and tried to sweep him away. Nigel Ridgely and Violet Quinn, who had both taken off their hats as soon as they'd entered the hot tunnel, now looked like a pair of drowned rats.

The downpour stopped just as suddenly as it had started, and from somewhere overhead a baking hot sun began beating down on them instead. Angus undid the top buttons on his coat to stop himself from suffocating in the sudden heat, but the end of the tunnel was now, thankfully, in sight.

He was just about to climb through the round door that led to the next chamber when the girl with the horse-chestnut-colored hair shot in front of him and pushed him hastily to one side.

"Watch out!" she warned as a large, hairy coconut fell from an overhanging palm tree, narrowly missing them both. It smashed open on the ground, exactly where Angus had been standing just seconds before.

"Wow . . . thanks!" he gasped. "I owe you one for that. Er . . . sorry, but I don't even know your name—"

"It's Indigo. Indigo Midnight," the girl said quietly from beneath her rain hat. She gave him a brief, embarrassed smile, but before Angus could say anything else, she'd climbed through the round door and disappeared into the next chamber.

Angus stepped gingerly over the smashed coconut, trying not to imagine what would have happened to his head if it had made contact with the hard, hairy nut. Indigo had just saved him from a serious concussion, or worse.

The lightning cubs climbed through the next round

door and entered a desolate, boggy moor, complete with wet grass, thick mud, and dense, swirling fog that tasted like the bottom of a swamp. Progress was painfully slow as they tripped, stumbled, and squelched their way over the soggy ground. And Angus couldn't help wondering what treacherous conditions they would have to face next. Would they be thrown into the middle of a vicious thunderstorm? Would they be required to catch a lightning bolt in a tin cup, in order to test the strength of the rubber in their boots?

"I really hope not!" Dougal blanched when Angus plucked up the courage to voice his concerns a few moments later. "Nobody actually catches lightning bolts at Perilous anymore. It's forbidden."

"But . . . what about the Lightnarium? Don't they experiment with lightning in there?"

"Yeah, but that's different, it's all controlled and deliberate in the Lightnarium." Dougal stumbled in the fog. "It's not like catching lightning bolts from a real live thunderstorm like they used to back in the olden days."

"Then why did they make us sign a declaration saying we wouldn't attempt to catch any on our own?" Angus

asked, not sure if he felt slightly disappointed or highly relieved by this unexpected news.

"Who knows?" Dougal shrugged. "All I know for sure is that there was some sort of horrible accident years and years ago, down in the lightning vaults, and since then, nobody at Perilous has been allowed to catch them."

"The lightning vaults?" Angus asked.

"Yeah, when the Exploratorium was first built, Philip Starling and Edgar Perilous wanted to discover everything they could about lightning and how to control the stuff, you know, stop it from destroying any more towns and cities. They weren't crazy enough to build any lightning towers here on Imbur, though, especially after what happened with the Great Fire, so they had the lightning vaults tunneled deep inside Perilous instead," Dougal said, wiping his foggy spectacles with his sleeve. "They did loads of seriously dangerous experiments down there, blasting storms into a thousand pieces. They also had the biggest collection of fulgurites in the world."

Thanks to Uncle Max, Angus already knew that fulgurites were formed when a bolt of lightning struck sand, melting the grains together and leaving a perfect cast of a lightning bolt behind.

"There was also supposed to be something really dangerous in the vaults," Dougal added with a gulp. "Something huge and horrible that nobody could control."

"Like what?" Angus asked, shivering.

"Haven't got a clue," Dougal said. "But I do know there was a terrible accident one night, somebody died, and the vaults were sealed up forever. Actually, we're not supposed to know the vaults even exist. I only know about them because I overheard my dad talking to Principal Dark-Angel once, ages ago. Dad's the only historian on the island these days," he explained, lowering his voice to a whisper. "He's written loads of books about the terrible turnip blight of 1899 and stuff like that. Anyway, he was asked to write a modern history of Perilous, and Principal Dark-Angel came to the house one night to give him some background information, and she just started talking about the vaults. I was sitting on the stairs, and I accidentally overheard her talking. I don't suppose I—"

"*GRRRRRRR!*"

"What was that?" Angus stopped dead in his tracks, feeling all the hairs on the back of his neck stand up on end.

"I dunno." Dougal gulped beside him. "But whatever it

was, it didn't sound very . . . vegetarian, did it?"

A moment later, Catcher Mint had gathered them all together into a tight group, a worried expression on his face.

"Sorry about the growling, everyone," he said, hastily doing a head count. "I was under the impression that the fog yeti had been shipped back to its natural habitat, in the freezing marshes, but well . . . perhaps we'd better just get to the other end of the tunnel before I say any more." He glanced over his shoulder warily. "It's probably best if you don't go wandering off by yourselves under the circumstances . . . just in case it hasn't had breakfast yet."

"Breakfast?" Dougal spluttered as they moved off again, at a much quicker pace. "They've sent us in here with a yeti that hasn't had its breakfast yet?"

"What is a fog yeti?" Angus asked, not entirely sure he wanted to know.

"It looks a lot like Dewsnap." Percival Vellum snickered. "Only without the stupid specs."

"You're so hilarious, Vellum. I'm splitting my sides with laughter." Dougal frowned as the twins pushed roughly past.

The fog continued to grow thicker and thicker, swirling around them until eventually Angus could hardly see his own hand in front of his face.

"So what happened about the lightning vaults, anyway?" he asked the dense patch of fog beside him, which he was fairly certain was still occupied by Dougal.

"Oh . . . yeah, well, my dad wasn't allowed to put any of the stuff Principal Dark-Angel told him in his book."

"Can we go and look at them?" asked Angus eagerly.

"That's just the thing," Dougal said. "They've been lost for so many years now that nobody knows where they are. My dad thinks they were never real in the first place, though. He says they're probably just another Perilous myth, like the *Forgotten Book of Grudge-Bearing Blizzards.*"

Dougal's voice was suddenly drowned out by another bloodcurdling growl that seemed to fill the entire tunnel. This one sounded much closer than the last. The fog parted for a second, and Angus caught a brief glimpse of an apelike creature stalking along behind them. It was vast, hairy, and unmistakably yeti shaped. Angus and Dougal both broke into a sprint as the end of the tunnel came into view up ahead of them.

In the next section of the tunnel, they were plunged into a frozen wasteland of deep snow, slippery ice, and forbidding rocks. Angus, who was still drenched from their experience in the rain forest and who had already been chilled to the bone by the dense fog, could now feel his toes freezing inside his boots as flurries of thick white snow swirled around them.

Nobody spoke much in the freezing tunnel. Angus kept his head down against the wild wind, half expecting to stumble across a hungry polar bear at any minute. Thankfully, the only wildlife he encountered was a small colony of blue penguins, who were all huddled together behind a large igloo. He was forced to dive sideways suddenly as a team of husky dogs came hurtling out of nowhere, pulling a large sleigh piled high with cold-looking lightning catchers dressed in yellow coats.

"Where did they come from?" he gasped, brushing himself off as the sleigh disappeared into the snow once again.

"That's one of the polar expedition teams," Catcher Mint explained, helping several other trainees onto their feet.

"They come in here to acclimatize for a week or two before setting off to study glacial rainbows and ice storms, among other things. Lightning cubs do not start dogsled training until their sixth year. You will, however, learn a great deal about snow. For example, snow is formed in the lowest part of the earth's atmosphere, called the troposphere, where up to two hundred ice crystals gather around a single speck of dirt, eventually creating a snowflake. But don't be fooled by snowball fights and snowmen," he warned. "A snowstorm is one of the most hazardous conditions you will ever work in as fully qualified lightning catchers. There will be avalanches to deal with, invisible snow holes, giant twelve-sided snowflakes. . . ."

Angus glanced warily above his head, imagining a snowflake the size of a mattress falling from the skies.

"If you ever get caught out in a sudden blizzard, you will find an emergency pair of inflatable snowshoes rolled up and tucked under the cuff of your rubber boots," Catcher Mint continued. "The shoes inflate automatically when placed on your feet. Shaped like the head of a tennis racket, they help distribute your weight over a wider surface area, preventing you from sinking into the deepest drifts."

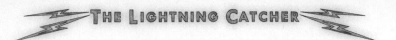

"He could have told us about those earlier," Dougal grumbled.

As they finally reached the end of the frozen wasteland, both Angus and Dougal were extremely pleased to discover it was also the end of the treacherous weather tunnel itself.

"Anyone with faulty earmuffs or leaky coats should report to me now," Catcher Mint said as a collective sigh of relief swept around the chamber. "Those of you needing rubber boot repair kits should go straight up to the supplies department. The rest of you can take the stairs on your right and down to the kitchens for some well-earned breakfast!"

Angus and Dougal headed straight for the staircase, before Catcher Mint could decide to send them back through the tunnel again.

The kitchens themselves were vast, with several fireplaces and two long serving tables set against the far wall, both of which were stacked high with great tureens of porridge, mountains of toast, and a giant pyramid of sausages and bacon. A gaggle of cooks was rolling dough and frying eggs next to the roaring open fires, and a number of impressive pillars shaped like palm trees stretched all the way up to the vaulted ceiling.

Angus and Dougal found an empty table and peeled off their weatherproof coats with numb fingers, feeling immensely hungry all of a sudden.

"If that's what they make us do on our first day here, we'll be wrestling polar bears with our bare hands by the end of the week," Dougal predicted, stabbing a mound of juicy sausages with a fork. "I thought we'd be doing a lot more reading—you know, studying the science of weather and that sort of thing."

"I'm just glad we didn't have to wrestle the fog yeti with our bare hands," said Angus, piling his own plate with bacon and feeling that his first morning as a lightning cub had definitely lived up to his expectations.

6

DANKHART

Angus discovered the following morning that he'd been assigned to a lightning catcher in the experimental division by the name of Sparks. Two other trainees would work with them: Dougal Dewsnap and Indigo Midnight, the girl who had saved him from a falling coconut. And it was Indigo who stepped forward briskly and knocked on the door to the experimental division to announce their arrival, before Angus and Dougal had even made it across the marbled floor of the Octagon.

"She's a bit enthusiastic, isn't she?" Dougal said, surprised. "Mind you, that could turn out to be a good thing in this place."

"What do you mean?" Angus asked, hurriedly scraping a stray blob of marmalade off his new tie.

"Well, with any luck, Indigo might volunteer for anything dangerous, and then we might graduate with all our limbs intact. It's odd, though. I've got a feeling I know her from somewhere." Dougal frowned, staring at Indigo as she hovered by the door. "I recognized her name as soon as I heard it yesterday, I just can't remember why. . . ."

At that moment, a harassed-looking lightning catcher answered the door with what appeared to be a tall copper funnel strapped to the top of his head.

"Yes, what is it?"

"Er." Angus faltered, trying hard not to stare at the funnel. "We're supposed to come and find Catcher Sparks. We're the new lightning cubs."

"Names?"

"Dougal Dewsnap, Indigo Midnight, and Angus Doomsbury," said Angus, still feeling self-conscious about his false name and flushing as he said it.

The lightning catcher's eyes, however, had fallen on Dougal, and they narrowed instantly with suspicion.

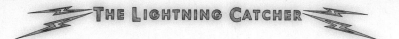

"Oh, it's you again, is it?" he said in a haughty tone. "I've got something for you."

He ducked behind the door and reappeared two seconds later with a brown paper bag.

"Just in case you feel like throwing up all over one of our machines again," he said, thrusting it toward Dougal. And Angus realized that it must have been Dougal who'd had an upset stomach on his tour of the experimental division. "Wait here while I fetch Catcher Sparks," the lightning catcher added, slamming the door in their faces.

"They really know how to make you feel welcome around here, don't they?" Dougal held the bag at arm's length with a disgusted look on his face.

The lightning catcher who came out to meet them a few minutes later was only marginally more friendly. Her long black hair was fastened tightly into a bun. She was dressed in a sturdy woolen shirt and matching leggings and a curious, close-fitting leather jacket—which looked tough enough to withstand a cannon blast. The jacket, which fell to her knees and had ten buckle fastenings up the front, had no sleeves or collar and was covered in stitched-up rips and tears, which looked like badly healed scars. There were six impressive lightning bolts pinned to her belt, Angus noticed as she stopped to consult a clipboard.

"What's that leather thing she's wearing?" he whispered, leaning closer to Dougal so he wouldn't be heard. Until now, almost everyone he'd seen had been wearing a shiny yellow weatherproof coat.

"It's called a leather jerkin. It's for protection," said Dougal solemnly. "And in this place, you definitely need it, with machines and storms going bonkers all over the place. I wish they'd given us one as well, just in case we—"

He stopped talking abruptly as the woman finally approached them with a stern look on her face.

"I am Catcher Sparks, and I will be your master lightning catcher for the duration of your training here at Perilous," she announced. "By choosing to become trainee lightning catchers, or lightning cubs, each of you has begun a difficult and dangerous journey, one that will test you to your limits. One that will show what you are truly made of."

She stared down her nose at Dougal, as if she was indeed trying to work out exactly what he was made of.

"Lightning cubs have been trained at Perilous since the first lightning catchers landed on this island. You are therefore following in the footsteps of some noble men and women. It is an honor and a privilege to work within these historic walls, and I will not tolerate any insolence, deliberate stupidity, or rule breaking under any circumstances, even those of a life-threatening nature. You, boy!" She suddenly jabbed a bony finger at Angus, and he noticed that his signed declaration was pinned to her clipboard. "Angus Von Dungbeetle, what was the most important thing you learned in the weather tunnel yesterday?"

"I . . . um . . . that you should never stand too close to a coconut palm." Angus said the first thing that came into his head, and then wished that he'd thought about it a bit harder first.

Catcher Sparks, however, made no comment.

"Indigo Midnight," she said, consulting her clipboard. "I understand that you are keen to work in the Lightnarium, if you eventually get three lightning bolts or more in your final examinations?"

"Yes, miss," said Indigo, in a barely audible whisper. "I

want to work with lightning like the great Philip Starling himself." She bit her lip as if worried that she might have said too much.

"Hmm. We shall see, Miss Midnight, we shall see."

Finally, Catcher Sparks turned her gaze to Dougal. "And you . . . are Dougal Dewsnap."

It was not a question. She glanced at the paper bag still clutched in his hand and gave him a withering stare.

"You will now follow me into the experimental division," she continued. "Do not touch anything if you are planning to retain all of your fingers until lunchtime."

"Have you noticed how they say that kind of thing a lot around here?" Dougal whispered, stuffing his own hands hurriedly into his pockets.

Angus was relieved to see that there was no sign of the storm vacuum on the other side of the large wooden door. There were definitely more gouges in the walls since the day before yesterday, however, as well as several new cracks running the full length of the floor. But the lightning catchers appeared to be gathered around a much smaller, less dangerous-looking machine this morning, working on it with rubber hammers and what

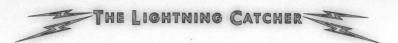
appeared to be the same flatirons his uncle sometimes used to tame his wild hair for special occasions.

Catcher Sparks led them quickly past the machine before Angus could get a proper look at it and shuffled them into a large workshop, closing the door behind them. Long coils of rusty wire and gleaming metal hung from the ceiling, along with a vast assortment of cogs, wheels, and double-ended bolts, which looked to Angus like they'd been wrestled from the neck of a colossal robot. A number of wooden workbenches had been arranged around the room, all of which were covered in oily rags and tools.

"Your first task as cubs will be to remove the buildup of earwax from the insides of these hailstone helmets," Catcher Sparks informed them, pointing to a large heap of copper helmets piled up in a corner, where three spoon-shaped instruments had also been arranged around a bucket. "I want to be absolutely certain that all three of you can tell one end of a hailstone helmet from the other before I let you loose on any of our more valuable pieces of equipment," she added firmly, catching the look of revulsion on Dougal's face.

"I shall be back at the end of the morning to inspect your progress. You may begin."

And she strode briskly from the room, the smallest hint of a smile on her face.

It was hot, sticky, disgusting work. And it was definitely not what Angus had imagined himself doing on his first day as a lightning cub. But as long as he kept his fingers at the far end of the gouging instrument, he found he could avoid making any actual contact with the earwax itself. It was impossible, however, to ignore the loud huffing and tutting noises that were coming from Dougal.

"This is the most disgusting thing I've ever done in my life!" Dougal eventually said, gouging out a thick yellow lump of wax and flicking it into the copper bucket, where it landed with a horrible squelch. "I thought they'd be giving us lectures on the theory of invention and stuff like that. I'd like to know what this is supposed to be teaching us about being lightning catchers."

"That you can get someone else to do your dirty work for you when you qualify?" said Angus. "Which won't be happening to us for years yet. Can you imagine how much earwax we'll have scraped up by then?"

"I'd rather not, thanks," Indigo said, making them both jump. She had been working quietly on her own pile of helmets and had hardly spoken a word to either of them all morning, although Angus got the distinct impression that she'd been listening intently to their conversation. She looked at them both now, for one embarrassed second, before turning hurriedly back to her work without saying another word. Dougal, however, continued to stare at her with a creased forehead, and Angus could tell that he was still trying to remember something about her.

"I can't believe we actually had to sit through three entrance exams to do this," Dougal muttered a few minutes later.

CLANG! Angus dropped his gouging instrument into the bucket and stared at Dougal. Nobody had mentioned anything to him about exams.

"E-entrance exams?" he asked.

"Yeah, did they make you answer all those stupid questions on yours about Brutus Beauregard, the famous Imburcillian weather forecaster and mud wrestler?"

"Er . . . ," said Angus uncomfortably, wondering all of a sudden if the incident with the storm globe at the ferry dock had, in fact, been some sort of secret test—in which case he'd definitely failed it. Miserably.

"Not that the exams mean all that much anyway. Because both the Vellum twins got in, and they've barely got enough brains between them to fill an eggcup." Dougal paused to wipe his gouging instrument on a sticky cloth. "I'd bet my last silver starling they only got into Perilous because their dad's one of the lightning catchers here."

Angus looked away guiltily, pretending to inspect his hailstone helmet for any hidden pockets of wax. Principal Dark-Angel had only allowed him to become a lightning cub because of his parents, too.

"What's a silver starling?" he asked, hoping to steer the conversation on to other things instead.

"Oh, yeah, I keep forgetting, you've probably never seen one on the mainland." Dougal rummaged around in his pocket, pulling out a collection of elastic bands and fluff-covered gumballs before he finally found what looked like a tiny silver pyramid with strange inscriptions engraved on every side.

"That's a starling," he explained, handing it over to Angus. "Named after the great Philip Starling, of course.

He and Edgar Perilous made up their own currency when they first came to Imbur. One starling will buy you a chocolate cream pie from Dingle's Bakery in Little Frog's Bottom; fifteen starlings will get you a ferry ticket over to one of the mainland ports."

"So silver starlings are money," said Angus, turning the pyramid over in his hands.

"Yeah, and if you've got more than a thousand starlings sitting in your pockets, then you've probably got pirates in your family somewhere!"

Beside him, Angus could see Indigo grinning.

They spent the rest of a very long day with the hailstone helmets, with Catcher Sparks allowing them a mere twenty minutes for lunch, which unfortunately included a sumptuous golden treacle tart.

"Looks a lot like melted earwax, doesn't it?" said Dougal, prodding the sticky pudding warily with his spoon.

The following morning, they arrived in the experimental division to find a mountain of muddy rubber boots waiting for them, each of which had to be hosed down, checked for punctures, and rewaxed. On Wednesday, Catcher Sparks left them knee-deep in fluffy blue earmuffs, which had to be shampooed, combed, and set in miniature rollers before being arranged under an enormous hair dryer.

On Thursday morning, however, they were ordered out of the experimental division by the frosty lightning catcher, who informed them that for two hours every week, they would be attending lessons on fog with the rest of the first-year trainees. Fog lessons took place in one of five astonishing weather bubbles. Made entirely of ornate steel and glass, bursting through the outer walls of Perilous like giant soap bubbles, the extraordinary classrooms appeared to float in midair, hundreds of feet above the ground.

"Whatever you do, don't look down!" Dougal warned as they entered the bubble and found two seats together.

Angus stared straight through the glass and steel beneath his feet, and instantly wished he'd taken Dougal's advice. A long way below them, a seagull soared on the breeze. And below the seagull . . . there was nothing but angry gray clouds. Angus gulped, hit by a sudden wave of vertigo.

"What's wrong with using a normal classroom, with a

solid stone floor?" he said, trying not to think about the terrifying drop below. After several anxious minutes, however, he was starting to believe that the bubble wasn't about to plummet to the earth with everyone in it. And by the time their fog instructor, Miss DeWinkle, arrived, he had plucked up enough courage to watch a flock of geese flapping past.

Miss DeWinkle was short and stout, with an impressive collection of double chins and ruddy cheeks.

"Fog," she announced as she came bounding into the bubble with frightening enthusiasm, "is a wonderful enigma, a beautiful, mysterious phenomena; it is also one of the most exciting forms of weather you will ever study at this Exploratorium. And the weather bubble is the perfect place from which to observe its unique qualities. Over the next few months, you will be introduced to all seventeen different types of fog . . ."

"There's seventeen types of fog?" Dougal whispered.

"Yeah, Edmund Croxley told me all about them on my guided tour," said Angus, glad to know something useful for a change. "There's amusing fog and confusing fog, and waist-high whistling fog or something."

"Whistling fog?" Dougal stifled a laugh behind his hand. "And I thought all it did was make your socks soggy."

"Shouldn't we be having lessons on lightning bolts and blizzards and stuff like that too?" Angus asked, hoping someone might also teach them more about Edgar Perilous, Philip Starling, and the exciting history of London's lost lightning towers.

"'Fraid not." Dougal shook his head. "Looks like we're stuck with fog for the whole year."

". . . you will explore the dazzling beauty of the foggy morning," Miss DeWinkle continued at the front of the class. "You shall observe the hypnotic power of the swirling mists, with the help of your weather watches. In the meantime, however, there are fog lamps and foghorns to come to grips with."

Despite Miss DeWinkle's obvious enthusiasm, Angus quickly decided that fog was duller than a week of wet Sundays, and as Miss DeWinkle launched herself into a long and tedious lecture on the history of the foghorn, he found his attention drifting.

This was the first time he'd seen the other cubs, apart from the odd glimpse at mealtimes, since they had each

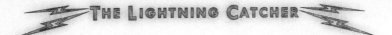

been assigned to their own lightning catchers. Nigel Ridgely was sporting a sunburned neck and ears, and Angus guessed that he'd been sent up to the roof, to clean thermometers and empty out slimy buckets of water. Indigo was sitting next to Nigel, and she gave Angus a brief smile before staring down at her notes again.

Millicent Nichols and Jonathon Hake were both looking rather pasty and dazed, and he decided that they must have gone to the research department. He was just wondering if anyone had been unlucky enough to get Gudgeon as their master lightning catcher, when something small and soggy hit him hard on the back of the neck with a splat.

"Ow!"

He spun round in his seat to see Pixie and Percival Vellum doubled over with silent laughter at the very back of the weather bubble, a ruler and a row of paper pellets lined up on the desk in front of them.

"Yes, what is it, Doomsbury?" Miss DeWinkle had stopped talking and was now watching him. "Do you have something interesting to say about the invention of Septimus Scrimshaw's silent foghorn?"

"Er . . . no, miss," Angus said, turning to face

the front again and rubbing the back of his neck.

"Then I suggest you stop gazing around the weather bubble and take some notes," Miss DeWinkle added tartly. "I will be setting a test on Mr. Scrimshaw's groundbreaking invention in your next lesson, and anyone scoring less than eight out of ten will find himself copying out every single one of Arthur Atkinson's 'Five Hundred Mistical Thoughts on Fog.'"

Angus reluctantly pulled his workbook and a pen toward him, still smarting as Miss DeWinkle returned to her notes.

"What's up with you?" Dougal mumbled under his breath.

"Vellums." Angus glared over his shoulder at the smirking twins, and he sincerely hoped that they had both been assigned to the Lightnarium.

The rest of the lesson passed at a snail's pace. Septimus Scrimshaw, it seemed, had taken an exceptionally long time to invent his silent foghorn, especially as he had become hard of hearing toward the end of his life, and Angus was extremely glad when the bell rang and their first fog lecture finally came to an end.

"We shall continue on our journey through the fascinating history of the foghorn next lesson," Miss DeWinkle shouted above the noisy babble of voices. "Before you go, however, I'd like you each to take a copy of the *McFangus Fog Guide* and study it closely."

Angus looked up quickly.

"The *McFangus Fog Guide* will be your constant companion during your first year at Perilous," Miss DeWinkle said, holding up a copy of the book to show them. "It will guide you through your first no-way-out fog, it will shield you from the sudden, clammy dangers of the wet-dog fog, and if you are extremely lucky, it will reveal to you the elusive and sometimes deadly mysteries of the great invisible fog itself!"

Angus took a copy from the pile that was being handed round the room, passed the rest on to Dougal, and studied the front cover with interest. The *McFangus Fog Guide* was bound in smart emerald-green leather with gold lettering across the front. Inside, on the first page, there was a large warning printed in red ink: *Danger! Invisible fogs can be deadly—approach with caution.* On the page opposite, the contents listed such interesting-sounding chapters as "What to Do When Fog Is Following You" and "Fog Mites: Truth or Travesty?"

Angus turned the fog guide over in his hands, wondering if his mum and dad had finished helping Scabious Dankhart over on the other side of the island yet. And when he might be seeing them again. And, more importantly, if they could somehow fix it so that he and Dougal never had to attend another fog lecture.

There were plenty of things that Angus did enjoy about being at the Exploratorium, however. For a start, he had discovered on his first day that Dougal's room was right next door to his, and that they were separated by what appeared to be a tiny hidden room. The room could only be accessed through a narrow door in Angus's bedroom, which had been concealed behind a moth-eaten wall hanging of a violent typhoon, and through an identical door in Dougal's room—behind a tall chest of drawers that had taken them over an hour to move. Due to the fact that the hidden room had been littered with old newspapers and candy wrappers and covered in muddy footprints when they'd first discovered it, they'd quickly nicknamed it the Pigsty.

The room itself was long and narrow and barely wide enough for the two battered armchairs, the small round table, and the copper kettle and chipped mugs that had been left behind by its previous occupants. There was a small fireplace and an even smaller window, and it was extremely enjoyable indeed just to sit there with a hot mug of cocoa after a long day of scraping toenails from the inside of somebody else's rubber boots, discussing everything they'd learned about Perilous so far.

It was common knowledge, for instance, that Catcher Brabble, who worked in the Lightnarium, had been struck by lightning fifteen times. Nobody, however, seemed to know what was hidden behind the door to the Inner Sanctum of Perplexing Mysteries and Secrets.

"There's loads of rumors flying around about top-secret inventions and killer rain clouds," said Dougal one evening as they discussed the fascinating subject. "Or maybe—hey, maybe it's completely empty, and that's the big secret!"

Angus also enjoyed mealtimes, since they gave him an excellent opportunity to watch the other inhabitants of the Exploratorium. Both he and Dougal had been very surprised to learn from Catcher Sparks, however, that there were just sixty trainees at Perilous in total.

"This is an extremely busy Exploratorium, Doomsbury," she had explained rather huffily. "We simply haven't got time to tackle wayward blizzards and hurricanes, and train hundreds of cubs, all at the same time."

Angus had already seen most of the older trainees laughing and joking their way along the stone tunnels and passageways. They also occupied some of the noisier tables at mealtimes and were constantly being shouted at by an irate lightning catcher called Howler.

"I won't tell you again, Grubb, Strumble, Follifoot—put those pet mice away! This is a kitchen, not a zoo!"

Angus was equally surprised to discover that there were over a hundred lightning catchers at Perilous.

"That guy rubbing the wart on his chin is head of the records office," Dougal told Angus one evening, while they were eating an extremely tasty dinner of mashed potato and juicy Imbur sausages. "His name's Thistle or Fristle or something. The guy sitting next to him is Jasper Heckles, he's friends with my dad, keeps coming round to our house to play cards."

"The woman pretending to listen to him has something to do with monsoons," Angus added, waving a forkful of sausage in her direction. "I heard some fourth years talking about her. Apparently everyone at Perilous hates her because she makes you camp out in the weather tunnel for eight whole days during your monsoon training. Her name's Miss Rill."

"Who's the lightning catcher sitting next to her, though?" Dougal frowned.

Angus almost choked as he realized that Dougal was staring straight at Felix Gudgeon.

"I—er, haven't got a clue," he answered quickly, looking away before Gudgeon noticed them both staring in his direction.

He'd done his best to avoid the gruff lightning catcher ever since the dramatic events at the ferry port, especially as Gudgeon was often seen around the Exploratorium with Principal Dark-Angel. And he had no desire to spend any more time with either of them.

Angus found the lightning catchers fascinating, especially as they often appeared in the kitchens with singed eyebrows or odd-looking contraptions clamped under their armpits, which tended to explode or burst into flames without warning. And he couldn't help imagining what it must have been like back at the very beginning, when Philip Starling and Edgar Perilous themselves had first come to the island and built the great Exploratorium.

He did not enjoy his trips to the library quite so much, however. Mr. Knurling, the new librarian, chased off any lightning cub who was foolish enough to enter his dusty realm, making it practically impossible to borrow any sort of book at all.

As the days passed, Angus also found it increasingly difficult to keep his promise to Principal Dark-Angel and lie about who he really was. Several times he toyed with the idea of telling Dougal that his real name was Angus McFangus and that both his parents were lightning catchers. He was also tempted, while he was at it, to tell him about the strange appearance of Gudgeon at the Windmill in the middle of the night, along with the trouble they'd had at the pier with the sinister men and the storm globe.

He'd already attempted it twice, in the privacy of the Pigsty, but for some reason the right words refused to come. Private conversations in the kitchens were too

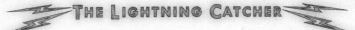

at-risk from eavesdroppers. In the experimental division, Indigo sat right beside them, scraping stubborn barnacles off submersible storm detectors or trimming the frayed cuffs off hurricane suits. And in the end, Angus decided he'd just have to wait for the right moment.

It came sooner than he'd expected, one Friday evening after dinner.

They were met just outside the kitchens by a sudden flood of trainees and lightning catchers, all heading in the same direction and talking excitedly.

"What's going on?" Angus said.

Before Dougal could answer, Edmund Croxley cut his way across the tide of people toward them.

"Ah, Angus, I've been meaning to have a quick word with you," he said, pulling them to one side and lowering his voice. "I hear you've been assigned to Catcher Sparks in the experimental division."

"Er, yeah. So?" said Angus.

"Well, I was wondering if there was any chance that you could get my fog aficionado badge back for me while you're in there, the one the storm vacuum swallowed. It's no good being a fog expert if you haven't got the badge to prove it, and quite frankly, people are starting to ask some very awkward questions."

"I'll, um, see what I can do," Angus said, not sure that he could do anything at all. The storm vacuum had been dismantled and was now lying in dozens of different pieces all over the experimental division.

"What's going on, anyway?" he asked, before Edmund could disappear into the crowd again. "Where's everyone going?"

"Oh, that," Edmund said in a superior tone. "Frogs in the courtyard, Angus, nothing to get too excited about, I can assure you. In fact, all of you first years really ought to be getting on with your homework instead of gadding about the Exploratorium at all hours of the—"

Before he could say any more, however, he was caught in the tide of bodies once again and was swept along the corridor and out of sight.

"What's so interesting about frogs in the courtyard?" asked Angus.

Dougal shrugged, hitching his backpack up onto his shoulder. "Only one way to find out."

There were ten different courtyards at Perilous. Some

were small and stuffed with scientific weather instruments for analyzing snowflake patterns and measuring wind speeds. Others were magnificent marble creations, overflowing with stone statues and Greek-looking urns. The courtyard that everyone appeared to be heading toward now was at the very center of Perilous. On any normal summer's evening, it would have been an extremely pleasant place to sit and digest dinner, perhaps while lounging beside the large granite fish pond, surrounded by pots full of wild strawberries. But it was obvious, as soon as Angus and Dougal had squeezed their way in, that there was nothing normal about this particular evening. This was due to the large cloud that had settled itself directly above the Exploratorium. Falling from it like rain were hundreds of small green frogs.

"What in the name of Perilous . . . ?" Dougal gasped.

Angus stared at the falling amphibians with his mouth hanging open.

The sky above had turned bilious green. The air around them was thick with a thousand startled croaks, along with a rhythmic *squelch-thud-hop* as the frogs landed in the courtyard and made a desperate dash for safety.

Some fell into the pond, while others somehow managed to cling to rain gutters and drainpipes, webbed feet paddling furiously in the air. A few unfortunate creatures hit the courtyard with a very unpleasant *SPLAT!*

"Urgh!" Dougal wrinkled his nose in disgust. "There's frog brains everywhere."

Most of the slimy creatures, however, had survived their fall and were now hopping madly around the courtyard. At least a dozen lightning catchers were chasing after the slippery creatures, attempting to scoop them up into buckets.

Angus stumbled back as Catcher Mint came diving toward them, flinging his bucket at a small, terrified huddle of frogs, which scattered at the last second and headed for the cover of a honeysuckle bush.

"Bother! Missed again!" Catcher Mint grumbled, before picking himself up and sprinting off.

"Stand back, Doomsbury, Dewsnap!" Catcher Sparks warned, hurrying past them with her own bucket, a stray frog clinging to the rim of her weatherproof hat.

"What's going on, miss?" Angus called after her.

"Nothing to be alarmed about, Doomsbury, perfectly

normal weather for this time of year," she said.

"There's nothing normal about it," Dougal mumbled.

"Yeah, I know, there was something in the news about showers of newts and frogs before I came to Perilous," Angus said. "I forgot all about it until now, but they've even been seen over Buckingham Palace. And that's definitely not normal."

"Maybe the experimental division is working on something top secret that they don't want the rest of us to know about?" suggested Dougal. "Maybe they've been training frogs to search for the great invisible fog itself, so we won't have to?"

Angus grinned. "Not exactly foggy at the moment, though, is it? Anyway, when I first met Principal Dark-Angel, she said something about finding out where the frogs were coming from and making them stop."

"Are you sure that's what she said?" Dougal asked, frowning.

Angus nodded. "Yeah, why?"

"Well, if they definitely didn't come from Perilous . . . there's only one other place on the island they could have come from—and that's Castle Dankhart."

Angus recognized the name immediately. According to Principal Dark-Angel, Dankhart was the person whom both his parents were helping with an important assignment. And according to Oswald Blott, the holographic storyteller, the Dankharts were worthless mongrels and cheats.

"Er, does the name Scabious Dankhart mean anything to you?" he asked Dougal.

"Of course it does!" Dougal raised his eyebrows in surprise. "Every person on Imbur knows who Dankhart is . . . due to the fact that he's a mad raving lunatic."

Angus felt his stomach churn. He had a horrible feeling he was about to discover the real reason he hadn't heard from his mum and dad in such a long time.

"What's wrong?" Dougal asked. "You've gone whiter than a wispy fog."

"Just tell me everything you know about Scabious Dankhart."

"There's no need." Dougal rummaged through his backpack and pulled out a thick volume. "Everything you need to know about the whole stinking family is in this book."

Angus read the title aloud. *"Famous Imburcillians—The*

Good, the Bad, and the Desperately Ugly."

Dougal smiled. "I borrowed it from my dad. I don't know why you want to hear about that old loony Dankhart, though. It's enough to give anyone nightmares for a week."

Angus skimmed quickly through the book, which was arranged in alphabetical order, until he reached the chapter called "The Dankhart Family: Vile, Violent, and Very, Very Nasty." He started reading.

> Secretive and powerful, little is truly known about the despicable Dankhart family other than the fact that they built Castle Dankhart more than five hundred years ago and have resided there ever since. Probably descended from a long line of pirates, they are rumored to possess a vast personal fortune, which includes gold coins, jeweled cups, and giant ingots.

"Descended from pirates?" Angus looked up, surprised.

"Well, yeah, if you believe the rumors." Dougal shrugged. "They're definitely devious enough, rotten to the core, my dad says. But that's not the scariest part." He pointed to the next paragraph.

Angus swallowed and continued to read.

As the Dankharts had gone to great, and often violent, lengths to establish themselves as the most feared family on the island, they took instant exception to the arrival of the lightning catchers in 1666. A terrible feud sprang up between them, the exact origins of which are uncertain, although it continues to this day. It is commonly believed that the Dankharts have also been responsible for some of the worst freak weather conditions ever experienced on this island and in various other places around the globe—including blizzards of black snow-flakes, black ice storms, and hailstone mon-soons. It is also believed that they are mean enough to try anything once.

"Dankhart knows almost as much about the weather as Principal Dark-Angel," Dougal explained. "He can whip up a thunderstorm quicker than you can say lightning bolt, only he's not interested in researching tornado patterns or drying up rainstorms like we are here at Perilous. He likes to use the weather as a weapon instead. There's a whole section of the library devoted to the Dankharts and the horrible things they've done with the weather over the centuries."

Angus felt his heart racing. Principal Dark-Angel hadn't mentioned any of this in her office.

"The lightning catchers try and stop him, of course, but every now and again he stuffs clouds full of frogs or something stupid," Dougal continued as a fresh shower of confused amphibians fell at their feet.

"What else do you know about him?" Angus snapped the book shut and handed it back.

"There's not much more to tell," Dougal said, "except he's only got one normal eye. He lost the other one in a hailstone accident, and it was replaced with a black diamond."

"A black diamond?" Angus said, surprised.

"Yeah, it probably came from one of his own personal diamond mines on the other side of the island. Gives me the collywobbles just thinking about it," Dougal said with a shiver. "Anyway, are you going to tell me why you want to know all this stuff about Dankhart all of a sudden?"

Angus swiftly decided that there would never be a better moment to tell Dougal everything. "Let's find somewhere more private first," he said, leading his friend back through the frog watchers toward the quiet of the deserted building. "Then I'll tell you exactly why I want to know."

7
THE LIGHTNARIUM

Nobody noticed when Angus and Dougal slipped back inside. As soon as the door to the Pigsty was closed behind them, Angus told Dougal everything that had happened since Gudgeon had escorted him from the Windmill in the middle of the night. The words came tumbling out of his mouth. It was a relief to finally tell Dougal the truth.

"So let me get this straight," Dougal said after Angus had finished. "Your real name is Angus McFangus, your parents are Alabone and Evangeline McFangus, and they're both senior lightning catchers—"

"Yeah, exactly! Only I didn't know that until a week ago.

They always told me they worked for some boring government department in London. But it turns out they've been
here at Perilous the whole time. I mean, they've written a
fog guide and everything."

"And now they're at Castle Dankhart?"

"Right, Principal Dark-Angel said something about
them staying with Dankhart while they helped him with
an important assignment."

"Hah!" Dougal snorted, eyes wide behind his glasses.
"Dankhart doesn't need anyone's help—unless he's finally
decided to get his lunatic brain fixed."

"Look, I would have told you all of this ages ago,"
Angus added, "but Principal Dark-Angel warned me not
to tell anyone my real name. She made it sound like I was
here on holiday until my mum and dad came back, and
that everyone would want to bring their relatives over if
they found out. Nobody even told me I was a lightning
cub until the night before the weather tunnel."

"You're joking!" said Dougal, sounding deeply
impressed. "The least they could have done was warn you
about the fog yeti! Although they could have warned the
rest of us about that one, too."

They sat silently for several minutes, with Dougal picking at a stray thread on the arm of his chair, a glazed expression on his face, and Angus rubbing his aching head, which felt like it had been squeezed through the inner tube of a bicycle wheel. It was clear to him now that Oswald Blott's description of the Dankharts had been by far the more accurate. It was even clearer that Principal Dark-Angel had lied to him and that his parents were in some sort of trouble.

"The thing I don't understand is what my mum and dad are doing at Dankhart's castle in the first place," he eventually said. "It doesn't sound like he needs any help with the weather."

"If the rumors about him are true, he can stir up a blizzard before you can reach for your snow boots," said Dougal. "Did Principal Dark-Angel say anything else about your mum and dad?"

Angus shrugged. "She just asked if they'd sent me any letters or messages through the mail lately. It sounded like she's been expecting something important to arrive, something that hasn't turned up yet."

"Well, did they send you any letters?" asked Dougal hopefully.

"Yeah, they did, as a matter of fact." And Angus pushed himself out of his armchair and went to fetch the last letter that his mum had sent.

He took it from a drawer in his bedside cabinet, where he'd stowed it on his first day at Perilous, and stared at it. He wondered, suddenly, if he'd missed some important word or sentence that would make perfect sense now he knew all about Scabious Dankhart, Perilous, and the lightning catchers. He scanned the letter, looking for any hidden hints or clues about secret assignments, but the letter, written on thick ivory paper, looked just the same as the first time he'd read it at the Windmill. He walked back into the Pigsty, disappointed.

"This is the only letter I've had from them in ages," he said, waving the envelope at Dougal, who was now perched on the edge of his chair.

"Well, what does it say?"

"I wouldn't get too excited if I were you. It's mostly just a load of boring family stuff," Angus said. "It says, 'Dear Angus, I hope you're well and not bothering your uncle Max too much while he is working on his inventions. It might be nice if you offered to wash up for him every now

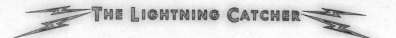

and again, and remember to thank him for taking care of
you. The weather here in London is fine—' Well, that was
obviously a lie, for a start, wasn't it?" Angus said, interrupting himself. "I bet they've been nowhere near London
all summer."

"Who cares?" said Dougal impatiently. "What does the
rest of the letter say?"

"Oh, yeah, sorry. It says, 'Your dad and I are both fine.
Sorry we've both been so busy lately, but you've been
the Koolest about it, as I was telling Taunt Pamela the
other day on the phone.' I think she means Aunt Pamela,"
Angus said, shaking his head at his mum's spelling mistakes, of which there seemed to be rather a lot.

"'. . . which reminds me, Angus,'" he continued reading,
"'I forgot to mention that she will be visiting us again during the next school holidays, I will have to try Very hard
to remember this time that she's allergic to your uncle's
snail-and-seaweed pie, Ands that Uncl Lars won't drink
anything but that revolting Trim Skim milk. That's all for
now. Make sure you eat your carrots and brussels sprouts,
and look after yourself. Love, Mum.'"

"And that's it?" Dougal asked, disappointed. "That's all

there is? There're no mysterious-looking symbols scribbled on the bottom of the page? No secret flaps hidden inside the envelope?"

"Nope, there's nothing, not even an accidental inkblot," said Angus, inspecting the letter closely in the dying light of the fire. "I warned you it wasn't exactly riveting."

He tucked the letter back inside its envelope, then spent the rest of the evening talking anxiously with Dougal about his parents and the mysterious assignment they had been sent to complete by Principal Dark-Angel.

The chaos caused by the frogs was far more widespread than any one at first realized, and for the rest of the night, small green amphibians could be heard hopping through stone tunnels and passageways. They were also caught hiding in cookie jars and cake tins by a startled Mrs. Stobbs, who had wandered down to the kitchens for a snack to settle her nerves.

By the following morning, some sort of order had been restored to most parts of the building. But as Angus and Dougal made their way up to the experimental division after breakfast, they were brought to an unexpected halt

outside the records office by a different sort of obstacle altogether. Piles of ragged paper had been stacked waist high in the corridor, almost blocking their path.

"Just step over it," a frazzled-sounding voice called from inside the office. "Only be careful not to tread on any of my dark blue folders. It's taken me hours to get them organized."

Angus poked his head around the door and found Mr. Fristle, the head of the records office, scrambling about the floor on his hands and knees. The office looked like it had been hit by a tornado, with papers, folders, books, and files all ripped to shreds and scattered about the room like piles of confetti at a party.

"Er . . . isn't there anyone who can help?" asked Angus, feeling sorry for Mr. Fristle.

"Help? Nobody can help me!" wailed Mr. Fristle. "I'm the only one who knows where everything goes. It'll take me weeks to get this sorted out. I only popped outside yesterday for five minutes to have a look at the frogs, and when I came back, I found the place in this mess. Wet amphibians and their grubby little feet everywhere! They must have come in through one of the windows. I'll be picking them out of my trainee records from now until Christmas!"

Luckily, the weather took a turn for the better over the next few weeks, becoming pleasantly warm and sunny, with absolutely no sign of any more amphibious showers on the horizon. In the experimental division, however, Catcher Sparks continued to find an endless string of disgusting objects for Angus, Dougal, and Indigo to clean. She even threatened them with a pile of waterproof, snot-repelling handkerchiefs, which needed to be strung up and scraped off by hand. Angus could only imagine what horrors awaited them within the revolting hankies, and as he went up to breakfast that morning, he found he wasn't looking forward to the day very much at all. He was not surprised, therefore, to see Dougal, already halfway through his toast, waving at him anxiously from the far side of the kitchens.

"You'll never guess what happened!" he said before Angus had even sat down with his scrambled eggs.

"Catcher Sparks was only joking about the snot-repelling hankies?" he asked hopefully.

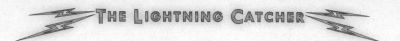

Dougal shook his head. "'Fraid not, but Miss DeWinkle came in ten minutes ago and put up a load of these posters. Here," he said, shoving Angus's breakfast to one side and unrolling a long sheet of parchment on the table. "Take a look at that!"

At the top of the parchment there was a drawing of a perplexed-looking lightning cub, about to be engulfed by a bank of sinister white fog. Beneath it, printed in bright red ink, were the words:

As the new FOG SEASON will shortly be upon us,

I have great pleasure in announcing

that this year, all trainees will be

participating in a series of exciting

FOG FIELD TRIPS,

details of which will follow shortly.

In the meantime, if you have any questions,

please see

Miss O. DeWinkle.

And happy fog watching to you all!

▲ ▲ ▲

Angus frowned. "I wonder what fog field trips are, exactly." He had a sudden image of himself standing utterly alone in a vast field surrounded by acres of menacing fog.

Still hungry, he pulled his plate back toward him and glanced around the kitchen, which now seemed to be buzzing with news of the field trips. Violet Quinn and Georgina Fox were discussing the subject nervously. A large group of fifth years were laughing loudly, studying the posters with great excitement. Edmund Croxley was in his element, talking with an air of superiority to a small crowd of second and third years. "Since I am the only trainee with fog aficionado status, Miss DeWinkle has already asked for my assistance, naturally. . . ."

"How come I've never heard anyone mention fog field trips before?" Angus asked, turning back to Dougal. It was Nicholas Grubb, however, a friendly fourth year with sandy-colored hair, who answered him.

"Because there hasn't been enough fog in the past few years to hold any," he explained, appearing at their table with a broad grin. Nicholas Grubb had already given them some valuable tips on how to stay on the good side of Catcher Sparks, who was also his master lightning catcher. "The forecasting department is predicting a bumper fog season this year, though, with prolonged periods of mist and murkiness. Principal Dark-Angel wants you first years to get a good grounding in the subject, plus it means you can get in some real practice with your weather watches. It can be dangerous—"

"Dangerous?" Dougal gulped. "W-what do you mean?"

"Sorry, can't tell you. DeWinkle would go bonkers if she found out." He grinned. "But stay well clear of anything with teeth, and you should be fine."

Angus forced himself to laugh, hoping it was a joke.

"DeWinkle wants everyone to fill in one of these forms and give it back to her as soon as possible." Nicholas handed both of them a sheet of paper, and then, with a friendly "See you later," hurried off to another table.

Angus read his form warily. It was extremely short and asked only for his name, age, and the identity of his master lightning catcher. There were just two other boxes to fill in. The first asked for any identifying marks he had on his body, such as scars, moles, or freckles; the second box appeared to be for any last messages for his family and friends, in the event that something went horribly wrong during the field trip.

"I'm not signing that!" Dougal croaked, holding his own form at arm's length, as if it might be hazardous. "How can fog be *this* risky?"

"Everything in this place is risky," Angus pointed out, scribbling his fake signature at the bottom of his form, before he could think too hard about it.

The second surprise of the morning came when they reached the Octagon fifteen minutes later, to find it buzzing with the chatter of familiar voices. They were met at the top of the stairs by the rest of the first-year cubs, all of whom appeared to be gathered around a lightning catcher. He was dressed in a long brown leather jerkin, littered with rips, tears, and broken buckles, and his bald head shone like a flesh-colored billiard ball under the glowing light fissures of the marbled hall. Angus recognized him immediately.

"Hey, that's Felix Gudgeon," he said, nudging Dougal in the ribs as they joined the back of the group. Indigo gave them both a shy smile.

"You mean the same Felix Gudgeon who practically

dragged you out of the Windmill in your pajamas?"

Angus nodded. "I wonder what he's doing here?"

"Who cares?" Dougal shrugged. "Whatever it is, it's got to be better than spending a whole day with somebody else's snot."

Angus wasn't so sure. His last meeting with Gudgeon had culminated in a lump the size of an egg on his forehead and several hours of unconsciousness.

"For those of you who don't know me," Gudgeon began a few moments later, bringing a swift and absolute silence to the Octagon, "my name is Felix Gudgeon."

For a split second, his steely eyes came to rest on Angus, but he gave no sign whatsoever that the two of them had ever met before.

"You won't normally see me around Perilous. I don't do teaching and I don't waste my time messing about with strips of seaweed and weather cannons. I work directly for Principal Dark-Angel herself, and this morning, she's instructed me to take charge of you lot. It's about time you stopped messing about with fog guides and tins of boot wax and saw what Perilous is really all about. That's why I'm taking you into the Lightnarium."

A shocked murmur swept around the marbled hall. Angus felt his skin tingle with anticipation.

"The capture of lightning bolts at Perilous was stopped long before any of you was even born, and for reasons you've got no business knowing about. However, some experiments are still performed under strictly controlled conditions inside the Lightnarium. Normally, you wouldn't be allowed in there until your sixth year as trainees, but I say you need to know from the start what the weather's capable of in the wrong hands. So I've arranged for the lightning experts to give us a small demonstration.

"Anyone who is too afraid to enter the Lightnarium should say so now." Gudgeon glared at each of them in turn, searching for any signs of weakness. "You'll be sent home immediately, and your place at Perilous will be given to somebody who deserves it."

A deathly silence followed this statement. Only Violet Quinn let a faint whimper escape her lips. Angus swallowed hard, hoping that nobody else could hear his heart, which was beating like a large drum against his rib cage. Behind Gudgeon's left shoulder, he could just make out the faded outline of the shimmering golden fire dragon,

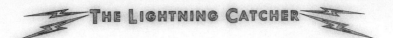
placed long ago on the door that led to the Lightnarium. He'd hardly given it a single thought since first arriving at Perilous. And he looked away from it now, before Gudgeon caught him staring.

"Right, then." Gudgeon finally broke the tense silence. "I want all of you dressed in lightning deflector suits and safety goggles, or you're not going anywhere." He pointed to a large box behind him that was filled with shiny garments.

It was like being swallowed by an enormous, slippery tent, Angus decided as he pulled a lightning deflector suit over his head and felt it fall to the ground around his feet. He barely had time to roll up the cuffs before they were following Gudgeon through the door and into a narrow stone passageway beyond, which had been blasted through the solid rock of Perilous with some extremely powerful explosives. At the far end of the passageway, just visible under the glow of a solitary candle, stood a pair of battered-looking safety doors made of thick, pitted steel.

"Once we get inside the Lightnarium, you're to stay close to me and DON'T TOUCH ANYTHING!" barked

Gudgeon as they gathered behind him. "If you mess up this morning, it might be the last thing you ever do, so pay attention!"

He swung the solid doors open wide and quickly disappeared inside. Angus shuffled in behind him, tripping over the hem of his lightning deflector suit, wondering what he was about to find—an enormous, cathedral-like hall perhaps, where hundreds of thunderstorms all battled against one another with great lashes of dazzling light? He wasn't disappointed. The Lightnarium was dimly lit, and for the first few seconds he could see nothing but the gleam of Gudgeon's bald head, but then, as his eyes grew accustomed to the semidarkness—

"Wow!" he gasped, staring around, trying to take it all in at once.

The Lightnarium was a vast cavern of a room with sheer, clifflike walls of lumpy stone. Just the height of it made his head spin. Ominous-looking storm clouds, all grumbling with menace, hovered just below the dome-shaped ceiling—from which there also hung some impressively long stalactites. A strong smell of sulfur lingered in the air and stuck unpleasantly to the back of his throat.

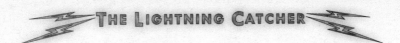

At the far end of the cavern stood a complicated array of enormous machinery that was clearly being used to generate the storm overhead. Thick metal coils, fifty feet tall, were humming and vibrating loudly.

"I'm not sure this is such a good idea," Dougal said nervously, appearing at Angus's elbow, his eyes magnified to several times their normal size behind his safety goggles. "What if something goes wrong while we're in here? What if we all get struck by lightning?"

"In your case, Dewsnap, it might be a definite improvement," growled Gudgeon. "We're expected down at the far end of the Lightnarium for our demonstration, so get a move on, you two. We haven't got all day."

Close up, the thick metal lightning generators were even more enormous. They cast a sinister shadow over them all as they were ushered behind a protective shield. The trainees huddled together in a tight group, waiting for the demonstration to begin. Gudgeon was approached immediately by a tall, bulky man with five lightning bolts clearly displayed on his own deflector suit.

"You're fifteen minutes late!" the man snapped, not bothering to keep his voice down.

"Hey, that must be Valentine Vellum," Angus said quietly. "Percival and Pixie's dad."

The resemblance was remarkable. It was easy to see where the terrible twins got their thuggish looks. They had clearly inherited the low brow line and long hairy arms from their dad, and all three of them bore a striking similarity to a family of gorillas. Valentine Vellum's pin-sharp eyes, however, were as cold and threatening as the blizzard section of the weather tunnel.

"Keep your beard on, Valentine." Gudgeon brushed him aside. "I had to get them all into lightning deflectors first."

"I was also under the impression that you were bringing a group of sixth years to this morning's demonstration," Vellum continued. "Not this sniveling bunch of whelplings."

"Principal Dark-Angel gave her permission, and that should be good enough, even for you, Valentine."

"And what's that supposed to mean?" Vellum glared at Gudgeon, his fists clenched into tight balls of white knuckles.

"You already know what it means," Gudgeon replied sharply, "but if you want me to spell it out for you again

in front of your great lumps of a son and daughter, I'll be happy to oblige!"

For a moment, Angus thought a fistfight was about to break out, but after a prickly pause, Valentine Vellum turned on his heel and marched toward the great machinery behind them.

"Make sure your lightning cubs keep well behind the safety shield," he ordered without looking back. "I will not be held responsible for any unfortunate injuries or deaths that occur while you and your whelplings are intruding on us."

Gudgeon merely shrugged and turned to talk to another, friendlier-looking lightning catcher beside him.

"What was that all about?" asked Angus.

"Dunno." Dougal shrugged. "But it doesn't look like they'll be sending each other birthday cards, does it?"

A few moments later, the demonstration finally began, with an impressive display of spider-shaped lightning that jumped aggressively from cloud to cloud above their heads, spinning a dazzling web of light. At such close quarters, the thunder that followed was deafening. Angus pressed his hands tightly over his ears, wishing he'd brought his earmuffs with him.

"Lightning tarantulatis," Gudgeon informed them as soon as the rumbles of thunder died away. "A single bolt of lightning tarantulatis contains approximately one billion volts of electricity, which is enough energy to power a lightbulb for three months, or to prod Miss Vellum's brain into action for a good five years."

Everyone giggled. Pixie Vellum, however, glowed the color of a freshly boiled beet.

"The lightning flash heats the air surrounding it to a temperature that is five times hotter than the surface of the sun," Gudgeon continued, his voice echoing loudly round the cavernous room. "The air nearby then expands and vibrates, forming the rumbling noise that we hear as thunder."

Angus adjusted his goggles, making sure the straps were covering his earlobes.

"Contrary to what you may think, lightning *can* strike in the same place twice. It is also one of the most dangerous and violent forces on this planet. No one can control it. No one can predict when or where it will strike next. If any of you ever find yourselves caught outside in a thunderstorm, I suggest you take cover immediately and wait

until it's passed. None of you should ever go looking for lightning on purpose, do I make myself clear?"

"He doesn't have to go on about it," said Dougal in an awed voice. "I'm never going outside again after this."

"You don't think this could be the lightning vaults, do you?" Angus whispered, staring around at the magnificent cavern and remembering what Dougal had told him in the weather tunnel about stored lightning bolts and dangerous experimentation.

But Dougal shook his head. "If you believe what Principal Dark-Angel said to my dad, the lightning vaults were lost years ago. No one knows where they are."

The demonstration continued with some tidal lightning, which snapped and crackled above their heads, rolling in great electric waves from one side of the Lightnarium to the other. Angus's favorite, however, was sky rocket lightning, which launched itself with a great burst from the ground, zooming straight up into the clouds, and was accompanied by a spectacular whooshing sound like a fireworks display. It was closely followed by some angry-looking forked lightning, which struck the ground directly in front of the shield with a blinding flash. Angus could feel millions of volts of electricity surging beneath his feet, and he took several swift steps back, along with everyone else, just to be on the safe side. Only Gudgeon remained standing exactly where he was, as if he was watching nothing more deadly than a football game.

With the final lightning strike, however, came something that nobody was expecting. A small blue ball rose up suddenly from the ground and hovered in front of them.

"Ball lightning!" said Gudgeon as everyone gasped. "An extremely rare phenomenon. It may look harmless, but it has the power to burn down entire buildings and char bones if it gets too close. And you're very lucky to see it."

"Lucky?" Dougal spluttered, his eyes now rounder than dinner plates.

"Yes, Dewsnap, lucky. There are still those in the scientific world who don't believe that this stuff exists."

The ball hovered a few feet above the ground, almost as if it was watching them through an invisible eye. Angus stared as little veins of white light arched and crackled across its surface.

"Tell your trainees to stand farther back, Gudgeon!"

Valentine Vellum ordered from behind them. "We've been having a lot of trouble with ball lightning lately. The last one burned our entire collection of research notes on lightning accelerators before we could stop it."

"Stay exactly where you are!" Gudgeon ordered, his face stern. "There are some who believe that ball lightning is attracted to movement. If any of you raises so much as an eyebrow, you'll have me to answer to. I suggest you attempt to catch it, Valentine, before it destroys something really important, like the notes on how you got those twins of yours into Perilous after they both scored less than zero on their entrance exams."

An extremely tense hush descended upon the Lightnarium as the strange, crackling ball began revolving toward the lightning cubs. It touched the corner of the safety shield and fizzled, sending out small sparks of blinding light. Angus was aware of some frenzied activity going on behind him, and he saw the glint of a metal box from the corner of his eye as it was moved hurriedly into position by six or seven lightning catchers.

The ball suddenly began spinning toward them at an alarming rate. Violet screamed and ducked as it shot a mini bolt directly at her head. Gudgeon pulled her out of the way by the wrist and stood between her and the menacing ball.

"If you're going to catch that thing, I suggest you do it now, Vellum!" he barked.

But before the lightning catchers could get anywhere near the strange ball of crackling electricity, it made a move toward Indigo. It floated on its eerie path past Angus, who had an odd urge to reach out and touch it. If he could just push it away from Indigo somehow, and toward the lightning catchers and their metal box, everything would be okay. . . .

He reached out his hands, mesmerized by the dazzling orb . . . and it was only then, as he gazed into its transfixing depths, that he saw it. Curled up deep within the ball was a creature he knew only too well; it was the same one that he'd discovered on the door to the Lightnarium in faded gold and flame, the same fiery creature that had been forcing its way into his dreams all summer. Only this time, it was no nightmare, and it was staring right back at him.

BANG!

Angus stumbled backward in surprise as the dragon burst out of the ball in an explosion of snarling teeth and talons. Its long, shimmering wings unfurled, blasting him with a surge of heat as it hovered beside the ball lightning. The creature held his gaze, dark eyes boring into his own, and suddenly, almost as if it had reached out and planted the thought directly into his brain, Angus knew that Indigo was in deathly danger.

"INDIGO! LOOK OUT!" he yelled.

Indigo stared at him, frozen to the spot with fear. Angus dived, pushing her sideways just as the ball lightning struck. A long streak of brilliant light snapped violently at the space where Indigo had been standing only seconds before, catching Angus on the arm instead.

"Arrgghhh!"

White-hot pain seared straight through his skin and shot deep into his bones, the room swam before his eyes, and he crumpled to his knees.

"Stand back, everyone! Let the boy breathe!"

Gudgeon's voice came floating toward him from what sounded like a very long way off. Angus blinked, opening his eyes slowly. A sea of faces swam into focus above him. And he was very surprised to find himself lying on the floor, with the whole class staring down at him like he was an exhibit in a museum.

"Can you sit up?" Gudgeon asked. He was looking at Angus with deep lines of worry etched into his craggy face.

Angus propped himself up on his elbow and winced with pain. He stared around the Lightnarium quickly, but all traces of the fire dragon and the ball lightning had disappeared.

"What happened?" he asked, his head feeling as if it had just been used as a human trampoline.

"The lightning got you in the arm," Gudgeon explained. "You lost consciousness for a couple of seconds, but you were lucky. Your lightning deflector took most of the sting out of it."

Angus looked down at his arm. The slippery suit had been ripped wide open, and somebody had tied a make-shift bandage around his elbow. Hot, sticky blood was oozing through it.

"But—what about the dragon?" he asked urgently.

"Dragon?" Gudgeon frowned. "What are you talking about?"

"It burst out of the lightning . . . it was going to hurt Indigo. Is—is she all right?"

"Calm down, Doomsbury," Gudgeon reassured him quickly. "Miss Midnight's a bit shaken, but she'll live. She's already been taken up to the sanatorium for a full checkup." Gudgeon helped him slowly to his feet, which wasn't nearly as easy as it sounded, since the floor seemed to be tilting sideways at a very odd angle. "You'd better come with me," said Gudgeon. "There's someone who'll want to have a word after what you just did."

Angus looked over his shoulder and caught a brief glimpse of Dougal's worried face before he followed Gudgeon toward the far end of the Lightnarium. The burn on his arm was beginning to sting painfully now, making him feel dizzy and sick, and he wondered if he was being taken to the doctor. Or was he in some sort of trouble for diving in front of Indigo like a lunatic?

They came to a halt outside a door at the end of the Lightnarium. Gudgeon glared down at him, knocked once, and stomped inside.

8
STORM PROPHET

Angus took a deep breath, which somehow made his arm sting even more. He then followed Gudgeon through the door and into a small room. After the cavelike dimness of the Lightnarium, he was surprised to see bright sunlight streaming in through a small window on the far wall. It hurt his eyes and made him blink. He was also amazed to see that the room was filled with an impressive collection of antique safety goggles of every shape and size, hanging from the ceiling on hooks; some were rose tinted, while others had been rubberized or coated in tough-looking leather. Angus instantly got the impression that hundreds of pairs of eyes were all watching him at once.

Sitting behind a desk in the center of the room was a bearded lightning catcher Angus had never seen before. His eyes resembled those of an owl and were a rich, tawny amber. His long, toffee-colored beard was braided down the middle and tucked inside his leather jerkin.

"Felix?" The man stood, looking puzzled, as they crossed the room toward him.

"You know who this boy is, Aramanthus?" Gudgeon asked.

"I certainly do, but I don't quite see why you have brought him—"

"I've brought him to your office," Gudgeon interrupted, "because Angus here has just saved another cub from a very nasty encounter with some ball lightning. Pushed her out of the way before it struck."

"Did he indeed?" A deep frown crossed the other lightning catcher's face. "Angus, would you mind if I took a quick look at your arm?" he asked. And before Angus could answer, he undid the bandage and carefully inspected the burn beneath it. "Lightning burns are a hazard of working in the Lightnarium, I'm afraid," he explained as he turned Angus's arm toward the light. "As are melted rubber boots, perforated eardrums, and bright purple spots before the eyes. I'm happy to say this burn does not appear to be too serious." He smiled kindly. "I must warn you, however, that it will feel rather sore for the next few days."

He opened a drawer in his desk and took out a jar of thick yellow gel that reminded Angus of wallpaper paste. He spread the gel generously over the burn, and Angus, who suddenly felt his muscles relaxing, realized that his whole body had been clenched tight like a fist ever since the ball lightning had attacked him.

"Thanks a lot, sir," he said, grateful.

The lightning catcher nodded, then turned back to Gudgeon. "Forgive me, Felix, but I still don't understand how Angus came to be facing a ball of lightning in the first place?"

"I'll give you one guess—it was that great bearded goat, Valentine Vellum." Gudgeon spat the name across the room. "If I didn't know any better, I'd swear he'd done it on purpose. I thought, under the circumstances, that you two might want a chat. And if the boy's not about to perish, I'd better get back out there, before Valentine

'accidentally' attacks any more trainees." And with a fleeting glance at Angus, he left the room abruptly, closing the door behind him.

"Why don't you take a seat, Angus?" the lightning catcher said, pointing to a comfortable-looking chair. Angus stayed where he was, however, wondering what there was to chat about.

"Please allow me to introduce myself," the man continued, sitting down behind his desk. "I am Aramanthus Rogwood."

Angus could just make out an impressive nine lightning bolts pinned to the front of his jerkin, hidden beneath the braids of his toffee-colored beard.

"Am I in trouble, sir?" Angus burst out anxiously, unable to stop himself. "Because I only pushed Indigo out of the way to stop her from getting injured."

"Trouble?" Rogwood looked confused. "Why on earth would you be in any trouble?"

"Well, I just thought that . . . because of what I . . . I . . ." Angus stumbled over his words and then stopped, feeling confused.

"Angus." Rogwood fixed him with a steady gaze. "I have

been at Perilous longer than I care to remember. During that time, I have managed to boil my own beard, wreck several hurricane suits, and fall down a flight of stairs, smashing a very rare and valuable collection of antique bottling jars in the process, and I have never been threatened with punishment once. Nobody is about to discipline you for saving your friend from a nasty injury."

Angus nodded, feeling extremely relieved. He lowered himself into the chair, limbs aching as if he'd just run a grueling underwater marathon.

"I would be very grateful, however," Rogwood continued, "if you could explain exactly what happened a few moments ago in the Lightnarium, even if some of the details may sound a little . . . far-fetched." The lightning catcher studied Angus with a thoughtful gaze, as if he could already tell exactly what had happened. But how could he possibly know?

Angus fiddled with the ripped sleeve of his lightning deflector for a moment, weighing the unhappy options now before him. If he told Rogwood about the appearance of the fire dragon, he ran the risk of being sent home for being completely delusional and seeing things that weren't

really there. If, however, he lied about what he'd just seen, if he tried to pretend he had merely pushed Indigo out of the way on an impulse, he might never discover what was going on or why he'd been having the strange visions in the first place.

His mind flashed back to the faded dragon on the door that led to the Lightnarium. Somebody at Perilous knew about the shimmering creatures. This had something to do with the lightning catchers. He was now sure of it. . . .

"I've been having these strange dreams lately, sir," he began, taking a deep breath and deciding he might just as well tell Rogwood everything. "They started when I was staying with my uncle over the summer—"

"Ah, and how is Maximilian these days? Still setting fire to his kitchen on a regular basis, I trust?"

"I . . . you know my uncle?" Angus asked, surprised.

Rogwood smiled, his amber eyes twinkling. "Indeed, I am lucky enough to know most of your family. I apologize for interrupting your story, Angus, but I happen to be very fond of your uncle; he once made me a rather ingenious mechanical moon phase calendar. But please continue."

"Oh, right, yeah . . ." Angus fought the temptation to ask more about the moon phase calendar. "Anyway, when I had these dreams, I always saw the same, er, thing," he said, reluctant to mention the word "dragon" too early in the conversation. "And then I saw another one of them when Edmund Croxley gave me a guided tour of the Octagon. It was on the door to the Lightnarium." He watched Rogwood's face for a reaction, but none came. "And today another one came bursting out at me, just before the ball lightning went for Indigo—"

"Another one of what, exactly?" Rogwood asked calmly.

Angus took another deep breath.

"Another fire dragon. It was hovering right next to the ball lightning and then I suddenly knew that I had to save Indigo, and if I hadn't pushed her out of the way . . . I know it sounds stupid," he said, realizing just how ridiculous it did sound, now he was saying it out loud. "But that's what happened."

Rogwood studied him for several long moments without speaking, an odd, almost sad expression on his face.

"Thank you, Angus, for describing what must have been a most distressing experience for both you and Miss

Midnight," he eventually said. "First, let me assure you that what you saw in the Lightnarium was every bit as real as that burn on your arm."

Angus stared at him, stunned.

"So y-you believe me, then?"

"Certainly. I have no reason for thinking you would make up such a story just to confuse and befuddle an old lightning catcher like me."

"But why can't anyone else see it if it's real?" Angus burst out. Gudgeon's puzzled reaction in the Lightnarium had made it obvious that no one else had caught even a glimpse of the dragon.

Rogwood knitted his fingers together in front of him and sighed. "I will do my best to explain, but first, would you care to join me in a mug of warm milk? It is the best cure I know for a nasty shock to the system such as the one you have just experienced." He stood up and went over to a small fire in the corner of the room, with a pan already simmering on it. He poured hot milk into two mugs and handed one to Angus.

"There have been other lightning catchers before you who have seen a very similar dragon, Angus," Rogwood said after a moment of silence. "It is a rare ability, however, and usually takes a number of years to show itself. It is very curious, therefore, that you have displayed such abilities, with no training, and at such a remarkably young age. I believe, Angus, that you are a storm prophet."

"A what?" Angus asked, swallowing more hot milk than he meant to and scalding the roof of his mouth.

"A storm prophet can sometimes predict what volatile weather is about to do, before it actually does it."

"You mean like a . . . a fortune-teller predicts things?"

"Along similar lines, yes." Rogwood nodded.

"But . . . I don't understand," Angus said, frowning. "What does seeing a fire dragon have to do with predicting the weather?"

"Soon after Edgar Perilous and Philip Starling came to Imbur and founded this Exploratorium," Rogwood explained, "it was discovered that some lightning catchers had a rare and natural ability to predict when violent weather might be of danger to others, and they were quickly given the name storm prophets. All of the storm prophets described how a fiery dragon appeared before them on such occasions, like a warning, but although they took part in countless experiments, some of them here in the Lightnarium, their abilities and visions have never been truly understood."

Angus shivered. What sorts of dangerous experiments had the storm prophets taken part in?

"One thing was clear, however," Rogwood continued. "Storm prophets did not see the weather as mere cloud or rain, hailstone or blizzard. Indeed, they could see beyond any flake of snow or gust of wind and sense the raw, elemental forces that lurked deep within the storm itself. And a fire dragon was the perfect vision, the perfect warning at such moments—a fearsome creature, trembling with the same power and violence that the storm was about to unleash."

Angus thought about the fire dragon that had appeared in the Lightnarium, and gulped.

"Some say this talent for storm spotting goes all the way back to the Great Fire of London itself," Rogwood explained calmly, "back to those heady days when lightning towers peppered the skies of that illustrious city, when the sheer scale and force of those vast towers caused an irreversible alteration in some of those who operated them."

"An . . . alteration?" asked Angus.

Rogwood nodded. "It is believed that these operators laid themselves open to such powerful forces of nature that over time, some of them were infused with the very forces they were trying to capture and control, and that this changed them—forever.

"Your own family, Angus, comes from a long line of lightning catchers. Indeed, they were among those who first came to Imbur from the ashes of the Great Fire itself. I believe that you may have inherited the skills of a storm prophet from your ancestors. The dragon appeared before you today as a warning that Indigo was in imminent danger. You pushed her out of the way before the ball lightning could strike and took the blow yourself, which, I might add, was an extremely brave thing to do."

Angus put his hot milk on the desk in front of him. His head was swimming once again. He didn't feel in the least bit brave.

"I realize all of this must seem rather odd," Rogwood continued, "when you are still spending your days repairing punctures in rubber boots. But it is nothing to be afraid of, Angus, if it is handled correctly. If you have no objections, I would like to talk to you further on this sub-ject at another time. I would advise you in the meantime, however, to keep this information to yourself." His owl-like eyes fixed upon Angus in warning. "It is not the sort of conversation that ought to be shared with your fellow lightning cubs over your breakfast, for instance. And now, I think we had better get that burn looked at properly by Doctor Fleagal."

Rogwood stood up before Angus could ask any more questions—of which he suddenly seemed to have hun-dreds. Such as, who else at Perilous could see fire drag-ons? And why could he, Angus, suddenly see them now, when the last ten years of his life had been entirely dragon free? And what if he didn't want to be a storm prophet at all? Was there something he could do to turn it off and go back to being normal again?

Angus followed Rogwood across the room. He knew that despite the warning, he would tell Dougal about everything that had just happened, as soon as he got the chance.

Talking to Dougal in private proved to be difficult, how-ever. At breakfast the following morning, they were joined at their usual table by Millicent Nichols, Jonathon Hake, and Nigel Ridgely, all of whom were extremely eager to talk to Angus about what had happened in the Lightnarium.

"Did it hurt when the ball lightning struck you?" Nigel asked, leaning across the table eagerly.

"Yeah, did you actually feel it going into your bones?" Jonathon Hake probed, staring hopefully at Angus's arm.

Angus mumbled a few words about not remembering much, his face shining with embarrassment. Then he stared down into his bacon and eggs until, one by one, his fellow trainees drifted back to their own tables.

He didn't get an opportunity to speak to Dougal as they made their way up to the experimental division either, since they were accompanied right to the door by an inquisitive Georgina Fox. And as soon as they slipped through the door itself, Catcher Sparks descended upon them both with two pairs of pink rubber gloves and an extremely stern look on her face.

"I'm surprised to see you here this morning, Doomsbury, after your adventures in the Lightnarium," she said, glaring at him angrily. "Catcher Vellum took great delight in telling me about it yesterday evening, and I must say that I am extremely disappointed by your reckless behavior. You were specifically told by Gudgeon and Catcher Vellum himself not to do anything without their permission while in the Lightnarium, and yet you chose to ignore the warnings of both."

"But, miss, I—"

"You would do well to remember the declaration you signed on your first day here, Doomsbury," Catcher Sparks continued, her nostrils now white and somewhat flared. "And to pay close attention in the future to any safety instructions issued to you by a lightning catcher, particularly one who is used to dealing with lightning bolts on a daily basis."

"Yes, Catcher, but I—"

"If you choose to ignore any of *my* warnings, there will be no second chances. You will be sent straight back to the mainland before you can say 'cloud-busting rocket launcher,' do I make myself clear?"

"Yes, miss." Angus nodded and stared down at his shoes, which was easier than trying to argue.

Catcher Sparks finally seemed to feel that she'd said

enough on the subject, and she straightened the buckles on her jerkin, her nostrils slowly returning to their normal shape and size. "Now, I've got a special job for you two this morning," she snapped. "Come with me, if you please."

She led them straight past a new rain-measuring device with an enormous vibrating funnel that was being worked on by several tired-looking lightning catchers, and all the way across to the farthest corner of the experimental division. Here the body of the storm vacuum had been detached from its sucking arm and was crouched on the floor like an enormous spider.

"I want this vacuum bag emptied out entirely before the end of the day," Catcher Sparks ordered, handing a pair of pink rubber gloves to each of them. "We are hoping to test the storm vacuum again tomorrow morning, and we cannot do so if the collection bag is full. One of you will have to crawl inside and pass the contents out to the other. And don't give me that look, Dewsnap," she added tartly, catching the expression of utmost disgust that had flashed across Dougal's face. "Being a lightning catcher isn't all about watching flashy displays of lightning tarantulatis,

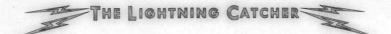

and the sooner the two of you get that into your thick skulls, the better."

Dougal exchanged dark looks with Angus.

"Any nuts, bolts, or other pieces of equipment you come across in the storm vacuum should be set to one side for cleaning. Any fluff, dirt, or other items of rubbish can be discarded, and try not to breathe in too much dust while you're working. I don't want Doctor Fleagal to be pestered with any more unnecessary injuries." She shot a disapproving look at Angus. "Miss Midnight will not be joining you this morning, so it will be up to the two of you to complete the task by yourselves."

"Is Indigo all right, miss?" asked Angus.

"She is a little shaken by yesterday's unfortunate incident. Doctor Fleagal is keeping her in the sanatorium for a little longer so she may rest."

And without another word to either of them, Catcher Sparks strode away.

"Anyone would think you'd deliberately broken into the Lightnarium and set off at least a hundred thunderstorms on purpose, the way she's talking about it," Dougal said, scowling after her. "You don't think Indigo is hurt, do you?"

Angus shook his head. He'd caught a brief glimpse of Indigo in the sanatorium the previous afternoon. She had been sitting on a bed, looking rather pale and shocked, clutching what looked like her own mug of steaming hot milk. But he'd seen no sign of any injuries. She'd given him a faint smile as he'd been swept toward Doctor Fleagal's office by Rogwood.

"So what did happen yesterday, anyway?" Dougal finally asked as soon as Catcher Sparks was safely out of earshot. "You should have seen Gudgeon's face when that lightning bolt hit you! I think he thought you were dead. Mind you, the rest of us thought you might be dead as well. I'm quite glad you're not, though," Dougal added, grinning. "Going to fog lectures on my own would have been really boring."

"Er, thanks . . . I think." Angus smiled.

"I knocked on your door loads of times last night, but there was no answer."

"That's because I was still in the sanatorium," Angus explained.

He had in fact, spent an extremely lonely and troubling day in the sanatorium. Doctor Fleagal, who had turned out to be a short, stout, chatty sort of man, had insisted on telling Angus several stomach-churning stories about an infestation of something called crumble fungus, which had broken out at the Exploratorium many years ago, while he dressed the burn on Angus's arm.

He had then ordered Angus to lie quietly on a bed, where there had been nothing for him to do but stare at the ceiling and imagine himself as a fortune-teller at the fair, complete with a crystal ball and gold hoop earrings, telling total strangers that they were about to be drenched by a bad-tempered monsoon or chased around the island by a hurricane. And he had been unable to shake off the uncomfortable daydreams until the doctor had finally released him at ten o'clock that evening.

He quickly described the events in the sanatorium to Dougal, leaving out the part about the gold hoop earrings.

"Yeah, but I still don't get why you dived in front of Indigo in the first place," Dougal said as soon as Angus had finished. "I mean, how did you even know the lightning was going to strike out at her like that?"

Angus glanced over his shoulder. Catcher Sparks was busy on the other side of the room, grappling with what looked like a huge weathervane. He took a deep breath and plunged into a hurried explanation about the appearance of the fire dragon. Dougal's eyebrows shot higher and higher up his forehead as he listened, and when Angus finally described the startling conversation he'd had in Rogwood's office afterward, Dougal could contain himself no longer.

"Rogwood says you're a *what*?" he gasped.

Several of the lightning catchers suddenly stopped what they were doing and looked around. Catcher Sparks glared over at them both.

"Shhhhhh! Keep your voice down, will you?" Angus hissed, pulling on the pink rubber gloves up to his elbows and kneeling down at the mouth of the storm vacuum, trying to look as if he was doing something useful. "I don't want everyone knowing about it."

"Sorry," Dougal said, kneeling down hurriedly beside him. "It's just, well . . . if Rogwood's right . . . I mean, a storm prophet!"

"Why, what's wrong with being a storm prophet?"

"Nothing, really, it's just . . . most people think they're a bit of a joke, actually," said Dougal, grinning. "They turn up every year at the Little Frog's Bottom summer festival wearing huge gold earrings and head scarves, pretending they know loads of mystical stuff about doomed lightning bolts and cursed rain. But I've never heard any of them talking about fire dragons before. . . . Real storm prophets are supposed to be pretty rare, though, according to my dad."

Angus felt his stomach lurch.

"Has your dad told you anything else about them?" he asked.

"Only that hundreds of years ago there were loads of genuine storm prophets around. Dad says they were a bit like weather forecasters, only they didn't need charts and wind socks to tell them what the weather was going to do, they just sort of knew it, by instinct or something. And I don't think there's anything you can actually do about it if you are one. Storm prophets are just born that way; it's a bit like being left-handed or having big feet. Are you sure Rogwood wasn't just pulling your leg, though?" Dougal asked, looking at Angus oddly over the top of his glasses. "I mean, my dad said they all died out ages ago, and as far as anyone knows, there haven't been any real storm prophets on the island for centuries now."

Angus thought back to the meeting in the lightning catcher's office and the sad look that had settled on Rogwood's face. "He definitely wasn't pulling my leg. I don't see how I could be any kind of weather prophet, though," he added. "I mean, I didn't even know about Perilous until a month ago, did I?"

"None of us has ever seen an invisible fog before either, but that doesn't stop Miss DeWinkle from going on about how dangerous it is to get caught out in one without your weather watch. I reckon there is one way of finding out for sure if you're a real storm prophet or not," said Dougal, suddenly looking shifty. "It won't be easy, Catcher Sparks'll go mental if she catches us, but I think I can . . ."

Dougal's voice suddenly trailed away to nothing as a dark shadow fell across the storm vacuum. Angus looked up quickly to see Catcher Sparks towering over them both, her arms folded, her nostrils flaring once again with rage.

"IT HAS BEEN FIFTEEN MINUTES SINCE I TOLD YOU TO START EMPTYING THIS STORM VACUUM," she bellowed, making them both jump. "WHAT ARE YOU TWO WAITING FOR—CHRISTMAS?"

It was easily the most revolting job they'd done so far. Worse, even, than removing earwax from the hailstone helmets or scraping somebody else's toenails from the depths of a smelly rubber boot. Angus crawled into the mouth of the vacuum bag first, a cloud of fine dirt and fluff forcing its way into his mouth and up his nose and swirling round his head like a swarm of dusty bees. The storm vacuum had sucked up half the contents of the experimental division, it seemed; there were ratchets and screwdrivers, rusty nails and rubber boots, a Band-Aid that had clearly been sucked straight off someone's finger—along with the scab it had been protecting. There was also an impressive collection of technical drawings (which had been ripped to shreds), as well as a handful of weather watches (smashed to smithereens) and a ham-and-pickle sandwich that was starting to get moldy.

For a long time, neither of them spoke. Angus did his best to push a mangled chair, several table legs, and what appeared to be a voluminous pair of spotted underpants back through the mouth of the storm vacuum, but it was tricky work. As unpleasant as crawling around inside the vacuum bag was, however, Angus felt it was far more enjoyable than what was going on inside his own head. Images of fire dragons came leaping into his mind, blazing with ferocious heat, making him feel dizzy. He couldn't help hoping that Rogwood might have made a mistake. After all, how could he, Angus McFangus of Budleigh Otterstone, Devon, be a genuine storm prophet when, according to Dougal's dad, none had even existed for hundreds of years now? Besides, he had never been able to predict so much as a gust of wind, never mind rainstorms or tornadoes or lightning strikes. And he crawled around the confines of the storm vacuum, hoping that he'd never see another fire dragon again.

Even more unsettling was Dougal's strange behavior throughout the rest of the day. On several occasions, as Angus struggled to drag a heavy bag of sand or a large copper kettle through the mouth of the storm vacuum, he emerged into the room, puffing and panting, only to find that Dougal was nowhere to be seen. When he did eventually appear again, there was an odd clanking noise coming from under his bulging sweater, which Dougal refused to discuss. It wasn't until the end of a very long day that Angus finally found out what his friend had been up to.

They ate a hurried dinner in the kitchens, then made a quick exit down the spiral stairs to the Pigsty. Only when both doors were closed firmly behind them and the curtains had been drawn across the window did Dougal remove two glass spheres from under his sweater and show them to Angus.

"Storm globes?" Angus said, recognizing them immediately. "But . . . where did you get those from?"

"I borrowed them from the storage cupboard in the experimental division, of course. They were stuffed in a box at the back of a shelf, so I don't think anyone will notice that they're gone. It took me a couple of tries to get them down without somebody walking in and catching me."

Angus stared at the dusty globes. "But what have you borrowed them for?" he asked, still puzzled.

"I got the idea from you, actually, after what happened with Gudgeon at the ferry port. It's the nearest thing we can get to a real live thunderstorm without actually getting ourselves killed in the Lightnarium," Dougal explained. "If we can make this globe produce a thunderstorm, with a bit of lightning tarantulatis thrown in for good measure, and you see the fire dragon again . . . well, it's like I said. At least you'll know then once and for all whether you're a real storm prophet or not."

Angus gulped. He wasn't sure he really wanted to know—once and for all. But Dougal had clearly gone to a lot of trouble on his behalf, risking the severe displeasure of Catcher Sparks and a possible overnight stay in the storm vacuum if he'd been caught.

"But . . . won't people hear it if we set a storm globe off in here?" he said, glancing around the tiny room and thinking of the likelihood that they would flood half the Exploratorium if they smashed a globe anywhere indoors.

"That's the brilliant part of the whole plan," Dougal said, looking immensely pleased with himself. "You don't have to smash a globe to get it to produce a storm. You can do it without anyone else knowing."

Angus picked up one of the glass spheres, wiped a thin layer of dust off the surface, and studied it with interest. He had been extremely curious about storm globes ever since the incident at the pier. This particular globe, however, appeared to be totally empty.

"What are we supposed to do with it?" he asked,

turning it around in his hands and admiring it.

"All storm globes contain an assortment of Swarfe weather crystals, which react with the natural heat from your hands to produce any kind of weather you can think of. We don't learn how to use them properly until our fourth year, so I'm not exactly sure of the details . . . but it can't be that hard to work it out!" Dougal looked hopeful and perched himself on the arm of a chair. "This one's probably been sitting in the cupboard for a while. It might be a bit sluggish to begin with, so you'd better give it a shake, just to help get it started."

Angus shook it carefully. At first nothing appeared to happen, but then, slowly, out of nowhere, clouds began to form inside the sphere, getting thicker and darker until eventually rain fell from the miniature weather system and collected in a tiny gray puddle at the bottom of the globe.

"Brilliant!" Dougal said, sounding pleased. "At least we know it still works."

After another twenty minutes, Angus had discovered that the incredible globe could produce any type of weather he thought of, depending on how he held the glass sphere in his hands. By cradling it in one hand only, he could conjure up a freezing blizzard; by cupping it tightly in both palms, he could bring on a balmy summer's day, complete with buzzing insects and a shimmering heat haze. He could also fast-forward or rewind his way through storms at any speed, or pause the weather alto- gether for as long as he felt like it, and count individual drops of rain or frosted flakes of snow as they floated in the orb.

"I'm definitely putting one of these on my Christmas list," Angus said, gazing at the amazing globe as it pro- duced a dazzling rainbow.

They spent several minutes watching a miniature hurricane rage inside the globe, and quite a few more listening to the rumblings of a dark thunderstorm as it brewed within the glass.

"Go on then," Dougal urged when the storm seemed ready to burst. "Close your eyes and tell me if you see anything dragon shaped."

Angus had been having such a good time putting the storm globe through its paces that he'd almost forgotten why Dougal had borrowed it in the first place. And he closed his eyes reluctantly. All he could see for a moment was a vision of himself with his eyes closed, looking ridiculous. He tried to think about the storm globe instead. He could feel the thunderstorm within it beginning to gather momentum. Then, all of a sudden—

"Wow!" Dougal gasped. "Forked lightning."

Angus felt a surge of heat travel through his left thumb and guessed that a miniature lightning bolt had struck the glass directly underneath it. It was an odd sensation, like having his thumb dipped in hot melted wax.

"Well . . . did you see anything?" Dougal asked.

Angus hesitated, searching the inside of his eyelids nervously for any suspicious-looking creatures. He opened his eyes and glanced around the room, quickly making sure that there were no dragons lurking behind the curtains.

"No!" he said, feeling immensely relieved. "I didn't see anything."

"Well, that proves it then, doesn't it? You can't be a storm prophet, or you'd be seeing dragons all over the place by now."

But the words had barely left Dougal's mouth when it

happened. From the corner of his eye, Angus caught one heart-stopping glimpse of the fiery scales and steak-knife teeth that could only belong to yet another fire dragon. It shimmered briefly in the air, a dazzling warning of danger, before—

"Ouch!" Angus yelped as a second bolt of lightning struck him out of the blue. A searing heat shot right through the palm of his left hand. He dropped the globe hastily, and it smashed into a hundred tiny slivers of glass all over the floor.

"Oh, no." Dougal backed away nervously as dark wisps of an angry storm rose up from the shattered glass. "That definitely wasn't supposed to happen!"

"Quick! We've got to get it outside before it starts raining on us," said Angus, darting over to the window and throwing it open wide.

Cool air rushed in. Wisps of storm began to spin above their heads ominously. Angus grabbed a copy of the *McFangus Fog Guide* and began to waft the cloud toward the open window. Dougal seized a cushion from his chair and joined in. Wafting a stubborn storm cloud in a direction it didn't want to go, however, proved to be practically

impossible. After several moments of frantic flapping, it simply refused to budge.

"This book's useless," Angus panted, dropping it on the floor in disgust. "We're going to need something much bigger!"

"Or a really good excuse about why we've flooded the whole Exploratorium," said Dougal, wiping beads of sweat off his brow.

For the next few minutes it looked as though the storm might win the battle, as Angus and Dougal used everything they could think of—weatherproof coats, pillows, and moth-eaten wall hangings—to disperse the angry storm cloud. Matters were not helped when Angus accidentally kicked over both their mugs of cocoa, splashing the sticky drink everywhere. Or when Dougal somehow managed to slice the entire cloud in two with a poorly aimed swipe.

"Quick, stop the other half of that storm before it slips under the door and escapes into the corridor!" he yelled, chasing after it with a large paper bag.

But finally they managed to force the storm through the window, just as the first few drops of rain began to fall.

"Phew! I thought we'd had it when I sliced that thing in half!" said Dougal, slamming the window shut and collapsing into a chair.

"Yeah, remind me not to put one of those on my Christmas list after all, will you?" Angus frowned, inspecting the tiny burns on his hands. "I think I'd rather take my chances in the Lightnarium than go through that again."

Dougal smirked. "You might have to if Principal Dark-Angel ever finds out what we've been up to."

Angus wandered to the window and watched the storm cloud as it slowly began to disperse in the evening breeze. With one final fizzle of lightning, it disappeared completely—taking all traces of the faded fire dragon with it.

9

FOG MITES

The unexpected appearance of yet another fire dragon put Angus in a very bad mood for the rest of the evening.

"Yeah, but you only saw it for a couple of seconds, so it doesn't really count, does it?" Dougal offered consolingly as they swept up the shattered glass and tidied the Pigsty.

But Angus couldn't shake the uncomfortable feeling that any sighting of the dragon, no matter how brief, merely confirmed the fact that there was something different about him, something odd that he definitely didn't want anyone else to hear about, and he swore Dougal to secrecy.

The following morning at breakfast, he was met at his usual table by Indigo Midnight, who hovered beside him awkwardly, chewing her lip.

"Hi," she said, giving him a faint smile. "Is it all right if I sit down for a minute?"

Angus shuffled his chair around to make room for her, noticing as he did so that there were dark shadows under her eyes. This was the first time he'd seen her since the sanatorium, and Indigo still looked rather pale and shaken.

"Listen, I just wanted to thank you for what you did," she said with a tremble in her voice.

"Oh, er . . ."

"I couldn't believe it when the lightning shot out at me like that." She shuddered. "If you hadn't shoved me out of the way . . ."

Angus shifted uncomfortably in his seat. The image of a fire dragon flashed before his eyes.

"Forget it, I owed you one anyway," he said, in what he hoped was a jokey-sounding voice. "After you saved me from that coconut in the weather tunnel and everything."

Indigo gave him an anxious smile. "How's your arm? Does it hurt much?"

"Nah, it's fine," Angus lied. The burn had been sting-ing quite a bit since he'd woken up that morning. "Doctor Fleagal says it'll heal by itself if I leave it alone."

Indigo nodded, her hair falling over her eyes. She pushed it out of her face impatiently, and Angus got the distinct impression that she was about to say something else, something she found deeply awkward and embarrassing, judging by the crimson blush that was now creeping up both sides of her neck. Before she could speak again, how-ever, Dougal pulled up a chair, said a cheerful good morn-ing to them both, and sat down with a steaming plate of sausages in front of him.

Indigo stood up without uttering another word and returned swiftly to her own table.

"Was it something I said?" asked Dougal, puzzled. "What did she want, anyway?"

"I'm not sure . . . but I think there's something she's not telling us."

"Well, there's definitely something I'm not remember-ing about her." Dougal frowned, pushing his glasses up his nose. "I just wish I knew what it was. It's probably got something to do with my dad, though, and the research he's done for one of his books. It's the only reason I'd know her name."

"Why don't you just ask her about it?" Angus suggested.

But Dougal shook his head quickly. "No way. If my dad's done any research into the Midnights, it's because they're pirates, or swindlers, or because they caused the Great Imbur Beer Riots of 1901, and I'm definitely not asking her about that."

Angus glanced over at Indigo, finding it very hard to believe that she, or her family, could ever have been involved in the kind of things Dougal was describing.

As the days drifted slowly by, all visions of the fire dragon stopped once again. Angus clung to the hope that Rogwood might have made a mistake about him, that the chances of him being a real storm prophet were remote, and that he'd acted on nothing more than pure instinct in the Lightnarium.

He was worried about his parents, however. Why were they even at Castle Dankhart in the first place? Why hadn't Principal Dark-Angel mentioned the fact that Scabious Dankhart was a weather menace? And when would he see his mum and dad again?

Meanwhile, in the experimental division, Catcher Sparks gave each of them a copy of *Pocket Book of All-Season Weather Words* by Cecil Doldrum, which they were supposed to study and learn. It referred to strange-sounding things such as crepuscular rays, Gulf Streams, and mistrals, which Angus had never heard of, as well as anvil zits (which had something to do with thunderstorms) and graupel (a combination of snowflakes and ice pellets). There were also custard winds, killing frosts, and kilopascals. And a whole section on isobars that made absolutely no sense whatsoever.

"It's all to do with atmospheric pressure and weather maps," Dougal tried to explain one evening in the Pigsty, grinning from ear to ear. "This is brilliant! I wish we could do more reading and less cleaning. I mean, this is real scientific stuff about the weather!"

A week later, Angus found himself with even more to occupy his brain. A huge notice appeared in the kitchens one blustery morning, revealing that the fog field trips would take place on the wild and gloomy Imbur marshes, beyond the town of Little Frog's Bottom. Fog fever gripped the Exploratorium in earnest, and a flood of outrageous rumors quickly followed.

Reports that Crowned Prince Rufus, a member of the Imbur royal family, would be disguising himself as a lightning catcher—just so he could take part—swept around Perilous like wildfire. But they were nothing compared to the story that Principal Dark-Angel had ordered that a whole troop of fog yetis be released onto the marshes to liven things up a bit.

"Only sixth years and above have been trained to deal with the hairy creatures," Theodore Twill, a loudmouthed sixth year, informed tables full of the most anxious lightning cubs one lunchtime. "But the best way to scare off a yeti is to—"

"Hey, Twill, I can tell you how to scare a yeti!" Nicholas Grubb called as he hurried past the tables with a group of sniggering friends. "Just try looking in the mirror!"

Dougal grinned; Angus tried hard not to laugh as Theodore stomped off, fuming. But he'd been listening to Twill's advice with a growing sense of unease. To add to his anxiety, he also discovered, from Edmund Croxley, that the only way to get off the towering rock upon which Perilous sat, and out into the Imbur marshes, was via an extraordinary contraption called a gravity railway. This alarming mode of transport involved being lowered down the near-vertical sides of the rock on a cable in an old-fashioned carriage. Just the thought of it made Angus feel light-headed.

"But you must have ridden in it when you first arrived here," Dougal said, looking surprised, when Angus eventually admitted he wasn't looking forward to the experience.

"I was unconscious, remember? They could have catapulted me up here with a giant rubber band and I wouldn't have known anything about it."

The subject of what the foggy trips might involve now occupied almost every conversation at the Exploratorium. It was a subject that Miss DeWinkle also addressed during their very next lesson. She came bouncing into the weather bubble wearing a sickly pink sweater over the top of her leather jerkin, and matching rubber boots.

"Good morning, everyone!" She beamed, a smile pinned to her round face.

It was a cold, damp morning outside, with the first hint of autumn blowing through the chilly stone tunnels and passageways of Perilous. A watery-looking sun was hiding stubbornly behind the clouds, refusing to come out. Despite the gloomy weather, however, spirits were running high inside the weather bubble. Everyone ignored the arrival of Miss DeWinkle and continued to discuss an interesting new rumor, which had surfaced only that morning. According to Juliana Jessop, a bossy fifth-year trainee, Principal Dark-Angel had decided to treat everyone who took part in the field trips to a whole month's supply of candy from Balthazar's, the most famous chocolatier on the island.

"I said GOOD MORNING!" Miss DeWinkle bellowed, slamming down a large pile of books on her desk, and a startled hush fell around the bubble. "That's more like it. I realize the field trips are causing a great deal of excitement, especially after some of the more ridiculous rumors that have been circulating. But we are here to discuss the subject of foghorns, in case you have forgotten."

"Not much chance of that, is there?" Dougal mumbled, opening his backpack and reaching inside it for his workbook.

"You will all now open your McFangus guides at the beginning of chapter two and—"

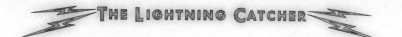
"But, miss," Nigel Ridgely interrupted from the front row before she could get any further. "Couldn't you tell us something about the field trips first? Nobody's told us anything yet."

Angus looked up from his desk, where he'd been busy trying to conceal an interesting book on the experimental division and their most spectacular mishaps within the pages of his fog guide.

"Haven't any of you read the excellent chapter in your McFangus guides about them?" Miss DeWinkle asked, sounding disappointed.

There was a general mumbling and shaking of heads. Angus understood why. Despite the fact that it had been written by his parents and had a number of exciting chapter headings (such as "How to Outwit a Wispy Fog"), the fog guide made for extremely dull reading. Even Dougal, a keen appreciator of books, had given up after the first few pages.

Nigel Ridgely tried again. "I bet you could tell us loads more about the field trips than any book." Behind him, Violet Quinn and Millicent Nichols nodded enthusiastically.

"Oh, goodness." Miss DeWinkle beamed, looking flattered. "Well, I suppose I have taken part in more field trips than anyone else at Perilous. I remember a particularly gripping season some years ago, involving a desperate dash through a field of giant fogcicles . . ."

Angus and Dougal grinned at each other. It was almost impossible to picture Miss DeWinkle—with her short, dumpy legs and wobbling double chins—doing anything so energetic.

"And it certainly couldn't hurt to give you a few of the basic facts," she added, happily abandoning her lecture notes now and propping herself on the edge of her desk. "According to Perilous records, the first fog field trip was a complete accident. In 1739, a lightning catcher called Neville Loxley set out from this Exploratorium in search of some giant hailstones, which had been bombarding various parts of the island for several days. Having taken a wrong turn on the far side of Little Frog's Bottom, however, he inadvertently found himself stumbling about the Imbur marshes instead. It was there, among the desolate wetlands, that he discovered some of the most rare and fascinating fogs known to man, including howling, poisonous, and contagious fogs, to name but a few. Elated by his discovery, he set about taking numerous samples and making detailed notes. Sadly, after wandering about the marshes for five days, he became hopelessly lost, not to mention delirious, and had to be rescued by a team of lightning catchers. By all accounts, he was never quite the same again. But it was such a significant episode in our history at Perilous that we still celebrate his magnificent discoveries each year on Neville Loxley Day."

"Imagine if we discovered a brand-new fog," Dougal whispered. "They'd have to name a day after us, too—or maybe even a whole Snap-Fang weekend!"

"Fog field trips have been a traditional part of lightning cub training ever since," Miss DeWinkle continued. "As lightning catchers, you will spend more than three entire years of your life studying different varieties, collecting samples, and dealing with fog emergencies as they arise around the globe. So it is crucial that you learn how to work in it without suffering from a severe case of fog disorientation."

"I think I might be suffering from that already," Dougal whispered, forcing Angus to hide a smirk behind his McFangus guide.

"Or even vapor sickness," Miss DeWinkle continued, giving them both a hard stare. "Dangerous, devious, and extremely tricky, fog is impossible to navigate without rigorous training. The purpose to these field trips, therefore, is threefold. First, to introduce you to as many different types of fog as possible, while the fog season lasts. Second, to ensure that each of you learns how to use your weather watch correctly. And finally, to teach you how to tackle even the thickest confusing fog, with the aid of your *McFangus Fog Guide* and without collapsing into a quivering heap. There will be perils concealed deep within the dense mists," Miss DeWinkle warned dramatically. Dougal stopped smiling abruptly, the color draining from his face. "There will be bumps, grazes, shocks, and surprises. I guarantee you will never forget the excitements of your first fog season. And that is what makes the field trips one of the most popular events in your training calendar."

"What kind of shocks, miss?" Nigel Ridgley asked, looking rather worried.

"It wouldn't be much of a surprise if I told you, now would it, Ridgley?" Miss DeWinkle chortled, her chins wobbling. "I can tell you, however, that there will be four field trips in all, spread over the next two months. Precise dates will only be given a few days before each trip begins. Older trainees at different stages of their fog training will be taking part in their own field trips, some of which may take place at the same time as yours.

"Now, if everyone will open their textbooks and answer the questions on page twenty-nine," she said as a groan swept around the room, "we must return to our lessons. And before I forget, I have just received a most promising weather report from our very own forecasting department." She waved a sheet of paper at them. "From the early hours of tomorrow morning, the whole island will be plunged into a thick fake fog, which often shows itself shortly before the real season begins. It will, however, give us the perfect opportunity to get in some vital practice for your field trips. We will be leaving Perilous no later than six o'clock tomorrow morning in order to catch the fog in its most unspoiled and pristine state."

"Six o'clock!" Dougal said, looking stunned. "But the kitchens don't even open until seven."

"I will expect you all to be awake, alert, and equipped

with your copy of the McFangus guide," Miss DeWinkle continued. "Wet weather clothes and rubber boots should be worn by everyone, please. And I suggest you all get an early night."

The next morning, they assembled bleary-eyed and yawning in the courtyard outside, and it looked like the forecasting department had predicted the weather with depressing accuracy. Angus could hardly see his own hand in front of his face. The thick fog swirled unpleasantly around his head, freezing his ears and making him wish he was back in his warm, comfortable bed. Dougal was too tired to even speak, and the rest of the group was fighting to keep their eyes open and clearly losing the battle.

None of them had taken Miss DeWinkle's advice about getting an early night. They had spent the entire evening in the kitchens discussing what shocks and surprises might be waiting for them on their field trips and hadn't gone to bed until just before midnight.

At six o'clock precisely, Miss DeWinkle bounded into the courtyard, looking annoyingly awake and cheerful.

"Good morning, everyone!" She beamed from beneath

a revolting hat of bile-green wool. She was carrying a pile of flashlights and immediately began handing them out to everyone. "Can't be too careful this time of the morning," she said, flicking her own light on and off to make sure it worked. "If any of you get lost, I suggest three flashes with your light as a distress signal."

"If I get lost out there, I'm not wasting my time with signals," Dougal said, shivering. "I'm yelling my head off for help."

Miss DeWinkle led the way out of the courtyard and into the thickest depths of the fog.

"Now, before we go any farther, this is an excellent opportunity to recap on the basics of how fog is formed."

"Recap?" Angus whispered. "You mean we've covered this stuff before?" He racked his brains trying to remember what Miss DeWinkle had told them, but it felt like the early morning fog had seeped in through his ears, leaving him befuddled.

"Fog is formed when warm moist air travels over much colder ground below, which is why it usually occurs during the autumn and winter months, and often after frosts, ice, or snow," she explained as they shivered before her. "If the warm air contains enough moisture, it will condense as it is cooled by the ground and form itself into one of the many fascinating types of fog that you have already been introduced to. There are those who insist that fog is simply a cloud created on the ground," she said, with obvious disdain, "but, in my opinion, that does not describe the sheer complexity of this most magnificent weather."

Angus glanced at his weather watch, which was smothered at that moment in pearly white swirls and was advising him to turn right around and head back inside again.

"Fake fog, such as the one you are now standing in, is thick and impenetrable one second, and vanishes completely the next, and is therefore not a proper fog at all. A true fog reduces visibility to half a mile or less. And on Imbur, it often leaves you with no more than a few feet to get your bearings. Running is therefore strictly forbidden in such conditions," she continued. "I would also advise taking small, measured steps, to avoid painful collisions. And if you feel disorientation setting in, staring at the ground often helps."

Two minutes later, they were split up into groups and

forced to practice walking through the fog in the correct manner.

"I said no running, Hake!" Miss DeWinkle bellowed as Jonathon collided with Millicent Nichols head-on.

She then instructed them to identify the unique characteristics of the fake fog, using their McFangus guides. It was cold work, with moisture droplets freezing their gloves solid and making their teeth chatter. And they quickly discovered that outside the nice warm weather bubble, all fogs really looked exactly the same.

"This is totally impossible," Dougal said after fifteen minutes of staring at the water droplets and trying to measure them for size and sogginess.

"Yeah, I know," Angus said, concentrating hard. "What are we supposed to do with the stuff once we've measured it, anyway?"

They weren't the only ones having trouble. Most of the class looked wet through, and miserable, and to make matters even worse, the mouthwatering smell of fried bacon began to drift toward them from the Perilous kitchens.

After another head-numbing half hour, Miss DeWinkle handed around small glass jars to everyone and instructed them to collect fog samples, so they could continue their studies back inside after breakfast.

"How are you supposed to know if you've got any in your jar, though?" Dougal asked, peering through the glass and giving it a shake.

Angus shrugged. "Stick your nose inside it, and if it smells like old turnips, you'll know you've probably got something."

"I'm not sticking my nose anywhere near . . . ouch! Geroff me!"

There was a tinkle of breaking glass as Dougal suddenly dropped his jar. Angus spun around to see his friend waving his arms frantically about his head and desperately trying to flick something off his ears.

"What is it, what's up?" he asked, concerned.

"Something just bit me!"

Angus frowned. "Bit you? But—OW!" he yelped as something flew in front of him and sank its extremely sharp teeth into the back of his hand. "What in the name of . . ."

Two more blurry shapes whizzed past him, heading straight for his ears. A second later, it seemed the whole class had been engulfed by a cloud of strange flying insects that buzzed menacingly above their heads and attacked at will. Pixie Vellum ran past them, screaming as a vicious horde jabbed at the back of her neck. Violet Quinn had a whole cloud of the nasty creatures stuck in her hair. Trainees scattered in every direction, trying to escape. Only Indigo, it seemed, was having any success at fending the creatures off, by whirling her scarf in a frenzied circle around her head.

"Don't panic!" Miss DeWinkle called. "It's probably just a swarm of fog mites. Harmless, playful creatures, just try to shoo them away nicely."

"Fog mites?" Dougal said in disbelief. "Fog mites are about the size of a pinhead and they . . . don't . . . have . . . *teeth*!"

Angus ignored Miss DeWinkle's advice completely and tried to keep the strange winged creatures at bay with his McFangus guide. He swung it wildly in every direction, catching Georgina Fox on the side of the head.

"Sorry!" Angus apologized, dropping his guard for a second and receiving a very nasty bite on the end of his nose.

A few minutes later, Miss DeWinkle ordered a hasty retreat back to Perilous, and Angus was pleased to see that whatever was attacking them in the fog had taken a particular liking to Percival Vellum, who was now covered in angry red marks like an outbreak of measles.

"How extraordinary!" Miss DeWinkle said, once they had reached the safety of the courtyard, where the fog had thinned to a watery mist. "In all my years as a fog instructor, I have never seen anything like it. I have never known fog mites to attack in such numbers before, and in daylight as well. I suggest those of you with bites follow me up to Doctor Fleagal in the sanatorium for some soothing lotion."

There was a disgruntled murmur as the entire class shuffled through the doors and back into the Exploratorium, before the swarm could return for second helpings.

Once inside, it seemed they were hardly any better off. Fog mites had forced their way in through every open door and window and were buzzing about the corridors in large, vicious swarms, attacking anyone in their path. Catcher Mint was jamming a hailstone helmet onto his head. At least a dozen lightning catchers, led by Gudgeon, went racing past them, with fishing nets.

"Get those fog mites away from the kitchens!" Gudgeon yelled. "If the blighters get into the food preparation area, we'll be scraping bits of sausage off the ceilings for weeks."

And as they rounded a corner to the kitchens, they were greeted by the sight of the entire cooking staff charging the length of the room, armed with heavy frying pans and long forks.

"Oh, Amelia! Thank goodness," Miss DeWinkle said as Catcher Sparks came marching toward them wearing a gauze mask and carrying a frying pan, upon which several mites had already met their ends. "Is Doctor Fleagal up in the sanatorium? My class has just been hit by a nasty swarm of fog mites."

"Fog mites my eye," Catcher Sparks said firmly, and she took a small glass jar from the pocket of her jerkin.

The jar contained a beetle with a distinctive pink zigzag across its back and a snorkel-shaped nose. It was buzzing angrily against the side of the glass.

"But that's an Imbur Island snorkel beetle. What's it doing here?" Miss DeWinkle said, sounding surprised. "It normally lives out in the Imbur marshes."

Angus and Dougal inched closer to the lightning catchers to try and get a better look at the jar, and to eavesdrop on what promised to be a very interesting conversation.

"Heaven knows how they got here, but we've got a whole swarm of the blasted things trapped in the weather tunnel upstairs," said Catcher Sparks, sounding unusually flustered. "Rogwood's sealing off the entire roof so they don't get into the weather cannon and accidentally set it—"

BOOOOOOM!

The explosion vibrated through the whole building, dislodging lots of dust and several birds' nests from the rafters above their heads. It was clear to everyone that the snorkel beetles had indeed found their way to the weather cannon.

"Oh, honestly," said Catcher Sparks, gazing up at the ceiling. "It's absolute pandemonium! If they get into any of the equipment in the Lightnarium, I dread to think what might happen. Really, this is worse than the newts and frogs."

"So you think the beetles have come from the same source as before?" asked Miss DeWinkle, lowering her voice.

Catcher Sparks drew her several steps farther away from the class before answering. Angus grabbed Dougal by the sleeve and followed, ducking behind a pillar where they could continue to eavesdrop without being caught.

"Of course they've come from the same source," Catcher Sparks said. "Do you know anyone else on the island who's capable of creating this much chaos?"

"But I don't understand it. What has Scabious Dankhart got to gain by bombarding us with these wretched creatures?"

"For goodness sake, Olivia, keep your voice down," Catcher Sparks hissed through her gauze mask. "We don't want the whole Exploratorium in a panic. But if you must know, Principal Dark-Angel believes it has something to do with his kidnapping of Alabone and Evangeline. . . ."

Angus felt his stomach swoop down into his rubber boots. He shot a sideways glance at Dougal.

"It was only after Dankhart kidnapped the McFanguses that the frogs and newts began falling over Perilous. There is no question that the two events are linked."

"But has nothing been heard from them yet?"

Catcher Sparks shook her head. "Not a word. It is almost certain that they are locked up in one of Dankhart's dungeons, I'm afraid. Principal Dark-Angel is doing everything she can. She has some hope that they may find some means of escape by themselves, but . . ." Catcher Sparks shook her head again and stared down at her feet. "Who knows if we shall ever see them again?"

Angus felt his insides freeze.

"To think that I was speaking to Alabone only a week before it happened," said Miss DeWinkle in a miserable voice. "He had just agreed to give my fifth years a special lecture on advanced fog navigation techniques, and then—" She sniffed and blew her nose loudly into her woolly hat.

"For heaven's sake, Olivia, pull yourself together. We have quite enough on our hands as it is without you falling to pieces," said Catcher Sparks, putting a consoling arm around Miss DeWinkle's shoulders. "Alabone and Evangeline are made of stern stuff. They have been in tighter spots than this before, and somehow found their way back to Perilous unscathed. That is precisely the reason why Principal Dark-Angel chose to give them this particular assignment in the first place. She knew that it would be risky, she knew that if any word of what they were looking for should get back to Dankhart . . . that if he ever got the chance to get his greedy, thieving hands on it . . ."

"Yes, but get his hands on what precisely?" Miss DeWinkle sniffed, recovering suddenly and dabbing at her eyes. "Principal Dark-Angel has been most secretive about the whole affair. Jasper Heckles from the forecasting department says she sent them to search for the *Forgotten Book of Grudge-Bearing Blizzards*."

"And you should have learned by now not to listen to Jasper Heckles and his ridiculous stories," Catcher Sparks snapped, adjusting her gauze mask. "It's got nothing to do with forgotten books or any such ludicrous thing."

"Then what is it, Amelia? Why has none of us been informed?"

"Because it is none of our business," Catcher Sparks said matter-of-factly. "And this is hardly an appropriate time for us to be having this conversation, either. I would advise you to get those first years up to the sanatorium before Doctor Fleagal runs out of soothing lotion." She swept past, frying pan held high, and disappeared into the chaotic kitchens.

Dougal looked anxiously at Angus, his eyes wide. But there was nothing either of them could say in the crowded hallway, and they stood in stunned silence until Miss DeWinkle led them up to the sanatorium.

10

A MIDNIGHT TALE

They spent the rest of a very irritable day shut up in the sanatorium, watching the progress of the fog through tightly closed windows and being told to keep out of the way by an irate Doctor Fleagal—who was treating endless snorkel beetle bites.

Any private conversation was impossible. Angus sat in a corner of the overcrowded sanatorium, focusing hard on a very ugly painting of a portly looking doctor with a rusty stethoscope and a handlebar mustache. He could feel Dougal glance anxiously in his direction every few minutes, but he was careful not to look back—careful not to think or feel anything that could possibly distract him from the horrible truth that had suddenly been laid before him.

His parents were being held captive in one of Dankhart's dungeons, maybe sitting on a cold stone floor with nothing but the rats to keep them company. They'd been there for weeks now, while he, Angus, had been learning all sorts of useless stuff about invisible fog and storm vacuums and cleaning other people's rubber boots. Principal Dark-Angel had known all along. And yet she'd looked him straight in the eye when he'd first arrived and told him some fairy story about his parents helping Dankhart with an assignment. But now he knew the truth. . . .

He was also painfully aware of just how little he himself had even thought about his parents in the past few weeks. Why hadn't he been pestering Principal Dark-Angel for news? Why had he been filling his head with fire dragons and field trips, wasting his time with hailstone helmets and weather tunnels, when his mum and dad had been imprisoned by a lunatic who filled fog with snorkel beetles? He hugged his knees tightly into his chest, hoping that Principal Dark-Angel, Gudgeon, or even Rogwood had planned a dramatic rescue and that both his parents would walk through the doors of Perilous before the week was out.

News reached them midafternoon that the fog was finally beginning to lift. But it wasn't until dinnertime that evening, when some sort of order had finally been restored and they were allowed to leave the sanatorium, that he and Dougal were able to talk.

"You ought to go straight to Principal Dark-Angel and demand to know what's going on," Dougal suggested as soon as they reached the noisy babble of the kitchens and found a deserted table in the corner. "I mean, they're your parents. You've got a right to know if some maniac's got them locked up in his dungeons."

Angus had already considered storming up to the principal's office and demanding that she tell him everything. But he knew exactly what would happen if he did.

"There's no point. She's already lied to me once. What's to stop her from doing it again?" He toyed with a soggy Yorkshire pudding on his plate.

Considering the damage caused by the beetles, it was a miracle they had any dinner at all. And even though they'd had nothing to eat all day up in the sanatorium but hard candy and hot chocolate, Angus found that the very thought of food made his stomach turn.

"Look, I'm really sorry about your mum and dad," said Dougal, fiddling awkwardly with his knife and fork.

Angus nodded, not trusting himself to speak.

"I just wish there was something we could do." Dougal sighed. "I wish somebody would tell us what's really going on." For hours now, Angus had been thinking the same thing, turning the facts over and over in his head, trying to understand what had happened. But only one thing seemed to be clear.

"That assignment's at the bottom of this whole thing," he said, pushing his food aside. "You heard what Catcher Sparks said. My mum and dad were looking for something when they were kidnapped, something that Dankhart desperately wanted to get his hands on. . . ."

"Yeah, but what?" said Dougal gloomily. "We've got no chance of getting anything out of Dark-Angel about secret assignments or Castle Dankhart dungeons."

"What's Dankhart's castle like, anyway?" asked Angus, amazed that he'd never asked this question before.

Dougal squirmed uncomfortably in his seat. "Well, it's a

bit hard to say, really. I mean it's not like Dankhart opens his doors every Christmas and invites the whole island over for a huge party, is it? Anyway, nobody would go even if he did. I . . . look, are you sure you really want to hear about this? Won't it just make things worse?"

Angus shook his head, knowing that it was impossible to feel any worse than he already did.

"Well," Dougal began warily, "it's all the way over on the other side of the island, across the mountains, so it's pretty impossible to get to, you can't even see it from here. But it sits on top of a big chunk of rock—"

"You mean it's like Perilous?" Angus burst out, surprised.

Dougal shook his head. "It's nothing like Perilous. It's supposed to be a creepy, crumbling old castle. There're loads of stories about it being haunted with pirate ghosts, but Dad reckons that's just the Dankharts spreading rumors to scare people off. He *has* got real crocodiles in his moat, though. And that's all I know." Dougal shrugged. "Apart from the fact that the castle's got loads of secret passageways and tunnels running underneath it for miles in every direction."

Angus stared down at the table, feeling more helpless than he'd ever felt in his life before. Why did Castle Dankhart have to be so impossible to reach? He had zero chance of trekking over the mountains by himself, and even if by some miracle he managed it, what would he do then? Knock politely on the castle door and ask Dankhart to set his parents free?

"Couldn't you ask your uncle Max what's going on?" Dougal suggested, breaking into Angus's thoughts. "He must know something."

Angus stared at Dougal, wondering why this brilliant idea hadn't occurred to him straightaway. "Yeah, you're right, thanks. I'll write to him tonight."

In the difficult days that followed, everything they did seemed to remind Angus of his parents and their dangerous predicament. When they sat down to eat in the kitchens, he imagined his mum and dad surviving on stale bread and water. When they were sent outside into the sunshine by Catcher Sparks to scrub a pile of mud-splattered coats, he thought of his parents shivering in their dingy dungeon, trying to keep themselves warm. At

night, his dreams were filled with creepy castles, maze-like tunnels, and giant scuttling rats.

It was just after he'd woken up from a particularly horrible rat-filled dream one night, his face covered in cold sweat, that he suddenly remembered the letter from his mum, the one that was now sitting at the bottom of his drawer. He scrambled out of bed, flicked on the light fissure overhead, and retrieved the envelope from underneath a pile of socks.

He climbed back under the covers and read the letter carefully, feeling extremely glad that he hadn't handed it over to Principal Dark-Angel. Had his parents been kidnapped just days or even hours after they'd mailed this very letter? A lump formed in his throat as he stared at his mum's scribbled handwriting.

And what if he never saw them again? What if this letter was the last time he ever heard from either of his parents? He'd never be able to talk to them about Perilous or show them the row of gleaming hailstone helmets that he'd cleaned in the experimental division. He also knew that he'd never, ever be able to forgive Scabious Dankhart for tearing his family apart.

He folded the letter carefully, grabbed the fog guide from his bedside table, and tucked the letter safely inside a chapter on contagious fog, deciding that from now on, he'd carry it around with him like a talisman of hope. As if doing so might somehow let his mum and dad know that he had not forgotten them.

Once the damage caused by the snorkel beetles had been cleaned up, life quickly returned to normal. Thankfully, Miss DeWinkle continued their lessons inside, with a series of extraordinarily boring lectures on the salty properties of deep sea fog.

Twice more, when Angus was sitting alone in the kitchens, Indigo made a beeline for his table with a worried expression on her face, clearly intent on talking to him in private. On each occasion, however, she appeared to change her mind at the very last minute and veered off quickly in the opposite direction, her face crimson with embarrassment.

In the experimental division, they were put to work by Catcher Sparks setting large numbers of beetle traps, just in case any of the highly destructive creatures decided to return. Unfortunately, however, the traps went off with a vicious *SNAP!* at the slightest movement. And although Angus could no sooner forget about his parents than he could about the looming fog field trips, he found it impossible to think about anything if he wanted to retain all his fingers during this highly tricky process. And he did his best to keep all thoughts of Dankhart and dungeons under tight control.

To his surprise, Angus woke up one morning almost two weeks later to discover that several icicles had formed on the inside of his bedroom window and that the rest of Perilous was completely covered in a thick layer of wintry ice and snow. He got dressed at double speed, pulling on an extra pair of socks to keep his feet warm, then darted up to breakfast, looking forward to a hot bowl of honey and porridge. When he reached the kitchens, however, it was to find them almost completely deserted.

"What's happened?" he asked, sitting next to Dougal and glancing round at the empty tables.

There were fewer people than normal, and most of them looked half asleep. One small group of third years sat quietly in the far corner. Edmund Croxley was yawning over his toast and marmalade. The usual lively chatter had been replaced by a library-like hush that made even the clink of knives and forks sound too loud. For one wild moment, Angus thought that the field trips must have started without them, before he remembered the exact dates had yet to be announced.

"Where is everyone?" he asked, helping himself to a slice of toast.

"Principal Dark-Angel's decided to give everyone the day off," Dougal explained, yawning lazily. "Catcher Howler made an announcement ten minutes ago. You just missed it."

"A day off?"

"Yeah, you know, when you're allowed to go back to bed and lie in until lunchtime, without anyone trying to get you struck by lightning or sucked into a storm vacuum." Dougal buttered a hot crumpet, grinning. "According to Edmund Croxley, they do it sometimes when it gets really cold. They let the roof freeze over on purpose so we can go skating. You've got to be careful not to crash into any of the machines and stuff, but it should be brilliant." He produced two pairs of gleaming ice skates from under the table, holding them up by their laces. "I got these from the supplies department before they ran out."

Angus stared at Dougal, feeling mildly shocked. He hadn't even considered the possibility of a day off.

"You do know how to ice-skate, don't you?" Dougal asked.

"No," Angus confessed. "But I've got a feeling I'm about to learn."

Half an hour later, Angus stood on the roof of Perilous, wrapped up in several warm woolly sweaters, as well as a hat, scarf, and coat to protect him from the icy wind that was blowing from the east. Almost half the roof now resembled a frosted lake that glinted and twinkled in the morning sunshine. Beyond it, the whole of Imbur Island lay before them like a vast iced cake, its tall, snow-capped mountains just visible in the distance.

Angus stared hard at the row of jagged peaks, hoping he might somehow catch a glimpse of Castle Dankhart, but he knew Dougal was right. The mountains rose up like a great impenetrable fortress, making it impossible to see anything.

A handful of older trainees, including Nicholas Grubb and his friends, were already racing each other up and down the ice.

"I'd make the most of it if I were you," Nicholas advised Angus, skating over to say a quick hello. "Last time the roof froze over, Principal Dark-Angel sent everyone back inside again after only twenty minutes."

"Why, what happened?" Angus asked.

"Somebody accidentally dumped a bucket of ice over Miss Rill, the monsoon expert." He grinned. "She wasn't very impressed, for some reason."

Several lightning catchers were already spinning round the roof on their skates with surprising skill. Angus gasped as Rogwood, with his beard tucked inside what looked like a long knitted sock, sped past them both, arm in arm with Miss DeWinkle.

"Morning, Doomsbury . . . Dewsnap!" Miss DeWinkle waved cheerfully as they hurtled around the ice with a swishing of blades and a flapping of scarves.

"Wow!" Dougal said in an awed voice. "You wouldn't think they had it in them at their age, would you?"

Angus, who had once witnessed his own white-haired

uncle roller-skating around the entire windmill to test out a massive wind sock, wasn't surprised at all. He was surprised, however, to find himself lying flat on his back only seconds after putting a first tentative foot on the ice. It didn't seem to matter what he did with his feet after that; as soon as he got anywhere near the ice, they shot out from underneath him in opposite directions and brought him crashing down. The only way he could stay upright for more than five seconds was by clinging to the leg of a hurricane mast.

Dougal was surprisingly good on his own skates and treated Angus to a display of small leaps and jumps, as well as an accidental attempt at the splits that made his eyes water and caused Angus to laugh so hard he spent several helpless minutes lying on his back, unable to move.

At lunchtime, several trays of hot soup were sent up from the kitchens. They helped themselves to warm crusty rolls, sat in the shelter of the weather balloon, and watched Mr. Knurling, the bad-tempered librarian, do an unsteady circuit of the roof, his stiff blond hair frozen into icy peaks by the wind.

"What are you two looking at?" he snapped as he went lurching past. "Haven't you ever seen a skating librarian before?"

"Yeah, but I've never seen one using his own rear end as a brake," Dougal mumbled as the librarian tripped a moment later and skidded past them both on the seat of his pants.

Mr. Knurling was followed onto the ice by Gudgeon and Principal Dark-Angel herself. It was one of the few times Angus had seen the principal up close since their first meeting in her office. She looked pale, drawn, and extremely annoyed when Mr. Knurling crashed straight into her, bringing them both down heavily on the ice.

"Doesn't look too happy, does she?" Angus grinned through his soup steam.

"That's not the only thing she's annoyed about, either," said Dougal. "I forgot to tell you earlier. Catcher Mint and Gudgeon were up in the supplies department this morning, while I was getting our skates, and they were talking about Principal Dark-Angel and the snorkel beetles."

Angus frowned. "But . . . the snorkel beetles happened weeks ago now."

"Yeah, but apparently a whole swarm of them got down a chimney and into the principal's office while we were all shut up in the sanatorium, and they made a real mess of the place, turned it upside down, went through her personal filing cabinet and everything."

"I didn't realize snorkel beetles could turn things upside down," said Angus, picturing the small winged creatures.

"They must be stronger than they look." Dougal shrugged. "Anyway, according to Catcher Mint, she's been in a horrible mood ever since."

Angus, on the other hand, felt the cold, fresh air lifting his spirits a little, and the sight of Mr. Knurling doing an accidental somersault while trying to get off the ice only improved his mood.

Over the next few days, the weather took a turn for the worse, with dull sheets of relentless rain blowing in from the west. Fortunately for Angus and Dougal, however, Mr. Dewsnap had just sent a large parcel of books over to help keep them amused during the long, dark evenings.

"Dad knows I'm a bit of a bookworm," Dougal explained, clearly embarrassed by the delivery. "Just do me a favor, okay? Don't tell anyone else? Percival Vellum already thinks I'm a total nerd."

"I'd rather be a bookworm than a great hairy moron," said Angus, showing his friend some support. And as the wind howled furiously outside, they spent some very enjoyable hours toasting marshmallows over the warm fire in the Pigsty.

Angus's favorite book was a weighty tome on famous Imburcillian inventors who had shocked the whole island with such radical ideas as the knitted umbrella and the self-cleaning toilet—which never really caught on due to a problem with projectile flushing. He couldn't help wondering how Uncle Max was getting on back at the Windmill with the blizzard catcher. He also wondered if his uncle had received the letter he'd sent, asking about his parents. There had been no reply from Budleigh Otterstone yet.

Dougal was rather taken with a fascinating book on secret codes and how to crack them, written by someone called Archibald Humble-Pea.

"Hey, listen to this," he said excitedly one evening, as Angus was attempting to toast ten fat marshmallows over the fire on an extremely spindly stick. "According to old

Humble-Pea, the last two pages of our fog guides are written in secret code. And if you take out all the words beginning with an M, and then read the rest of it backward, it tells you exactly what they've got hidden up in the Inner Sanctum of Perplexing Mysteries and Secrets. Quick, where's my fog guide?" Dougal searched hurriedly through a pile of books on the floor beside his armchair. "I bet you anything they've got the brains of some doddery old lightning catcher pickled up there in a jar. Wouldn't it be brilliant if we knew all about it—and nobody else did!" Dougal spent the rest of the afternoon with his head buried in the thick volume, frowning in concentration. The only thing he managed to decipher, however, was a very cryptic message about some books with "melting words."

"How are we supposed to know what that means?" Dougal frowned, finally snapping Humble-Pea shut in defeat.

At the end of the week, feverish rumors began to circulate that a large horse and a carriage bearing the name Balthazar's Chocolatiers had been spotted making a secret delivery of chocolate to Perilous, including a dozen giant chocolate rabbits, six life-sized, cream-filled giraffes, and half a ton of solid chocolate eggs the size of rugby balls.

What appeared to be a fact, however, was that a burly group of fifth-year boys had just been told they would be tackling their first fog field trip on the Imbur marshes in a few days. And the chattering noise in the kitchens reached near-deafening levels.

"If only we could find out more about what's happened on previous field trips, we might know what to expect on ours," Dougal said on Friday evening, as they trudged up to the Octagon to return their ice skates to the supplies department.

"I'm not sure I want to know," said Angus, frowning.

"Well, maybe we could get some hints about what Miss DeWinkle's got hidden in the fog. I mean, what if she really has a whole troop of yetis waiting to jump out at us?"

"Or a school of piranha mist fish," Angus added.

"Er . . . piranha what fish?" Dougal asked, looking alarmed.

"Juliana Jessop was telling everyone about it in the kitchens last night," Angus explained. "Apparently some idiotic lightning catcher brought a sample back from

Brazil, about a hundred years ago, and they escaped. I mean it could be a load of old garbage, but—"

Angus stopped abruptly as they reached the Octagon and crashed into Indigo, who had come around the corner at precisely the same moment, heading in the opposite direction.

"Oh, er . . . hello."

"Hi," Indigo said, smiling awkwardly at them both.

None of them could think of anything else to say. Dougal stared up at the marbled ceiling as if searching for inspiration, Indigo inspected the floor around her feet, and Angus studied the door of the experimental division closely, for no particular reason he could think of. He chanced a furtive glance at Indigo, who was chewing her lip, and who once again seemed to be on the verge of telling him something that caused her to frown deeply.

"Well, we'd better get these skates back to the supplies department," said Angus, when he could no longer stand the uncomfortable silence. "See you in the experimental division on Monday."

"Yeah, see you on Monday," Dougal added with a wave

as they skirted around Indigo and hurried away from her. "Not much of a talker, is she? I wonder what that was all about?"

"No idea, but if she doesn't spit it out soon, I think her head might explode."

They were just about to knock on the door to the supplies department when Angus felt a soft tap on his shoulder. He turned around to find Indigo standing behind them, this time with a determined look on her face.

"There's something I want to talk to you both about. Something I've been trying to tell you for ages now. . . . But can we go somewhere a bit more private first?"

Dougal glanced around the deserted Octagon. "This is about as private as it ever gets in this place," he said with a shrug.

Indigo seemed set on moving their conversation to another location, however, and they followed her back down the stone steps and battled their way into a small room, which was crammed full of rusty old umbrellas. She closed the door behind them and stared down at her trembling hands.

"There's something about—about my family that I want

to tell you both," she began, not looking at either of them directly. "Something you might find a bit . . . shocking."

"Your family?" said Angus, puzzled. This wasn't what he'd been expecting at all. "Er, wouldn't you be more comfortable talking to one of your girlfriends about that sort of thing? I mean, family stuff's private, isn't it?"

"Yeah, private," Dougal agreed, backing away from Indigo with a panicked look on his face.

"You don't have to look so worried." Indigo smiled weakly. "It's not like I want to discuss my great-aunt Cordelia's crumble fungus problems or anything."

"Your great-aunt's got crumble fungus problems?" Dougal gulped, looking both revolted and curious at the same time.

Thankfully however, Indigo didn't elaborate. She swept her hair out her eyes and took a deep breath before continuing.

"Look, this isn't something I normally go around telling everyone. But I just thought . . . after what's happened . . . that Angus really has a right to know."

Angus exchanged puzzled glances with Dougal, who grabbed a moth-eaten umbrella and held it like a shield, to protect himself from anything embarrassing Indigo might say.

"I mean, my mum made me promise not to tell anyone—ever. She said nobody would understand, that it's got to stay a big family secret. . . ."

"Big family secret . . . ," Dougal repeated, and a sudden change came over his face.

"It's not my mum's fault she comes from such a horrible family," Indigo continued in a rush. "She hated living there. That's why she ran away from home when she was fifteen and married my dad—"

Angus still had absolutely no idea what Indigo was talking about. Dougal, however, suddenly seemed to understand her perfectly. His eyebrows shot up, disappearing under his bangs, and his mouth fell open as he stared at Indigo with wide-eyed shock.

"Of course! Married at fifteen . . . big family secret . . . that's it!" he gasped, steaming up his own glasses in excitement. "That's why I recognize your name. I knew I'd remember it eventually."

Indigo bit her lip and fell silent, watching Dougal anxiously.

"My dad's got this huge wall chart in his study at home showing all the old families on Imbur," said Dougal. "It goes way back to the fifteenth century or something. He uses it all the time for research into his books and stuff, and I remember now seeing the Midnight family on it. Your dad's called Timothy Midnight or something, isn't he?" he asked Indigo.

"It's Thomas, actually," she said, still chewing her lip.

"Thomas, exactly. Anyway," Dougal continued, barely able to get the words out of his mouth fast enough, "the important point is that Thomas Midnight went and married Etheldra Dankhart. Which makes—"

"Which makes Scabious Dankhart my uncle." Indigo finished his sentence for him in a tremulous voice.

A ringing sort of silence followed this astonishing statement. Angus couldn't quite take his eyes off a crimson-cheeked Indigo. He stared at her, thunderstruck, a slow understanding beginning to creep over him. Scabious Dankhart was Indigo's uncle! That explained why Indigo had been so quiet, why she'd been so reluctant to speak to anybody and had stoutly refused to make friends. She'd been terrified that if anyone ever found out about her dubious family connections . . .

"My mum didn't ask to be born into the Dankhart family," said Indigo hurriedly. "She ran away from home and married my dad, he's a blacksmith in Little Frog's Bottom. She's never been back to that horrible castle since. We're Midnights now. None of us has anything to do with my uncle Scabious. It's not my mum's fault that her brother turned out to be such a despicable villain."

Angus and Dougal exchanged dark glances.

"Mum and Dad wanted me to go to a school on the mainland where no one's ever heard of the Dankharts, but I've always wanted to be a lightning catcher, ever since I was little, and I thought if I just worked hard and tried not to speak to anyone too much . . ."

"If Scabious Dankhart was my uncle, I think I would have taken your mum and dad's advice," said Dougal, staring at her avidly.

"So I'm just supposed to hide under a stone somewhere because my uncle's a villain?" There was a dangerous tremble in Indigo's voice now.

"I didn't mean that. . . ." Dougal looked terrified that she might actually start crying. "I just thought it might be easier somewhere else, that's all. I mean, you must have known that people would find out sooner or later."

"But Imbur's my home," Indigo said, almost pleading with them to understand. "I've got just as much right to be here as anyone else. And Principal Dark-Angel obviously agrees with me, or she never would have offered me a place at Perilous."

"There's no arguing with that," Dougal admitted, taking another cautious step away from Indigo. He cast a nervous glance at Angus.

"But I don't understand. Why are you telling us this now?" asked Angus. "I mean, we had no idea about your uncle or anything. You could've just kept it to yourself."

"Oh, but I had to tell you after what happened in the Lightnarium that day!" The words came bursting out of Indigo, and it was clear that she'd decided to explain herself, no matter what. "When I was in the sanatorium afterward, I overheard Rogwood talking to Doctor Fleagal about Alabone and Evangeline McFangus, and how their son, Angus, had just saved me from the ball lightning, and obviously I realized straightaway that they were talking about you." She looked at Angus with wide eyes.

"Then they started talking about the fact that my uncle Scabious had kidnapped your mum and dad from the Imbur marshes because of some special assignment they were working on for Principal Dark-Angel. . . . I know it was weeks ago now, but I've been trying to pluck up the courage to talk to you ever since. And I just thought . . . well, if there's anything I can do to help . . ."

"Yeah, there is, actually," Angus said, desperate all of a sudden for any new information she could give them. "Did you hear Rogwood say what my mum and dad were looking for?"

Indigo hesitated for a split second, and then nodded. Angus felt his heart leap into his throat.

"Rogwood said your parents had been sent to look for something really old, something that had been written years and years ago now and then lost. He said they were searching for an old map."

Somewhere in the back of his mind, Angus suddenly remembered the very first conversation he'd ever had with Principal Dark-Angel, on the day he'd arrived at Perilous, when she'd been extremely interested to hear about anything his parents might have sent him through the post, particularly anything resembling a map.

"Did you hear anything else?" he asked urgently. "Did they say what the map was for?"

But Indigo shook her head. "They must have gone into Doctor Fleagal's office after that and closed the door. But I remember my mum saying once that my uncle was obsessed with maps. He's got rooms full of them at Castle Dankhart. He spends hours just staring at them. She said it was like he'd lost something and he was desperate to find it again."

"Yeah, but desperate to find what, exactly?" Dougal said, frowning.

And they each stared around the room, knowing that the answer to that question was going to be harder to find than an invisible fog.

11

STORM GLOBES

"I bet you anything she goes around calling him Uncle Scabby when no one else is listening," Dougal mumbled darkly under his breath.

It was the morning after their conversation with Indigo. They were sitting outside in their favorite courtyard, enjoying the fact that they now had the whole weekend ahead of them. They were also enjoying some pleasant winter sunshine; the sky had turned a pale, inviting blue and the sun was beaming down upon them lazily. Despite the sunny weather, however, Dougal had been in a very dark mood since breakfast, and had not stopped issuing dire warnings about Indigo and the desperate troubles that a possible friendship with her would bring them. And Angus now realized why Indigo had been so reluctant to tell them about her unfortunate family connections in the first place.

"And I mean, well, she is a Dankhart, whether she likes it or not," Dougal continued, sitting on a stone bench next to the fish pond, shielding his eyes from the sun. "And everyone knows the Dankharts are a bunch of thieving, cheating pirates."

"Yeah, but Indigo's not just a Dankhart, she's a Midnight as well," Angus pointed out fairly.

"I see she's already got you fooled." Dougal squinted at him. "You'd better watch out, or she'll be inviting you round to Castle Dankhart for afternoon tea and scones, and you'll be banged into your own cozy little dungeon before you can say Uncle Scabby."

Angus sighed. He had absolutely no doubt in his mind that Indigo was as loyal to Perilous and the lightning catchers as either one of them. And that she'd bravely told them the truth about her mum's flight from the castle and her family's abhorrence of all things Dankhart. He was anxious to talk instead about her other startling revelation—the fact that his parents had been searching for a map. But what kind of a map, exactly?

He'd been turning it over and over in his head, racking his brains for half the night, but so far he'd failed to come up with any realistic possibilities. What could Dankhart be so desperate to get his hands on? Did he need some more gold, perhaps, or something that was hidden in the Inner Sanctum of Secrets that would make him even more powerful than he already was? But then he would hardly need a map to find his way through a door that was clearly marked in the Octagon. Nor, for that matter, would Principal Dark-Angel—who seemed equally keen on finding the mysterious map.

He'd also been thinking hard about the fact that Dankhart had kidnapped his mum and dad from the Imbur marshes, the very place where he was about to embark upon his first-ever field trip. What if his parents had left some tiny clue behind, something that would help rescue them?

"And who knows where all those secret passageways under Castle Dankhart lead to?" Dougal's voice broke into his thoughts once again. "I mean, there could be one going right to Indigo's parents' house in Little Frog's

Bottom. I bet she waits until everyone's gone to bed at night, then pulls back the carpet and—"

"Look, give it a rest, will you?" Angus muttered as he suddenly caught sight of Indigo herself cutting across the courtyard toward them.

Dougal glared at her sulkily as she approached. Indigo, on the other hand, looked far happier than Angus had ever seen her. Gone was the wary, guarded expression she'd been hiding behind since he met her; she now had a sparkle in her eyes and a bright, eager look on her face.

"I've been looking for you two all over the place." She smiled at them shyly, as if still testing out the idea of being friends. "Miss DeWinkle has just put up another notice in the kitchens. All first years have to meet in the entrance hall first thing tomorrow; they're finally telling us more about the field trips."

"Good." Angus smiled back at her. "At least we'll find out what we're up against now."

At five to nine the following morning, Angus, Indigo, and Dougal shuffled into the entrance hall, wearing their waterproof coats once again, to find Gudgeon waiting for them.

"On second thought"—Angus gulped—"it might be better if we *didn't* know."

The last time the gruff lightning catcher had taken them for a lesson, Angus had been struck by lightning. He exchanged dark looks with Dougal, wondering what dangers Gudgeon might be leading them into this time.

"Miss DeWinkle's asked me to tell you more about your first field trip," barked Gudgeon as the last few stragglers raced into the hall. "But you won't be going anywhere until I've checked that all your weather watches are working properly. So if it's accidentally been struck by lightning, dropped in a bucket of rainwater, or trodden on by your great clumsy feet, now is the time to come forward."

A nervous silence fell. Several lightning cubs twitched. Angus glanced at his own watch surreptitiously. At that precise moment it was showing him a collection of fluffy white clouds, one of which was shaped like an elephant. He wondered if that was normal.

"No damage to report?" Gudgeon finally broke the silence. "Right, we'd better see if you're telling the truth, then. Follow me and keep a close eye on what your weather watch is telling you."

"You don't think he's taking us into the weather tunnel, do you?" Dougal whispered anxiously.

Gudgeon turned and strode swiftly through the front doors and straight into the courtyard outside, where he took a sharp right and dived through a wooden door hidden in the wall. Down a narrow flight of steps they went. It was impossible to see where they were heading, however, as they were instantly engulfed by a dense, damp cloud.

They followed Gudgeon in silence, filing out onto a flat expanse of grass when they reached the foot of the stairs a few minutes later, the cloud still swirling around them.

"Right, Miss Midnight." The lightning catcher folded his arms and stared down at Indigo. "What type of cloud does your weather watch say we're standing in?"

"It—it says it's a stratocumulus cloud, sir," Indigo answered quietly, turning bright red. "Puffy and gray, it skulks around at low heights, trying to engulf people."

"Correct. Doomsbury." Angus flinched. "Give me a precise temperature reading. Quickly, boy!"

"It's, er, forty-two point eight degrees Fahrenheit, sir." Angus said, hoping he had the numbers the right way around.

Gudgeon nodded once.

"How many of you can see an orange glow on the surface of your weather watches?"

Almost every hand went up. Angus suddenly realized that his watch was virtually luminous.

"Orange is one of the few colors in the spectrum that can cut through fog here on Imbur, allowing you to read your weather watch even in the thickest no-way-out fog."

At that moment, however, the cloud finally lifted, and Angus felt his knees wobble. Without realizing it, they had just descended a daunting flight of stairs that wrapped itself around the outside of Perilous. And they were now standing in the strangest garden he'd ever seen. Cut directly into the tall tooth of rock, like a green wedge with a deep bottom lip poking out into the sunshine, it was covered in tall grass, luscious ferns, and long trails of ivy tumbling over the edge like a beard.

The Exploratorium towered a hundred feet above them. The Isle of Imbur stretched out before them, a colorful patchwork of green fields, woods, and towns.

"You are now standing in the cloud gardens," Gudgeon announced above a wave of shocked gasps and whispers. "Planted back in the 1800s so that lightning cubs would

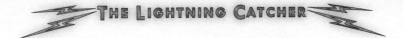

have somewhere to run about and let off steam. It's been closed for the last few months due to an invasion of poisonous Imbur hogweed. But as of today, it will be open for use during weekends and evenings until dusk."

"You mean we can come down here whenever we want, sir?" Nigel Ridgely asked.

"No one is allowed to enter the cloud gardens during blizzards, thunderstorms, gales, or showers of newts and frogs," Gudgeon warned. "But it's the perfect place to test the settings on your weather watches. Anyone who did not see an orange glow as we came through the clouds should go straight up to the supplies department after we've finished here and get their watch recalibrated.

"One of the aims of this field trip is to introduce you to as many different types of fog as possible," Gudgeon continued. "The best way to do that is to send you round a course, in teams of two. Although as one of you is allergic to fog and can't take part"—he glared down at a quivering Millicent Nichols—"Miss Midnight will be teaming up with Doomsbury and Dewsnap instead."

Indigo shot them both a shy smile.

"Because this is your first field trip," said Gudgeon,

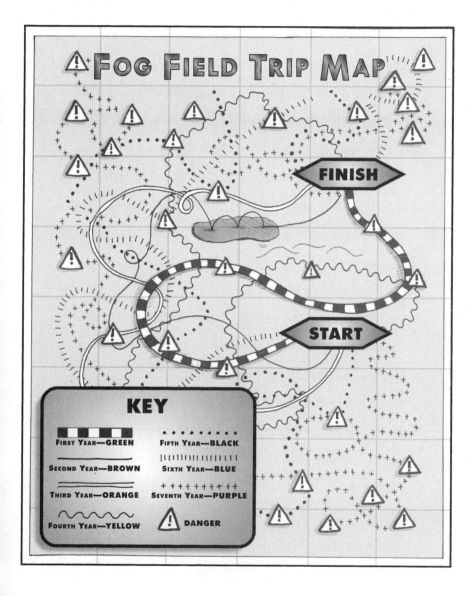

handing out maps to each team, "you will be tackling the easiest section of the course, marked in green."

Angus looked at the map. Sections had been outlined in green, brown, orange, yellow, black, blue, and purple, each with increasingly complicated-looking routes. The green course was much shorter than the rest, but it appeared to contain a dizzying number of mysterious obstacles, each of which came with its own red DANGER symbol.

"Let me remind you that this is *not* a competition." Gudgeon scowled at them. "There are no prizes for coming in first, so there's no point trying to beat everyone else to the finish line like a bunch of harebrained idiots. Right, each team should take a few minutes to study their maps before returning to the Exploratorium."

"Have they completely lost their marbles?" Dougal hissed, a wild, startled look in his eyes, as soon as Gudgeon's back was turned. "That course looks completely mental! I'm off to find Miss DeWinkle," he added resolutely.

"What do you want to find her for?" asked Angus.

"Because she's the one who made us sign that stupid field trip form, and I want it back . . . so I can rip it up and burn it!" And Dougal stomped off with a determined look on his face.

For a moment, Angus fought the urge to run after Dougal and rip up his own form. The field trip was going to be the hardest thing they'd tackled yet. But if it somehow took him to the very spot where his mum and dad had been kidnapped . . . if they had left even the tiniest hint or clue behind that would help . . . and he sprinted after his friend to try and talk some sense into him.

Before he could even begin to reason with Dougal, however, a large shadow fell across them both.

"What's the matter with Dewsnap?" a familiar voice sneered behind them. "He's not afraid of the big scary fog course, is he?"

Angus looked over his shoulder to find the Vellum twins looming over them like a pair of particularly ugly gargoyles that had recently fallen off a church. Ever since their first confrontation outside the weather tunnel, he had been doing his best to avoid the twins, but there was no escaping them now. Pixie was hovering behind her brother, her coarse hair tied up in ridiculous-looking pigtails. It wasn't a pretty sight.

"Dewsnap, you're not actually thinking of pulling out, are you?" Percival goaded, his gorilla-like arms swinging by his sides.

"You wish!" Angus said hurriedly, before Dougal could say anything. "As a matter of fact, we were just discussing our course strategy, weren't we?"

Dougal looked momentarily confused. "Were we? Oh, yeah, I mean . . . that's right, we were."

"I don't know about you two, but I'm really looking forward to it," Angus continued. "It should be a piece of cake after the kind of training we've got planned."

"The only thing you and Dewsnap will be practicing is how to fake double fainting fits before you cross the starting line." Percival grinned at his own joke. "Dewsnap will be screaming like a girl before the first whiff of fog even hits him."

"As if," Angus said, in what he hoped was a confident voice. "Actually, we were hoping the course would look like this. If it had been any easier it wouldn't have been worth doing."

His bluff worked. The corner of Pixie's mouth twitched, and the sneer on her brother's face slipped. Percival recovered quickly, making up for his lapse by being even more revolting than usual.

"You can brag all you want, Dungbeetle, but you three have got no chance of getting through this course first," he said.

"But Gudgeon just told us it isn't a competition." Indigo appeared beside them, frowning. "It doesn't matter who comes in first."

"Don't be so idiotic, Midnight. Of course it matters. The Vellums have been beating everyone on that course for hundreds of years, and we're not about to stop now. You could call it a family tradition, and Pixie and me intend to carry on the winning streak."

Indigo snorted, surprising everyone, including herself.

"What's so funny, Midnight?" Percival glowered.

Indigo blushed furiously, but she faced Percival with a defiant look. "Winning streaks don't count if you have to bully your way to victory. The only thing you two could win without cheating is a who's-the-biggest-numbskull? competition."

"Just watch it, Midnight," said Pixie, when she finally realized that she'd just been insulted. "You'd better talk nicely to me and my brother, or we could get all three of you thrown out of Perilous, just like that," she added, with a thick snap of her pudgy fingers. "Our dad works here. He's really good friends with Principal Dark-Angel, and she'll do anything he tells her to."

"Oh, yeah, I almost forgot about your dad," Angus said. "He looks after the Perilous sewers or something, doesn't he?"

Dougal let out a huge guffaw of laughter. Indigo was overcome with giggles. Pixie, however, poked Angus hard in the chest. "You'll be laughing on the other side of your face when we beat you."

And with that, the twins retreated to the other side of the cloud gardens, muttering.

In the days that followed, the first groups of older trainees began to leave Perilous to complete their own field trips. They returned at the end of each day nursing a spectacular variety of bruises and cut lips. Clifford Fugg, a popular sixth year (who could squash a whole custard tart into his mouth while reciting the alphabet backward), was rushed up to the sanatorium with a broken wrist, instantly renewing wild tales of roaming fog yetis, and testing Dougal's courage to the breaking point.

"If Clifford Fugg's been injured, I'll never make it through that course alive!" he wailed at least once a day. "Why can't I be allergic to fog too?"

In the meantime, Angus decided that he'd search as much of the marsh as possible during their own field trip, under the cover of the fog, hoping to unearth even the tiniest hint or clue that his parents might have left behind. If he could somehow find the exact spot where they'd been kidnapped, if he could just sense their faded presence in the marshes, maybe then he'd know how to help.

Getting through the fog course without injury, however, was going to be virtually impossible, and he was extremely glad when Dougal and Indigo offered to help.

"Indigo can take charge of navigation and make sure we get through the course in one piece," Dougal decided as all three of them sat quietly together, discussing the plan. "I'll study the McFangus guide, so we'll know how to tackle any fog we run into," he added, looking faintly sick at the notion of fog. "And then all you have to do is search for clues."

"Thanks." Angus nodded, feeling immensely grateful to them both. He knew the chances of finding anything in the swirling mists were remote, that Rogwood and the rest of the lightning catchers must have searched the marshes right after his mum and dad were kidnapped. But after weeks of feeling utterly helpless, he also knew he had to try.

It was four days after their unexpected visit to the cloud gardens that Indigo made an interesting discovery, one that she was convinced could help them get through the fog course. And it involved a trip to the library.

The library at Perilous was large and sprawling, with a glass-domed ceiling at the top and a majestic spiral staircase leading up to an impressive balcony.

"Just remind me what we're doing in here again?" Angus whispered as they crept between the dusty shelves.

Thanks to Indigo, they had managed to sneak past Mr. Knurling—who was skulking about among the reference books—and make their way quietly up the spiral staircase to the balcony without being caught. Dougal had been kept behind in the experimental division by Catcher Sparks to reorganize a cabinet full of antique storm snares, which he'd somehow managed to knock over.

"Miss DeWinkle was talking to Catcher Sparks in the girls' corridor this morning," Indigo said, "about some old field trip training manuals that might have been left in the library by Ernest Elbow."

"Er . . . what's been left in here by who, sorry?" asked Angus.

"Ernest Elbow. He was a famous lightning catcher. He worked in the Inner Sanctum of Secrets about seventy years ago. He also took part in loads of field trips, until he got a bit of an injury," Indigo explained as they tip-toed between the bookshelves, making as little noise as possible.

"What kind of an injury, exactly?" Angus asked, frowning.

"A shattered kneecap or a severed earlobe or something like that." Indigo shrugged. "Does it matter?"

"It might." Angus felt a rush of nerves. "Just don't tell Dougal about this Ernest what's-his-name, okay? Or he'll be threatening to tear up his form again."

Indigo grinned at him over her shoulder. "Anyway, Miss DeWinkle said he wrote a whole series of training manuals after that. She also reckons they're still buried in the library somewhere. And if we could just find out for sure if anyone's ever encountered any piranha mist fish before, I'd feel much happier. . . ."

Angus had to admire Indigo's spirit. But he was fairly sure that the only way to deal with such dangers was with the aid of a large baseball bat—or a tub of extra-powerful piranha poison. He was just about to suggest that they try to get their hands on as much of the stuff as possible, when something small and circular shot through the glass ceiling above them with a crash, leaving a perfectly round hole in the large dome.

Indigo gasped, tripping over a pile of dusty books that had been left carelessly on the floor. Angus recognized the falling object instantly.

"I don't believe it!" He rushed to the edge of the balcony and peered over the railing as a dozen more holes appeared in the ceiling above. "Those are storm globes."

"Storm globes?" Indigo stood beside him, clutching the rail. "But I don't understand. What are they doing in the library?"

"They're getting ready to rain." Angus frowned as, far below them, scattered far and wide across the library floor, the miniature storms were released from their shattered orbs.

Fortunately, most of the storms were no bigger than the dumplings they had eaten the night before at dinner, and they produced nothing more than puddles of halfhearted rain before they fizzled out completely. One storm, however, was much uglier than all the rest, and appeared to be gathering itself into a great, dark mass.

"Er . . . I think we'd better get out of here," Angus said. "Getting caught in one of those storms is no picnic, trust me."

"Oh, but—what if it's dangerous?" Indigo grabbed his arm. "What if there's been an accident in the experimental division or something?"

But Angus had already spotted a suspicious-looking dark cloud hovering directly above the glass dome of the library. "I bet you anything this has something to do with your uncle Scabious. He must be bored with the showers of newts and frogs—"

"What—so now he's sending storm globes instead?" Indigo said. "But why?"

Angus didn't answer. The storm had almost doubled in

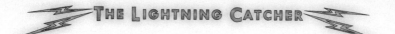
size during this brief conversation, and he grabbed Indigo by the sleeve and tried to drag her down the spiral staircase instead.

Indigo resisted. "Shouldn't we find Mr. Knurling and warn him?"

Angus cast a quick glance around. Mr. Knurling was nowhere to be seen. "He must have made a run for it already. Come on!"

They hopped gingerly over the shattered globes when they finally reached the bottom of the staircase, and ran toward the library doors. As they slipped outside and into the hallway, however, they were met by another, even uglier storm. The seething cloud rumbled in front of them—almost as if it could sense their presence and was keen to start raining on them as soon as possible.

Angus flattened himself against the wall and attempted to squeeze his way past without the storm noticing, but before either of them could reach the long passageway beyond, there was an ominous grumble of thunder, and—

"Back to the library!" Angus yelled as the storm suddenly unleashed its full fury.

Indigo yanked the door open and they tumbled through

it, vicious hailstones the size of golf balls bouncing off the backs of their necks. The storm burst into the library behind them. With one colossal thunderclap, it collided with the other dark cloud, forming a terrifying superstorm.

"Quick, try and hit the hailstones before they hit you!" Angus shouted, pulling a heavy dictionary off the shelf closest to him and swinging it around his head like a baseball bat, sending frozen missiles flying in every direction and breaking inkwells, glass cabinets, and windows in the process.

Book after book turned to pulp in his hands, but it was no use. The storm grew more violent still, with strong gusts of icy wind forcing them to retreat behind reading chairs and under homework tables—until there was only one place left for them to hide.

"We've got to get under Mr. Knurling's desk!" Indigo shouted, scrambling under the large mahogany desk on her hands and knees and dragging Angus with her. They waited, shivering, hoping that the storm would blow itself out. But it howled happily above their heads, raging so violently now that the legs of the librarian's desk began to tremble under the large weight of ice that had collected on top of it.

"We can't stay here! This thing's about to collapse," Angus yelled above the fury. "We've got to make a run for it!"

"No, wait!" Indigo pulled him back by his sweater. "I—I think it might be stopping."

Indigo was right. The storm was finally running out of steam; its deadly pellets of ice were now the size of peas. Less than a minute later, it was all over. The remains of the storm hung briefly above their heads, looking wrung out and exhausted, before it quickly melted away to nothing, and a strange hush fell over the dripping library.

Angus removed several lumps of ice from his right ear and crawled out from under the desk to survey the damage.

Books had been ripped from their shelves and flung across the floor. Large piles of melted hailstones had formed icy puddles, some of which looked deep enough for a colony of Imbur seals to take a plunge in.

"The library's ruined!" Indigo gasped, standing beside him. Her neck and arms were covered in angry-looking ice burns.

Angus gulped. "It's just lucky there was no one else in here."

"Oh, but . . . look," Indigo whispered, pointing to a thin trail of shattered glass that led to a crushed monocle on the floor. There were also signs that someone had been scrambling desperately for cover. "Mr. Knurling!" Indigo turned a funny shade of green. "He was still in the reference section when the storm struck. He never got out."

"Where is he? He must be buried under a pile of books . . . or hailstones. Quick, we'd better split up and see if we can find him before he suffocates."

It was a miserable job. Angus picked his way through the soggy mass of books. Every now and again he found a snow directory or a volume on famous old lightning catchers that could be hung up to dry. But the rest of it was beyond repair.

Nor was there any sign of the missing librarian. And Angus was just beginning to wonder if they might need some help finding him when something odd caught his eye. Lying in the middle of a particularly large pile of books was a shiny black object. He bent down and tapped it with his knuckles. It twitched.

"Over here!" he called to Indigo. "I think I've found him!"

The shiny object turned out to be a shoe, which still had a foot inside it, and a moment later they had uncovered the librarian. He was lying flat on his back, his eyes closed, stiff hair flattened by the storm.

"You don't think he's—oh, he's not dead is he?" Indigo gasped.

"I think he's just unconscious." Angus inspected a large lump on the librarian's forehead. "One of us had better go for help, though. We'll never be able to carry him on our own."

"I'll go!" Indigo volunteered, getting swiftly to her feet.

"Just—be as quick as you can, will you?" said Angus as she began to pick her way across the debris. "He looks really bad."

With Indigo gone, it was eerily quiet. Angus looked down nervously at the librarian, who still showed no signs of movement, his arms and legs spread-eagled over a large pile of books. It was obvious that he'd been trying to save some of the rarer ones from being damaged by the storm. Among the books that were poking out from underneath him were several on how to create your own thunderstorm, and some extremely risky reading material about hurricanes that Angus would never normally have been allowed to see.

Angus picked up another volume, glancing at the title on its faded cover . . . and suddenly he felt the blood drain from his face.

The book had been bound in plain brown leather and was quite unremarkable in every way, except for the ten words that were printed across its front cover.

Angus read the title slowly, hardly daring to breathe, hardly noticing the tight lump of excitement that had suddenly formed in his throat. Because finally he knew . . . he knew exactly what his parents had been searching for on their secret assignment; he knew what the missing map would lead them to, if they ever managed to find it; and he understood why Indigo's uncle was so desperate to get his hands on it. It all made perfect sense. He took a deep, steadying breath and read the title once again.

A Holographic History of the Lightning Vaults, by Philomena Whip-Stitcher.

12

THE FOG FIELD TRIP

It was only after Indigo had returned with Catcher Sparks, two additional lightning catchers, and a stretcher that she and Angus were finally free to leave the library. They quickly discovered that it wasn't the only room at Perilous to have been hit by a wave of storm globes, and they picked their way through the soggy tunnels and passageways with difficulty.

Storm globes had burst through almost every window and glass ceiling, causing chaos at every turn. Angus caught a brief glimpse of four lightning catchers fending off a blizzard with some flaming torches at the end of a long tunnel, and a mini tornado had wrecked the entrance to the lightning catchers' living quarters.

"We were extremely lucky they didn't do even more damage," Catcher Howler, an expert on wind, explained to a group of fellow lightning catchers as Angus and Indigo slipped their way past. "Winds of up to three hundred miles per hour, violent columns of rotating air, totally out of control. I dread to think what would have happened if it had broken into the experimental division and grabbed hold of the cloud-busting rocket launcher."

The kitchens were awash under three feet of water, with tables and chairs bobbing about like fishing boats in a harbor. And it wasn't until the waters had subsided a bit and they were helping themselves to a hot dinner, a few hours later, that Angus finally got a chance to tell Dougal and Indigo of his amazing discovery.

"It all makes sense, when you think about it," he said as they waded their way across the kitchen in their rubber boots. "What's the one thing that Dankhart would love to find? What's the one thing that could make him more powerful than anyone else?"

"The lightning vaults!" said Dougal.

"Exactly!"

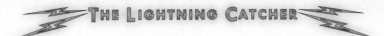

"But the lightning vaults don't exist," Indigo hissed, checking over her shoulder for eavesdroppers, as she always did before they discussed her villainous uncle. "They're just a myth, a story made up by old lightning catchers to frighten their grandchildren."

Angus raised an eyebrow at her. "Says who?"

They found an empty table and wiped it dry with some fresh napkins, and for the next few moments none of them spoke as they tucked into plates heaped with roast potatoes and chicken pie. Now that he had actually found something that might help lead him to his parents, Angus suddenly had his appetite back, and he shoveled another slice of pie onto his plate before he'd even finished the first one. Indigo however, merely picked at her dinner.

"Wha's up wiv you?" Angus asked, potatoes and gravy dribbling down his chin.

"Nothing. It's just, well, nobody's ever seen the vaults, have they? So how can you be so sure they exist all of a sudden? I mean, Principal Dark-Angel's—"

"Principal Dark-Angel's hardly likely to run around Perilous shouting about it, is she? And anyway, she told your dad about it, remember?" said Angus, turning eagerly to Dougal.

"Yeah." Dougal nodded. "She told him not to go blabbing to everyone else about it."

"And what if she only said that because she knew all along that the lightning vaults were real? Look, this book's got something important in it," Angus said, patting the holographic history, which he'd smuggled from the library and concealed beneath his sweater. "Why else would the librarian have been trying to save it?"

"Oh, dear," Indigo said, biting her lip.

"What now?" Angus and Dougal both asked together.

"It's nothing, really, but, well—I feel a bit guilty, actually," she said, her cheeks flushing. "We've all been a bit unkind about Mr. Knurling, but he must really like being a librarian after all. I mean, look at the way he tried to save those books from the storm. What if he notices that the holographic history is missing when he recovers?"

"He won't," said Angus. "That library's totally waterlogged. Plus it's going to be weeks before anyone sorts through all those soggy books on the floor."

Dougal nodded in agreement. "Knurling will just think it got destroyed in the storm."

As soon as they finished their dinner, they headed straight up to the deserted weather bubble to hear what the holographic history had to say for itself. As no girls were allowed into the boys' corridor, it was impossible to invite Indigo into the privacy of the Pigsty.

Thankfully, the large steel-and-glass bubble had escaped the ravages of the storm globes and was one of the few rooms left at Perilous that was still warm and dry.

"A real holographic history," said Dougal when Angus finally removed it from his sweater. "My dad's told me all about these, but I never thought I'd actually see one. They're really, really rare, you know."

"Yeah? Well, I've already seen one in Principal Dark-Angel's office, and they're also really, really noisy, so we'd better close the door or we'll have half of Perilous in here wondering what's going on."

Dougal closed the inner door quickly, sealing the bubble tight. They then found three seats at the far side, placed the book in front of them where they could all see it, and began at chapter one. As soon as Angus turned to the first page, he was surprised to find it occupied by the familiar figure of Oswald Blott. Oswald had abandoned his fancy pantaloons and was now wearing a straggly blond wig and red velvet dress that failed to conceal his hairy chest. He was obviously trying to pass himself off as the Philomena Whip-Stitcher named on the front of the book, but he had merely managed to make himself look ridiculous instead. His voice, however, remained the same, and it echoed magnificently around the empty bubble.

"Beware the power of the mighty lightning bolt!" he boomed with a dramatic flourish that made all three of them jump. "Beware the dark and rumbling skies and take cover in your potting shed, or in your chicken coop—unless you be wearing boots made of the finest Indian rubber. So warned Edgar Perilous when he first came to the fair Isle of Imbur, saving the smelly peasants from their slovenly ways. For it was here—after watching London burn to a crisp—that he and Philip Starling, determined that some good should arise from the smoldering ashes of the Great Fire, decided to master and control this most vicious force of nature. And they began to build the only lightning vaults known to exist in the world.

"Greater than the mystical pyramids of Egypt, more wondrous than the ancient gardens of Babylon, nobler than the mighty Greek Acropolis . . ."

"Goes on a bit, doesn't he." Dougal grinned.

". . . more bewitching than the great stones of Henge, the lightning vaults were carved deep within the rock of Perilous, and noble experimentation began within. Lightning bolts, violent and mighty, transformed the ground in the vaults into sheets of magnificent glass that sparkled like melted emeralds. Others were split, vanquished, captured and hung from the ceiling like giant bats, their secrets plundered and their power overcome for the good of all mankind."

Oswald beckoned them closer and lowered his voice to a faint murmur, as if he too was afraid of being overheard.

"But dark days were ahead. Not all men who faced the power of the lightning bolt could be trusted to honor it, and a tragic incident occurred one bleak and stormy night. Crimson blood flowed through the mighty vaults, and Edgar Perilous ordered that they be sealed forever. And their location was slowly forgotten in the pearly mists of time."

Oswald adjusted his wig, which had slipped over to one side of his head, and then hopped to the center of the holographic square before continuing. "Many have tried to find the lost vaults since those desperate days, but without the secret map to guide them, none will succeed," he concluded in a superior tone.

"The secret map!" Dougal stared at Angus, his mouth hanging wide open. "I don't believe it. You were right, that's got to be what your mum and dad were looking for."

Angus felt excitement surge through him.

Oswald Blott took a deep breath before he continued. "To learn more about the map and hear what terrible secrets lay within the fabled vaults, I suggest you turn to the beginning of chapter two immediately—unless you be a filthy peasant, and then I demand that you shuffle off back to your turnip growing, and release me from your beer-stained grip!"

Angus turned hastily to the beginning of chapter two, but the holographic square was filled with water and the only thing they could hear coming from it was a strange sort of gurgling noise, as if Oswald was attempting to continue his narrative from the bottom of a fish tank.

"I don't believe it," Angus wailed, flicking quickly through the remaining chapters. "The rest of the book's the same. The storm ruined it!"

He held the book on its edge and gave it a shake, hoping that the water would simply trickle out by itself, but nothing happened.

"What are we supposed to do now?" he groaned, his head whirling. "How are we going to find out what happened to the map without Philomena Whip-Stitcher to help us?"

Angus listened to Oswald/Philomena's narrative each night before he went to sleep for the next week, muffling the storyteller's booming voice under his bedclothes and hoping that the rest of the chapters might miraculously dry themselves out, but it was hopeless. Except for chapter one, Oswald's voice remained nothing but a fishy gargle.

Meanwhile, in the rest of the Exploratorium, the cleanup operation had begun in earnest. It took a full five days before they could go to the kitchens without their rubber boots. All lightning cub duties in the experimental division were temporarily suspended until a particularly stubborn hurricane could be pried out of it using great numbers of emergency storm bellows. In the Octagon, the door to the Inner Sanctum of Perplexing Mysteries and Secrets, which had received quite a battering from a mini typhoon, was being repaired with extra locks and lengths of wood.

Mr. Knurling was making good progress and had suffered only a mild concussion—which was more than could be said for the library itself. Now that the floors had been mopped dry and the remains of the storm globes removed, the full scale of the devastation was plain for everyone to see. And the ancient collection of books was almost beyond repair.

Dougal, who was particularly upset by this destruction, quickly volunteered all three of them to help clear up the mess, which also gave them an excellent opportunity to discuss everything they had learned from the holographic history.

"Dankhart must have found out somehow that my mum and dad were looking for the map of the lightning vaults, right?" Angus said one evening as he shoveled up a pile of mushy dictionaries. "So I bet you anything he waited until they'd actually discovered where it was before he kidnapped them."

"Hang on a minute, though," said Dougal, frowning. "If Dankhart did manage to steal the map from your mum and dad, why haven't we heard about it?"

"Actually, Dougal's got a point," said Indigo, who was on her hands and knees flattening out a pile of historical newspapers. "If Dankhart had broken into the Exploratorium with the map and uncovered the lightning vaults, there'd be a huge rumpus. Not even Principal Dark-Angel could keep something like that quiet."

"So you don't think that Dankhart has the map?" said Angus, his shovel suspended in midair.

"No, or like Indigo says, the whole Exploratorium would know about it," Dougal reasoned. "And watch what you're doing with those dictionaries, will you?" he added, looking upset. "You're flicking soggy words about everywhere."

"What? Oh, sorry." Angus lowered his shovel carefully, still following his train of thought through to its logical end. "So where's the map now, then? I mean, Principal Dark-Angel definitely hasn't got it, or she wouldn't have asked me all those questions about what my mum and dad had sent me through the mail lately. And the only letter they've sent me in months is that boring one about my other aunt and uncle. So I definitely haven't got it either. . . ."

He glanced around the devastated library, with the faint hope that he might somehow see a secret-looking map poking out from behind one of the bookshelves, just waiting to be discovered. But he knew that his chances were depressingly slim.

Due to the damage caused by the storm globes, all fog field trips had been postponed until further notice. But as Angus and Indigo entered the kitchens one evening for dinner a few days later, they were met by the sound of excited chatter and the news that their own trip had now been scheduled in three days' time. This also meant that Angus could finally put his plan into action and search the marshes for any clues his parents might have left behind. He began to feel a nervous leap of excitement whenever he thought about it.

"Three days!" said Indigo, playing with the apple crumble in her bowl. "And we still don't know if we're going to run into any schools of piranha mist fish. If we'd just had a bit more time to find out . . ."

"Yeah, but how could we? Half the Exploratorium's been knee-deep in the mess from the hurricanes and typhoons for days, hasn't it," reasoned Angus. "At least everyone else is in the same boat—"

"Not quite everyone, Dungbeetle," came a familiar thuglike voice from above them.

Angus swung around to see the Vellum twins towering over them once again. They were both wearing the smuggest smiles he'd ever seen.

"Tell us what you're talking about, Vellum, or go away and bug somebody else," Angus snapped.

"I'm talking, Dungbeetle, about the fact that some of us have already been practicing on the actual fog course itself," said Percival. "Should be a piece of cake, now we've been around it a few times."

"You've done what?" said Indigo, jumping angrily to her feet. "But nobody's allowed, not before the actual field trip."

Percival shrugged. "You can do anything you feel like, Midnight, when your dad's a senior lightning catcher."

"But that's cheating!"

"Call it what you want." Percival grinned. "It won't change the fact that Pixie and me will have finished that course before you three have worked out where the starting line is."

"Yeah? Well it won't change the fact that neither of you has the brains of a fog mite, either," said Angus.

Percival clenched his fists and looked as if he was about to pick a fight. But the presence of several lightning catchers at a table close by seemed to bring him to his senses.

"Brains have got nothing to do with getting round this course, Dungbeetle," he sneered. "It's all about courage, which means that you three should easily come in last. See you on the fog course, losers!" He and Pixie wandered off, snickering.

"Oh, that settles it!" Indigo slumped down into her chair, glaring after the twins. "I know Gudgeon said this isn't a competition, I know we're going to be busy looking for clues. But we've got to beat those two hairy morons, even if it's the last thing we ever do."

Angus swallowed hard, sincerely hoping that it wouldn't be.

▲ ▲ ▲

The day of the fog field trip dawned a dull and cloudy gray. Angus woke up much earlier than usual, feeling bleary-eyed. He got dressed quickly in his weatherproof coat and rubber boots, making sure he had the letter from his mum—which was still tucked safely inside his fog guide, like a talisman of hope. And he made his way up the spiral stairs, impatient to begin his search of the Imbur marshes.

The atmosphere in the Exploratorium was electric. Quite a number of lightning cubs, who were obviously feeling far too nervous to even attempt breakfast, were loitering anxiously about the corridors, chewing on their fingernails instead. Angus hurried past the kitchens with his own stomach churning and went straight up to the entrance hall, where they had all been instructed to gather by Miss DeWinkle.

It was clear that several groups of older trainees were also heading out to tackle their own sections of the fog course, and they stood talking in excited huddles.

"Good luck, Doomsbury!" Edmund Croxley waved as he passed. "And remember what your fog guide says . . . if in doubt—run!"

A number of lightning catchers, including Gudgeon, Catcher Sparks, and Principal Dark-Angel, had gathered to assist. It was the first time Angus had seen Principal Dark-Angel since the roof top ice rink. There were dark circles under her eyes, and it looked as if she hadn't had a decent night's sleep for a very long time.

"I think I'm going to be sick!" Dougal hissed as soon as Angus found him a few moments later. "I couldn't sleep last night, so I dug this out." He held up an old book entitled *Most Foul and Deadly Mysteries of the Imbur Marshes.* "Just listen to what it says about fog phantoms."

Angus frowned. "Fog phantoms?"

"Yeah, exactly." Dougal gulped. "'Known for their terrible boggy stench, fog phantoms lurk in the deepest marshy depths, waiting to pounce on the lost and unwary, some of whom have never been seen again.'" He snapped the book shut. "If fog is *this* dangerous, why are they sending us out into the middle of the stuff?"

"You're such a nerd, Dewsnap!" Percival Vellum snickered as he and Pixie pushed through the crowd. "Books won't save you now. You won't last five minutes out in those marshes."

"Just shut it, Vellum!" Angus glared angrily after the disappearing twins.

Dougal, however, looked doubly nauseous and kept his mouth clamped shut until Indigo found them.

At eight o'clock precisely, Miss DeWinkle, who was dressed for the occasion in a bright orange coat and matching earmuffs, herded everyone into the gravity railway carriage, which carried them straight down to the island below.

Angus gripped his seat tightly as the carriage plummeted toward the ground at an alarming rate, making him feel as if all his internal organs had been squashed inside one of the pickling jars that he'd seen on Principal Dark-Angel's desk. Clouds, birds, and big chunks of sky flashed past in a nauseating blur. He kept his eyes averted from Gudgeon, who was assisting Miss DeWinkle, and concentrated hard on a flickering lamp instead. He was extremely relieved when they finally reached the bottom with a surprisingly gentle bump.

"I wonder how we're getting out to the marshes," said Indigo as she, Angus, and Dougal staggered out onto solid ground again.

Her question was answered almost immediately by the arrival of several open-topped, steam-powered coaches, brass lamps and railings gleaming even in the damp weather. Due to the gloomy conditions, however, it was impossible to see anything of the countryside they were traveling through. And by the time they arrived at the start of their course on the marshes, they were already wet through. Boggy and desolate, the marshes were the least welcoming spot Angus had ever set foot in.

"I knew it! These are perfect conditions for fog phantoms." Dougal trembled as Miss DeWinkle beckoned them over to a row of green flags poking up through the marshy grass.

"Gather round, everyone!" she called. "And welcome to your first-ever fog field trip! I'm sure it will prove to be a memorable and enjoyable day!"

Angus and Dougal exchanged doubtful glances. Miss DeWinkle waited for all fidgeting to stop before she continued.

"There are just a few basic rules before we begin. Anyone caught deliberately taking a shortcut through the fog, or confusing their fellow lightning cubs with false directions, will be dealt with swiftly by Principal Dark-Angel. Any pushing, tripping, shoving, or attempts to scare one another witless will be punished with two weeks on pencil-sharpening duty in the research department."

Angus glanced over at the Vellum twins, who looked less than pleased, and he felt his confidence rise a notch.

"Remember that you are here to study and experience the perils of working in fog. This is not a race to the finish line. Running in such conditions is strictly forbidden," Miss DeWinkle warned. "Each team must also take great care not to wander onto any other part of the course, particularly those marked in black, blue, and purple. Those sections have been designed for more experienced cubs and are far too difficult for you to attempt. You must also collect one of these tokens"—she dangled a small, perfectly formed Perilous charm on a string—"at the end of each section, to prove that you have completed it. Now, decide which member of your team will be taking charge of the map."

Indigo, looking determined, clutched the map tightly.

"Fog guides and weather watches at the ready . . ."

Dougal, who still looked faintly sick, gripped the fog guide, which he'd now read at least a dozen times.

Angus glanced down at his weather watch, which was already glowing a luminous orange. A boggy swirl covered the entire surface. What else were they about to discover in the fog?

"Gudgeon will be starting teams off at two-minute intervals, so you don't all crash into each other. Good luck, everyone!"

The gruff lightning catcher emerged from behind them suddenly.

"Quinn, Fox, you're first," he barked as the two nervous-looking trainees stepped up to the starting line.

Angus caught a brief glimpse of Violet Quinn's face, which had turned the color of dishwater. A second later, the whistle blew, and their first fog field trip was suddenly under way. Pixie and Percival Vellum were next, followed by Nigel Ridgely and Jonathon Hake. Each team instantly vanished into the fog, from which no sound escaped.

"Doomsbury, Dewsnap, Midnight. You're up next."

Angus jumped at the sound of his fake name.

"This is it!" Dougal gulped as they followed Gudgeon to the starting line. "If I don't make it to the other end, it's been nice knowing you!"

Angus tried to smile back, but he could feel that his face was stuck in a horrible sort of grimace. Only his eyebrows moved. Indigo gave them both an anxious smile.

A second later, Gudgeon blew his whistle . . . and they were hurrying straight into a thick bank of fog. It hit Angus in the face like a cold, wet blanket and wrapped itself around his ears. He tried to remember exactly what Miss DeWinkle had taught them about taking small, measured steps.

Before he could check his weather watch, however, a low, earthy tunnel began to appear up ahead. It resembled the entrance to a giant rabbit burrow.

"There's a sign right next to it!" Indigo pointed to a luminous board, glowing at them through the fog. It read:

THE PASSAGE BEFORE YOU REPRESENTS ONE OF THE CELEBRATED FOG TUNNELS OF FINLAND, FILLED WITH NOTORIOUSLY TRICKY TUNNEL FOG. YOUR TEAM MUST NAVIGATE ITS WAY THROUGH TO THE OTHER SIDE TO EXPERIENCE THE CONDITIONS FIRSTHAND.

"'Tunnel fog,'" Dougal said, reading directly from the McFangus guide. "'An extra-thick fog that forms in damp underground spaces, concealing many hazards, such as rocks, tree roots, and uneven ground.'"

"Why's it extra thick?" asked Angus.

"Obvious, isn't it," Dougal said. "It's being squeezed through a narrow tunnel, so it gets all concentrated. Plus it hasn't got the room to swirl about like normal fog does."

Angus stared into the mouth of the tunnel. Up close, it was obvious it ran directly under the marsh. The fog inside was thicker than custard.

"I'll go first," said Indigo, pushing her hair out of her face. "According to the map, the course heads north from here." She rolled the map and stuffed it in her pocket. "So as long as we follow the compass on our weather watches . . ."

Indigo took a deep breath, clambered inside, and disappeared into the gloom without a backward glance. Angus followed quickly, before he could change his mind. Dougal brought up the rear, grumbling loudly.

On and on the tunnel went. Angus tripped and stumbled blindly, hitting his head more than once on the low ceiling, swallowing great gulps of the terrible-tasting fog.

He finally reached the other end of the tunnel and collapsed in a sweaty, breathless heap. Dougal scrambled out behind him.

"Is it my imagination," said Indigo, collecting their first token from a box and pulling both her teammates upright again, "or is everything much creepier on this side of the tunnel?"

"You're not imagining anything. We've just walked straight into a spooky fog," said Angus, checking his weather watch quickly.

Dougal shivered. "According to the McFangus guide, spooky fog is most commonly found lurking in graveyards, deserted castles, and old ruins.' It can also 'induce feelings of fear and panic and the irrational belief that you are being followed.' You don't think we are being followed, do you?" He glanced warily over his shoulder.

The next illuminated sign instructed them to navigate their way through the ruins of an old house. Dark and forbidding, the gaping doorways dared them to enter. Angus led them silently into the heart of the ghostly ruins, desperately hoping they weren't about to come face-to-face with a colony of vampire bats. Spiderwebs floated through the air, and long stone columns poked up through the lumpy ground like gravestones, making all three of them feel extremely jumpy. Angus forced himself to peer through every doorway, to explore each nook and cranny searching for the tiniest hint that his parents might have visited this place before their kidnapping.

"What was that?" gasped Indigo as the ominous sound of snapping twigs echoed all around them.

"Arghhh!" Dougal yelled.

A tall, shadowy figure suddenly burst through the fog. Angus took several hurried steps backward as the sinister shape edged closer and closer.

"It's a fog phantom!" shrieked Dougal. "Fog phantom!"

"Don't be so ridiculous, Dewsnap," the phantom said, in a very familiar voice. Catcher Sparks emerged from the mist, equipped with an orange fog lamp. "I am simply here to hand you your next token and make sure you haven't gone wandering off into the bogs by accident. I suggest you stop gawping, Dewsnap, and get a move on."

"That was scarier than running into a real phantom," said Dougal, still shaking as they raced off again a moment later. "Who else do you reckon they've got lurking about in here?"

Angus shuddered, hoping they weren't about to crash into Valentine Vellum.

On through the dreadful course they plunged. A dense patch of confusing fog sent Angus's weather watch haywire—it would show him nothing but flocks of pink flamingos, no matter how hard he shook it—and it only started behaving itself again when they'd left the confusing fog behind. Dougal almost passed out in a panic when they skirted the edge of an invisible fog; for several minutes he was unable to locate his own elbows. But it was a thick no-way-out fog that caused them the most problems.

Round and round in circles they went, desperately searching for a way out. Angus could barely find his own feet. And with each passing minute, he felt his spirits sink. Searching for clues about his parents was utterly impossible. He could have walked straight past Scabious Dankhart himself without even realizing it. He had more chance of finding a needle in a fog stack.

But it was only as they scrambled up the steep slopes

of a marshy hill that things started to go really wrong. Angus had almost reached the top when he was met by the size-ten boot of another lightning cub, who accidentally kicked him in the nose.

"Ow!" he howled as pain shot through his skull. For several seconds, he could see nothing but bright, silvery stars dancing before his eyes. Then the sound of snickering reached his ears.

"If I'd known it was you, Dungbeetle, I would have kicked harder." Percival Vellum jeered down at them from the very top of the hill.

"You did that on purpose!" Angus yelled, blood gushing from his nostrils. He grabbed the hanky that Indigo offered him and pressed it to his nose.

"You'll have a hard time proving it, Dungbeetle. Especially when I tell DeWinkle how my boot accidentally slipped . . . such a tragic accident. Your team's never going to win this now," he gloated. "You might just as well give up and go running back to DeWinkle."

"Get lost, Vellum! We're not giving up because of you!"

"Suit yourself." Percival shrugged. "With any luck, one of the fog phantoms might get you instead."

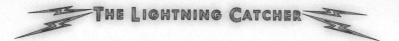

"We've already met one of those," said Dougal. "And it wasn't half as ugly as you!"

Percival scowled. "What have I told you about trying to be funny, Dewsnap? Just for that . . ." He grabbed the entire pile of tokens that had been placed in a box at the summit and stuffed them into his pocket. "You've got no chance of winning now, not when me and Pixie will be the only team to finish with all our tokens."

Dougal gasped. Angus took a wild swipe at the smirking twin and missed.

"But you can't!" Indigo shrieked. "We'll go straight to Miss DeWinkle, we'll tell her everything!"

"Oh, boo hoo, Midnight, it'll be far too late by then! Me and Pixie are going to beat everyone else on this course, and there's nothing you can do to stop us. We've got an important family tradition to continue."

"Yeah, the tradition of being a lying, cheating thug, you mean!" Dougal shouted.

Percival smirked. "See you at the finish line, losers!" And before they could stop him, he slid down the other side of the hill, where Pixie was apparently waiting for him, and vanished.

"Is your nose all right?" asked Indigo as they took the last few steps to the top of the marshy mound.

"It's fine!" Angus said angrily, still trying to stop the bleeding. "I'm not letting Vellum cheat his way round this fog course. We've got to get those tokens back! Come on!"

Angus led the charge down the hill. He tore after Percival, fueled by his own disappointment and his throbbing nose, determined to stop the twins from cheating their way to triumph. He forced his legs to move faster, ready to wrestle Percival to the ground, if he had to, and steal the tokens back.

The mist parted. The twins were barely twenty feet ahead of them.

"You're never going to catch me, Dungbeetle! Not with those puny legs!" Percival yelled over his shoulder. But he was breathing heavily, rapidly losing ground.

Angus ran harder. He reached out, grasping at the tails of Percival's coat.

"Hey! Geroff me!" Percival yanked his coat free.

Angus stumbled. He picked himself up again quickly. All he needed was just one last burst of speed . . .

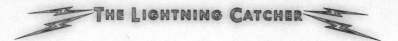
The fog came out of nowhere, almost knocking him over sideways. It rolled in from his left and swallowed him up completely. In less than a second, Percival Vellum had disappeared.

"No!" Angus stopped dead, gasping for breath as the sound of snickering faded into the distance. He stared at his watch, which informed him that he'd just been engulfed by a tropical fog. Strangely warm, it had a faint smell of coconuts.

"I've lost Vellum!" he told Indigo and Dougal when they bumped into him seconds later. "We've got to get out of this tropical fog and find him again."

"I don't remember reading anything about tropical fog in the McFangus guide." Dougal flicked hurriedly through the dog-eared book. "It must be really rare. Yeah, all it says here is that due to its high droplet density, it's wetter than most, and . . ."

"What?" asked Angus impatiently, dabbing his bloody nose.

Dougal gulped. "If you believe the legend, it's also the type of fog most favored by—"

"PIRANHA MIST FISH!" Indigo yelled suddenly, as a

large school of tiny, silvery fish came shimmering toward them.

"RUN!" Angus shouted, forgetting all about Percival Vellum, not caring which direction they sprinted as long as they escaped the terrifying fish. He charged blindly through the fog, trying not to lose sight of Indigo. Dougal darted behind them, tripping over every clump of grass.

"ARGGHHH!" Dougal dived to the left as the fish suddenly lunged, fins flicking, razor-sharp teeth ripping into his rubber boots. "Get these things off me!"

Angus doubled back, swiping the worst of the nibblers out of his way. He hauled Dougal onto his feet and dragged him off in a new direction, crashing straight into a petrified Georgina Fox.

"Ow!" she wailed.

"Sorry!"

"Who's there?" Dougal plowed into them both, causing a sudden pileup.

"Ooofff!"

"Oh, no! I've dropped my fog guide! It's got my mum's letter inside. . . ."

Several seconds of severe confusion followed before

Angus finally got his bearings again and somehow managed to retrieve his fog guide—by which time the fish had reorganized themselves into a solid, glimmering dart. Angus grabbed Dougal and raced in the opposite direction, accidentally falling over Indigo, who had come back to search for them both.

"This way!" she shouted, dodging frantically from side to side, trying to shake off the fish.

But the fish ripped at anything they could get their teeth into, shredding the lightning cubs' weatherproof coats, hats, and scarves and swimming perilously close to Angus's ears. It was only after Indigo made them double back on themselves, outmaneuvering the nibbling creatures, that they finally escaped.

They stopped, gasping for breath, in a surprisingly fog-free clearing.

"I've definitely . . . got vapor sickness." Dougal sank to his knees, clutching a stitch in his side. "Either that, or I've swallowed some mist fish."

Angus sat on the boggy ground, gulping down great lungfuls of air. There was no chance of finding Percival Vellum now. No chance of discovering anything useful about his parents. The entire field trip had been a complete and utter disaster.

"Where are we, anyway?" he asked, wondering if there was any possibility that they were still following the green route.

Indigo studied the map between her trembling hands. "We've gone way off course, thanks to the fish."

"We've wandered onto the wrong course, you mean!" Dougal turned pale. He pointed to a row of small blue flags. "Only sixth years are supposed to do the blue section."

Indigo nodded. "Dougal's right, we've come too far to the east."

"Yeah, and landed ourselves right in the path of a fognado, whatever that is," said Angus, looking at his watch. It showed a confusing swirl of dense mists heading rapidly toward them.

"A fognado?" Dougal hissed. "Oh, no!" He searched desperately through the McFangus guide until he came to a page covered in red warning symbols. "'A fognado,'" he read, "'is among the most deadly forms of fog in existence. Formed in freak weather conditions, it sucks in all other fog around it, creating a giant, suffocating whirl. Any lightning catcher caught in it is at serious risk of broken limbs or even death, unless equipped with a storm snare. The only other way to tackle a fognado is to leave the area *immediately.*' Which is what we should be doing right now, before that thing rips us to pieces!" A giant whirl of fearsome fog appeared behind them as he said it. "Come on!"

Suddenly they were running again. Angus had only taken a few steps when it happened. A fire dragon leaped before his eyes, a blinding flash of talons and claws, its great fiery scales burning with intense heat. Angus staggered to a stop. At the exact same moment, Percival Vellum darted blindly onto the sixth-year course. Seemingly dazed and confused by his own flight from the mist fish, he was now standing directly in the path of the fognado. And the fire dragon hovered, like a shimmering mirage, above his head.

There was no time to think. No time to shout a warning. Angus turned and ran full pelt as the fognado, twisting and turning with frightening speed, hurled itself toward Percival.

"Doomsbury?" Percival looked around in confusion as Angus made a desperate lunge. "Get away from me, you—"

CRASH!

Angus shoved him out of the fognado's path and forced him to the ground as the fognado went roaring past, only inches above them. It wailed and moaned, ripping furiously at their hair and clothes, almost sucking them both off the ground and high up into its swirling mass. Angus clung to the tough, marshy grass with the very tips of his fingers as the fognado attacked everything in its path like a powerful, out-of-control vacuum cleaner. The ground trembled beneath him. The air felt strangely thin, as if the fognado had sucked that up too, leaving him with nothing to breathe.

Slowly, slowly, the noise began to fade. Angus waited, fingers still gripping the grass tightly, only looking up again when he was sure it was safe. The fognado was disappearing into the distance at last, but all around them the ground had been pummeled and battered by the ferocious storm.

"Oh, thank goodness!" Miss DeWinkle was charging

toward them, looking appalled, her earmuffs trailing behind her. "First years on the sixth years' course . . . a fognado! You all could have been killed!"

Shouting broke out everywhere as more lightning catchers flooded the course, searching for any other stray trainees. Angus's ears were ringing. Beside him, he was dimly aware that a trembling Percival Vellum was being checked over for injuries by Miss DeWinkle.

"You'd better come with me." Gudgeon was suddenly helping Angus back onto his own wobbly legs. "Before that thing comes back and flattens us all."

And the gruff lightning catcher led him back to the watery mists at the edge of the marsh, where the open-topped coaches stood waiting.

13

INDIGO'S BIG IDEA

By the following morning, the entire Exploratorium had heard how Angus had accidentally stumbled onto the wrong course and saved Percival Vellum from a deadly fognado. He now found it impossible to walk anywhere without other lightning cubs, many of whom he'd never spoken to before in his life, stopping him to hear more about the fantastic tale. He left out all mention of fire dragons, of course, putting his quick thinking down to his weather watch.

"Cool!" Nicholas Grubb slapped Angus heartily on the back the next time he bumped into him. "If I'd almost been flattened by a fognado, though, I'd be laying it on thick, you know, asking DeWinkle for time off and stuff."

Angus, however, found the whole experience very uncomfortable.

"But it's brilliant!" Dougal said one lunchtime, after Angus had just been forced to tell Edmund Croxley and a bunch of his friends what had happened. "You've just made Percival Vellum look like a total idiot—I mean, after all the boasting he's been doing about being fantastic on the fog course! Anyway, I'd make the most of it if I were you. By this time next week, everyone will have forgotten about it and you'll be back to gouging earwax out of hailstone helmets with the rest of us."

Miss DeWinkle instructed him to stand up and give the whole class a proper account of the incident at their next fog lesson. Angus mumbled his way through it as quickly as possible, feeling hot and embarrassed.

Percival Vellum himself was maintaining a very low profile, for once, and had taken to skulking about the stone tunnels and passageways wearing a chunky scarf, to hide his face.

"He could have thanked you for saving his life, at the very least," said Indigo one day as she, Angus, and Dougal passed the glowering twin on their way to the experimental division.

"Yeah, but it's not very good for his image, is it?" said Dougal wisely. "Being saved from a fognado by someone half his size."

There were two things that troubled Angus far more than the attention he was now receiving, however: his complete failure to find any clues about his mum and dad out on the Imbur marshes, and the reappearance of the fire dragon. The disturbing dreams he experienced each night about his kidnapped parents had also become horribly entwined with visions of the frightening creature, giving him the worst nightmares ever.

"But being a storm prophet is a good thing. I mean, that's how you saved me from the ball lightning," said Indigo earnestly as they discussed it quietly at dinnertime a few days later.

Now that Indigo was spending almost all her time with him and Dougal, Angus had decided to tell her about his odd visions so he could talk freely on the subject with them both. Indigo had accepted without question the revelation that he might be a storm prophet, for which he was extremely grateful.

"I know Percival Vellum can be a bit annoying some-times—" she added.

"A bit?" Dougal spluttered, accidentally spraying half the table with rice. "Oops, sorry! But Percival Vellum's the most obnoxious cub on the planet."

"Even so." Indigo flicked a soggy grain of rice off her sleeve. "If Angus hadn't pushed him away from that fognado . . ."

"Yeah, but why am I the only one seeing fire dragons?" Angus whispered. "There must be other people at Perilous who can trace their families right back to the original storm prophets too."

"So?" Dougal looked puzzled.

"So why aren't they all jumping about and saving people from stuff as well?"

Just to add to his worries, Angus discovered a day or so later that a note had been slipped under his bedroom door. It was from Rogwood. Unfortunately this came at the end of a very long afternoon in the experimental division. Angus, Dougal, and Indigo had been cleaning out a pile of blocked storm bellows and had just spent several hours up to their elbows in stinking, slimy grease. He sat on his bed, pulled off his socks—which now smelled exactly like the blocked storm bellows—and quickly read the note.

> Dear Angus,
> I realize you must be busy with your trainee duties, now that the excitements of the fog field trip are over, but I require a brief meeting with you in my office, five o'clock tomorrow afternoon.
> Please wait in the Octagon, where I will come to collect you. Do not enter the Lightnarium on your own.
> Yours sincerely,
> A. Rogwood

Angus folded the note with a frown and shoved it under the spare storm globe at the bottom of his sock drawer. He'd been expecting this. News of the fognado had spread through the stone tunnels and passageways of Perilous like an outbreak of crumble fungus. Gudgeon and Miss

DeWinkle had also witnessed the incident. He was certain, therefore, that Rogwood would have heard every exciting detail. But would Rogwood have guessed at the appearance of yet another fire dragon? Was he now going to tell Angus more about the storm prophets?

Angus didn't have to wait long to find out. At ten past five the following day, he was escorted once again through the Lightnarium by the bearded lightning catcher. It was the first time he'd set foot inside the cavernous room since the incident with the ball lightning, and he was very relieved to find that this time there were no dark rumbles of thunder or violent flashes of lightning overhead. As they entered Rogwood's office, however, he discovered something much more unsettling. Principal Dark-Angel, Valentine Vellum, and Felix Gudgeon were all waiting for him with extremely serious expressions on their faces. He gulped nervously as Rogwood closed the door behind him.

"Ah, Angus, how nice to see you again." Principal Dark-Angel smiled rather thinly. "Please take a seat and tell me how you are finding your stay at Perilous?"

"Er," said Angus, feeling confused. "It's very interesting, thank you."

"Good, good, I am pleased to hear it. I trust Catcher Sparks and Miss DeWinkle are keeping you busy?"

Angus didn't answer. Instead he chanced a swift glance over his shoulder at Valentine Vellum, and instantly wished he hadn't. The lightning catcher was scowling at him, a muscle twitching on his low, gorilla-like forehead.

"Angus, I have asked you here this afternoon to discuss the strange visions you have been experiencing lately," said Principal Dark-Angel, catching him off guard. "Rogwood has explained to me about the incident in the Lightnarium with the ball lightning, and considering your recent actions on the fog field trip, he believes you must have had another . . . episode out on the Imbur marshes."

Angus swallowed hard. It had been bad enough talking about imaginary dragons in front of Rogwood, but with Catcher Vellum in the room? If Percival or Pixie ever found out about this, they'd have him laughed out of the Exploratorium.

"As you already know," the principal continued, "it is Rogwood's opinion that you may possess the abilities of a storm prophet—"

"Forgive me for interrupting, Principal," Valentine

Vellum spat, as if unable to contain himself, "but I fail to see how an eleven-year-old boy could possess any such abilities. Everyone knows it takes a strong mind to visualize the fire dragon, and if you ask my opinion, this boy—"

"But I don't recall anyone did ask for your opinion, Valentine," barked Gudgeon. "So why don't you keep your big trap shut until somebody asks you to speak?"

"Yes, thank you, Felix," Principal Dark-Angel snapped, scowling at both of them. "But Valentine is quite correct. It is precisely those abilities that we are here today to test."

"T-test?" asked Angus, not liking the way the conversation was going.

"Catcher Vellum has kindly agreed to carry out a number of experiments with you in the Lightnarium, Angus," Principal Dark-Angel explained. "They are designed to test any abilities you may possess as a storm prophet, and to help us decide what is to be done about them."

"But . . . why does anything have to be done about them?" asked Angus, shifting nervously in his seat. "What sorts of tests, anyway?"

"They will involve the use of a low voltage lightning bolt, but it's nothing to be alarmed about, I can assure you," said Principal Dark-Angel quickly. "Catcher Vellum will be extremely careful, and we will have Doctor Fleagal standing by, of course."

Angus glanced swiftly over his other shoulder; he hadn't even noticed the doctor standing there in the shadows. For the first time, he also saw a table in the far corner of the room, where a number of long-handled instruments (each with a sharp-looking probe attached to the end of it) had been laid out carefully and polished to a high shine. Next to the instruments sat a pile of clean bandages and a bottle of disinfectant. Angus gulped, feeling quite convinced that he'd be much safer smashing a large storm globe over his own head than he would be in the hands of Valentine Vellum.

"No!" he said, turning back to face the lightning catchers. "I don't think I want to do any tests, thank you."

The mole on Principal Dark-Angel's cheek twitched. She looked at him for a long moment.

"Perhaps I have not explained myself clearly. Storm prophets are gifted with a rare ability, but if that ability is allowed to go unchecked, it may . . . develop in the wrong direction."

"The wrong direction?" Angus asked, puzzled.

"Angus, I merely wish to help you," she said. "There is much a storm prophet must understand, much you simply cannot learn for yourself."

"I'm not letting anyone strike me with lightning . . . er, Principal," said Angus, folding his arms across his chest. From the corner of his eye, he was sure he could see Gudgeon grinning.

"I'm afraid I did warn you this would be a waste of time, Principal. The boy is obviously afraid," said Valentine Vellum, a sneer crossing his lips. "These tests call for absolute precision and cannot be performed on a subject who is squirming about in his seat."

"And you've only decided Angus here needs testing at all since he saved your great dollop of a son from blundering straight into a raging fognado," growled Gudgeon. "You should be grateful to the boy, Vellum, not plotting to injure him."

"I've never heard anything so ridiculous," Vellum spluttered.

"Ridiculous, is it? You've already tried to kill the boy once with that ball lightning of yours!"

"If you are suggesting that I can control the path of a lightning bolt and set it loose on trainees who I do not like—"

"I'm suggesting that you and that lightning of yours are a bad combination."

"That is enough!" Principal Dark-Angel shouted above them both. "You will conduct your petty personal arguments in your own time and not waste any more of mine. Aramanthus, what do you have to say about all of this?"

Angus had almost forgotten that Rogwood was even in the room. He had remained silent throughout the conversation so far, but all eyes turned to him now as he stroked his long, toffee-colored beard thoughtfully.

"I say it is simple. These experiments cannot be performed without Angus's permission, and since he has just refused to give it, I see no point in continuing this meeting any further."

Gudgeon grunted in agreement. "And that's the most sensible thing any of you lot's said all afternoon."

"I believe there are other ways of exploring the talents of a storm prophet," Rogwood added calmly. "Experiments with lightning, even those of the low voltage kind, are far too risky to conduct on an eleven-year-old boy, especially when we do not have the permission of his parents. As I have said before, I think it would be far wiser to await the return of Doctor Obsidian and consult him on a matter in which he alone has considerable expertise."

Valentine Vellum frowned at Rogwood. Principal Dark-Angel, however, appeared to be considering his words carefully.

"Very well, Aramanthus, we will allow Doctor Obsidian to determine our next step, once he returns to the Exploratorium. If you will kindly escort Angus back across the Lightnarium? We do not want him to miss his dinner." She stood up and peered down at Angus, a strangely disappointed expression on her ghostly white face.

"Valentine Vellum wanted to do *what* to you?" Dougal gasped as Angus related the whole incident to him later that same evening. He'd found Dougal sitting in the Pigsty after dinner, absorbed in his favorite book by Archibald Humble-Pea and attempting to decipher yet another of its secret codes. The book lay abandoned on the floor now, however, as Dougal listened intently to what Angus had to say.

"Vellum had a whole table of instruments already laid out," Angus explained, shuddering at the thought of it. "It sounded like he was planning to strike me with some lightning just to see what would happen."

"You're kidding." Dougal's eyes were now as round as saucers. "I can tell you what would have happened. You'd be half dead by now! I reckon it's like Gudgeon says. Vellum's an ungrateful jerk, even though you've just saved Percival from being flattened by a fognado, and he's managed to fool Dark-Angel with some ridiculous story about testing your brain."

"He might have gotten his own way, too, if it hadn't been for Gudgeon and Rogwood. Principal Dark-Angel seemed pretty keen on the idea."

Dougal let out a low whistle. "Still, it sounds like you should be safe enough now, until this Doctor Obsidian guy comes back to the Exploratorium. But all the same . . . I'd definitely sleep with your door locked from now on if I was you. You don't want to wake up in the middle of the night and find Valentine Vellum trying to zap your brains with some lightning tarantulatis."

"Yeah, I think I will." Angus nodded. But he also couldn't help wondering what the tests would have shown. Would they have revealed that he definitely was some weird kind of weather prophet? Or would they have proven, beyond any doubt, that he was nothing but an ordinary lightning cub after all? And what exactly had Principal Dark-Angel meant about his abilities developing in the wrong direction?

In the excitement of the fog field trip, Angus had almost forgotten about his duties as a trainee, and in the days that followed, he found it extremely difficult to concentrate on his work in the experimental division. Especially as it had now reached an all-time low, and they were cleaning and repairing an entire collection of moldy old armpit warmers (normally used on polar expeditions) that Catcher Sparks had discovered festering at the back of a storage cupboard.

To make matters worse, a letter had finally arrived from Uncle Max—ripped to shreds and hanging in tatters, with a sticker from the Imbur Island post office informing him that it had been "slightly damaged during transit." Angus, however, decided that "ravaged by a pack of hungry wolves" would have been a far more accurate description. He'd done his best to stick the ripped pieces back together again, but it was still impossible to read. And any hopes he'd had that Uncle Max might tell him more about his kidnapped parents had been dashed.

Instead, he now found his thoughts returning, almost hourly, to the holographic history, which was showing definite signs of drying out. Angus had high hopes that they would soon be able to listen to Philomena Whip-Stitcher's riveting tale in full—which, if they were lucky, might lead them straight to the missing map, and then to the lightning vaults themselves. Dougal, however, seemed less certain.

"I wouldn't get your hopes up too high if I were you," he warned one evening as they were sitting in the Pigsty. They had just spent a particularly revolting day in the company of the armpit warmers and were now attempting to tackle a series of homework questions on deep sea fog, assigned by Miss DeWinkle. The holographic history was on the table in front of them, its damp pages steaming

gently in the heat from the fire. "I mean, that book took quite a battering from those hailstones, didn't it? So there's always a chance it might never dry out again."

"Yeah, but it's already managed to say a few new words today," Angus said, watching as Oswald/Philomena squeezed a trickle of water out of his blond wig and hung it up to dry. "And okay, so we can't actually understand what any of those words are yet, but I bet it's only a matter of time."

In the meantime, Miss DeWinkle had finally moved on to the subject of invisible fog. They spent hours in the weather bubble poring over the McFangus guide, trying in vain to understand the mysterious properties of the elusive substance and how to tell if it was creeping up on you in the Imbur marshes.

It was while they were being lectured one afternoon on the great invisible fog of 1912—which had descended upon the unfortunate town of Little Frog's Bottom, concealing its whereabouts for a full three days before anyone could find it again—that Perilous was drenched by a sudden and unexpected shower of newts. The skies outside turned a damp and wriggling black, and the tiny creatures landed with a disturbing *thump* against the glass and steel of the bubble above their heads.

"Looks like your uncle's at it again, doesn't it?" Dougal mumbled quietly, so nobody but Indigo and Angus would hear him.

Relations between Dougal and Indigo had definitely improved since the first field trip, but Indigo was still reluctant to discuss her uncle and looked deeply uncomfortable whenever the subject came up.

"Shush, will you?" she hissed. "You know I don't want anyone else finding out about my family. I promised my mum I wouldn't tell . . . and if the Vellums overhear us talking . . ."

She glanced over her shoulder. Luckily, Pixie and Percival were both staring blankly into space at that moment, drooling. But Indigo continued to look troubled for some time after that.

At the end of their lesson, when it had finally stopped raining amphibians and they were stuffing their fog guides back into their bags, they saw Catcher Sparks enter the room and draw Miss DeWinkle to one side for a private chat. Angus, Dougal, and Indigo packed their things away as slowly as possible, trying to overhear.

"I've just met Aramanthus outside Principal Dark-Angel's office, and his room has been completely ruined by the newts," said Catcher Sparks, looking flustered.

"Oh, goodness, poor Aramanthus!" Miss DeWinkle shook her head. "Is there anything we can do to help?"

"I doubt it. He went outside when the newts started falling, to collect some samples for Principal Dark-Angel, and when he got back to his office, the horrible creatures had come in through the window and turned everything completely upside down. His entire collection of antique safety goggles has been smashed to pieces, including the pair worn by Hortence Heliotrope."

"But you can't mean—not *the* Hortence Heliotrope," Miss DeWinkle gasped. "The famous lightning catcher who first discovered the existence of double-ended lightning bolts?"

"The very same." Catcher Sparks nodded solemnly. "But that's not the worst of it. A whole year's worth of notes on forked lightning have been ripped up and thrown around the room like confetti. . . ."

At these words, Indigo suddenly gasped. She covered

her mouth with her hand, but it was too late. Catcher Sparks had heard her. The lightning catcher swiftly turned around, her eyes narrowing with suspicion.

"And what, may I ask, are you three still doing here?" she asked, her hands resting on her hips. "This lesson ended almost five minutes ago."

"Er, we're not doing anything," said Angus, pushing Indigo and Dougal hastily toward the door. "We were just leaving, Catcher Sparks."

"Well, hurry up and leave a bit faster," she said, watching them with beady eyes as they darted past. "And make sure you close the door on your way out, Doomsbury."

"What did you have to go and gasp like that for?" asked Dougal as soon as they'd left the weather bubble behind. "We might have heard something interesting if she hadn't noticed us standing there."

"Oh, but we did hear something interesting!" said Indigo, her face shining with excitement. "And I think I've just realized something really important—but I can't tell you out here in the middle of the hallway. Come with me." She dragged them down a dark and deserted-looking tunnel to their left.

The tunnel came to a dead end, and they concealed themselves in the shadows of a broom closet.

"Come on then, spit it out," said Dougal grumpily, removing his right foot from an empty bucket. "What's so important that you could only tell us in the presence of mops?"

Indigo ignored him and beamed at them both. "I think I finally understand why Dankhart's been bombarding us with newts and frogs and storm globes," she announced as loudly as she dared. "It was something Catcher Sparks said just now about Rogwood's office."

"Go on," Angus urged. He shot a warning look at Dougal to keep quiet and let her speak.

"Well, if Dankhart's trying to get his hands on the map of the lightning vaults . . . wouldn't it make sense for him to come looking for it himself?"

Dougal snorted. "I think we might have noticed if Scabious Dankhart was wandering around Perilous, rummaging through people's drawers, searching for a missing map."

"Not if we were busy fighting off a swarm of snorkel beetles or storm globes, we wouldn't," said Indigo. "None of us would have noticed if a whole herd of elephants had gone stampeding through the Exploratorium juggling pineapples while that was going on."

Angus stared at her, understanding dawning on him like a thousand-watt lightbulb being flicked on inside his head.

"Indigo, that's brilliant . . . you're brilliant!" he gasped. "I don't know why we didn't think of it sooner. That's exactly what Dankhart's been doing."

Indigo smiled at Angus, looking extremely pleased with herself.

"All this time he's been sending distractions," Angus continued, "and while everyone's been busy trying to fend off frogs or catch fog mites, he's been turning Perilous upside down looking for the missing map. Remember the snorkel beetles?"

"Of course I remember the stupid beetles," said Dougal, scowling.

"While we were all shut up in the sanatorium and Catcher Sparks and everyone else was running around with nets and frying pans, Principal Dark-Angel's office was trashed."

"And I'd like to meet the snorkel beetle that could destroy a whole filing cabinet by itself," Indigo added.

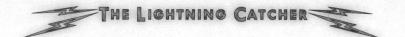

"There must have been somebody up in her office, looking through her things."

"And on the day of the frogs, when the records office
got wrecked," said Angus, turning to Dougal, "Mr. Fristle
told us that some of them must have gotten in through the
window and made a mess of things, but frogs couldn't
have caused that much damage on their own, could they?
Somebody else must have broken in and searched his office.
And now the same thing's just happened to Rogwood. . . .
You don't really think Dankhart is creeping around Perilous
looking through people's drawers, though, do you?"

He swallowed, wondering if the villain could be hiding
behind the mops and brooms at that very moment, ready
to pounce.

"How would we know even if he was?" asked Dougal
darkly. "Nobody knows what he looks like for sure, do
they? He doesn't exactly go around opening carnivals and
judging jam-making competitions and getting his photo
in the local newspapers."

"But your dad must have a book about the Dankharts
somewhere, with pictures and descriptions in it and everything?" said Angus.

Dougal shook his head. "Nobody's been stupid enough to write one. Everyone knows about his black diamond eye, of course, but he could have hidden it behind an eye patch or anything. If you really wanted to know what he looks like, you'd have to ask someone who'd actually met him. Or get a good look at one of his relatives and see if they've got any distinctive features that run in the Dankhart family, you know, like hooked noses or funny goggly eyes . . ." He tried to get a swift look at Indigo's eyes without her noticing.

Unfortunately, even in the gloom of the broom closet, it was perfectly obvious what he was doing. Indigo folded her arms ominously and glared at him.

"What are you staring at me for?" she snapped.

"There's no need to get your boots in a twist. I was just wondering, you know, if there was any family resemblance."

Indigo frowned. "I look like the Midnights, *not* the Dankharts."

"Yeah, but . . . you must know what your own uncle looks like?" Dougal insisted.

Indigo's nostrils flared, and Angus was suddenly

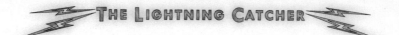

reminded of Catcher Sparks when she was about to force them, headfirst, into the storm vacuum.

"Er, just drop it, will you?" he advised Dougal swiftly, feeling that his friend might have pushed things too far already.

"But she can't seriously expect us to believe that her own uncle's never even popped round for a cup of tea in all these years," said Dougal, frowning. "You know, to catch up on all the family gossip, reminisce about old times at the castle. . . ."

The closet around them seemed to grow darker as Indigo took a deep, shuddering breath, fixing Dougal with an angry glare. "I'm only going to say this one more time. No mem- ber of the Dankhart family has EVER been invited into our home. And before you ask, Uncle Scabious has NEVER been a guest at any of my birthday parties, or dropped round with a sack full of presents at Christmas, okay?"

"Okay, okay, sorry I asked!" said an alarmed-looking Dougal, who finally had the sense to drop the subject.

14

THE SECRET MAP

"Should we tell Principal Dark-Angel what we've found out?"

"I bet you anything she already knows exactly what Dankhart's up to."

"Yeah, not to mention the fact that she'd probably make us search every inch of the experimental division for specks of storm fluff if we go charging up to her office. Just for knowing stuff we shouldn't."

"But what about the missing map? Do you reckon the lightning catchers are even looking for it?"

"'Course they are. That was the first thing Principal Dark-Angel asked Angus about when he arrived at

the Exploratorium, wasn't it?"

"That's the real reason she brought me here in the first place, you mean."

"Well, if they have found a map of the lightning vaults since then, they're keeping very quiet about it."

"If they've found so much as a missing mousetrap, I'll eat Percival Vellum's armpit warmers! Have you seen the look on old Dark-Angel's face these days? That's not the face of a happy principal."

And so their conversations continued over the next few days, going round and round in endless circles, until all three of them became irritable and snappish and Angus's head throbbed with sheer frustration. He also found himself staring out the windows, hundreds of times a day, half expecting to see another shower of newts or frogs falling from the skies. And he spent hours wondering what section of the Exploratorium Dankhart was planning to search next. Would he break into the sanatorium perhaps, or ransack the experimental division, or even rummage through the entire contents of every lightning cub's bedroom in his desperation to find the missing map? What if he actually found it? All in all, Angus decided that he'd never had so much to worry about in his life.

Philomena Whip-Stitcher's voice was growing clearer by the day, but it was still impossible to work out what she was trying to tell them about the fabled lightning vaults. And Angus was extremely glad that no one had realized yet that the holographic history was missing from the library. In the meantime, their only other option was to search for the missing map themselves—a task that was likely to bring them further problems, as Indigo pointed out one lunchtime, over cheese-and-pickle sandwiches.

"I mean, where would we even start if we did decide to go looking for the map ourselves?" she said, speaking directly across the table to Angus and only glancing at Dougal occasionally.

Dougal had been making an extra effort to be nice to Indigo, following their heated argument in the broom closet. Indigo, on the other hand, was still treating Dougal with caution, as if he might start spouting off about her uncle again at any minute. And a tense atmosphere remained.

"There are hundreds of hiding places all over Perilous," Indigo continued, "not to mention all the stone tunnels

and passageways, and it would be impossible to search every one of them. It could take us years to find the missing map."

Angus continued to keep a very vigilant eye on the weather, but all showers of newts, frogs, beetles, and storm globes had come to an abrupt halt with not so much as a single tadpole falling on the rooftops. And the skies cleared to a pale wintry blue. New posters announcing the next field trip of the season also appeared in the kitchens one morning, and fog fever gripped the Exploratorium once again.

"I am thrilled to tell you all that the forecasting department is predicting a rare occurrence of midnight fog in five days' time," Miss DeWinkle informed them with obvious enthusiasm during their next lesson in the weather bubble. Dark clouds had engulfed the ornate glass-and-steel classroom, making it feel like night had fallen several hours earlier than usual.

"Luckily, we will be able to observe this particular variety from the roof of our own Exploratorium. As I'm sure you have already read in your McFangus guides, midnight fog has only ever been encountered at midnight, hence its name. It is as black as a starless night, and it also happens to be one of the most exhilarating types of fog to work in."

"What's so great about wandering about in the middle of the night in a load of black fog?" Dougal mumbled, sounding less than thrilled at the prospect.

"Working in midnight fog has often been likened to entering an underground cave," said Miss DeWinkle, as if they were in for the treat of their lives, "and is a very similar experience to walking around with your eyes tightly shut. Without the proper light source, you will be unable to see your own hand in front of your face, or indeed the faces of those around you.

"Flashlights are all but useless in a midnight fog," Miss DeWinkle informed them cheerfully. "The only way to navigate your way through it effectively is by using candles, torches, and bonfires. Flames can be extinguished quickly in the thickest patches, so you must be extra vigilant. There'll be no maps or courses to follow this time, but that doesn't mean there won't be dangers. Several years ago, two first-year cubs got a bad case of rapid fog disorientation and had to be rescued from the top of a hurricane mast. So listen carefully to instructions,

and don't go wandering off. Your fog guides will also play a crucial role."

Angus quickly slipped his fog guide under his workbook so Miss DeWinkle couldn't see it. He'd been forced to make emergency repairs to the guide after it had fallen out of his pocket in the tropical fog and been severely trampled. It was now covered in sticky tape. Luckily, his mum's letter had come through the ordeal unscathed and was once again tucked safely inside the chapter on contagious fog.

"To get in some practice before the event, we'll be meeting tomorrow evening, in the cloud gardens."

A loud murmur swept around the room at this surprising news.

"As the occurrence of this fog is so rare," Miss DeWinkle continued, "we will be joined on the roof by a number of lightning catchers and trainees from other years who, for various reasons, have yet to see it."

"How will *any* of us know if we've actually seen it?" hissed Dougal.

At eight o'clock the following evening, Miss DeWinkle marched them down to the cloud gardens. It was so pitch black, Angus spent several moments rummaging through the pockets in his coat for his gloves before he realized the pockets actually belonged to Indigo.

"Sorry!" He grinned at her in the dark, remembering suddenly that she couldn't see him either.

"This is perfect practice for the midnight fog itself," said Miss DeWinkle as they stumbled along behind her through the dense gardens. "You must allow your eyes to adjust to the darkness. Let your other senses and your weather watches guide you."

"The only thing my senses are telling me is that I should have stayed up in the kitchens," Angus mumbled as he forced his way through a tall patch of sticky grass, which sprang back and whacked him in the face.

By the end of the class, the only person without bruised shins or cut lips was Indigo, who appeared to have better night vision than an owl.

In the days that followed, all conversation at the Exploratorium revolved around the looming field trip and the dangers that might be lurking in the midnight fog.

"There could be real fog phantoms, or ghosts, or giant flying yetis," Dougal pointed out as they discussed it

nervously in the kitchens. "I mean, nobody bothered warning us about fognadoes, did they? So what's to stop them from throwing in another surprise or two this time, just to liven things up a bit?"

Angus, Dougal, and Indigo therefore spent most of their free time in what was left of the library, trying to find anything useful about the tricky fog. It was just as Angus was creeping out of the mist, murk, and drizzle section late one evening (trying to avoid Mr. Knurling), that he bumped into Doctor Fleagal.

"Your mum and dad would both be very proud of the way you dealt with that fognado, young Angus, yes, very proud indeed," the doctor said, lowering his voice and giving Angus a knowing wink. "I'm sure they will be extremely interested to hear all about it upon their return to Perilous."

"Er, thanks a lot, sir," said Angus, somewhat taken aback. No other lightning catcher had ever mentioned his parents directly to him before, except Principal Dark-Angel and Rogwood. In fact, he had a strong suspicion that none of the others actually knew his real identity.

"I remember watching Alabone and Evangeline

compiling their famous fog guide, a number of years ago now, scribbling away in this very library late into the night, studying endless samples, consulting complicated droplet charts," Doctor Fleagal added, smiling kindly. "It was just after they'd returned from a rather adventurous journey to the celebrated fog tunnels of Finland."

"My mum and dad visited the actual fog tunnels?" Angus asked, astounded, trying to imagine his parents battling their way through the convoluted tunnels.

"Indeed. Evangeline had quite a close call, as I remember. She accidentally smashed her weather watch, got separated from your father, and had to find her way out again using nothing but a long piece of string and some earthworm trails."

Angus desperately wanted to hear more about this amazing story, but at that moment he spotted Mr. Knurling approaching them with a most unfriendly look on his face, and he quickly decided against asking Doctor Fleagal any questions. Even now, weeks after the incident with the hailstones, Angus wasn't entirely convinced that the librarian had recovered properly from his concussion—for which he seemed to blame Angus and Indigo.

Angus said good-bye to Doctor Fleagal and fled in the opposite direction.

When the day of the second field trip arrived, no one was looking forward to the experience, especially since Miss DeWinkle had just announced that they would be given an exam on it afterward. Angus, Dougal, and Indigo spent a tedious day up in the experimental division mopping up after a temperamental raindropometer, which kept leaking all over the floor.

"Well, looking on the bright side, at least we're not being sent out into the Imbur marshes again," said Indigo.

"Yeah, and if we get attacked by a school of piranha mist fish this time, we can just run back inside and barricade the doors," said Angus.

"It's not the mist fish that I'm worried about," Dougal mumbled darkly. "Theodore Twill's been telling everyone that midnight fog is famous for harboring giant bats."

Angus gulped, hoping that they wouldn't run into any— especially as it might trigger yet another appearance of the fire dragon.

Finally, at eleven thirty that evening, Angus, Indigo,

and Dougal made their way up to the Octagon, yawning sleepily. Despite their concerns about the midnight fog, it had been an enormous effort just to stay awake, hours past their usual bedtime. They were swept along the corridors on a tide of tired-looking lightning cubs, all dressed for a long session of standing around in the cold.

Even at this time of night, the roof was a hive of activity, and they were led carefully to the far end by an excited Miss DeWinkle. Candles and flaming torches had been lit so that they could see where they were going. A large bonfire was firing orange sparks twenty feet into the air and casting deep, flickering shadows across the roof. Clifford Fugg, who had made a full recovery after breaking his wrist on the first field trip, was standing with a small group of friends. A number of lightning catchers had also gathered. Principal Dark-Angel, Gudgeon, Rogwood, and Catcher Sparks were chatting happily beside the fire, enjoying freshly baked cookies. The kitchens had sent up several trays of late-night snacks for everyone.

"This is more like it." Dougal grinned, helping himself to three sausage rolls and a mug of hot chocolate.

Not quite so exciting, however, was the emergency

first-aid station that Doctor Fleagal had set up in the far corner. It was stocked with bandages and splints, and Angus looked away quickly, hoping that none of them would need to visit it.

A moment later, Miss DeWinkle called for attention, and a hush fell.

"Welcome to the second fog field trip of the season," she said, her eyes glittering. She was dressed for the occasion in a long silvery coat and knitted yellow hat. "Tonight you will experience the wonders of the famous midnight fog. Do not be alarmed when the fog first engulfs you; remember your training from the cloud gardens, and try not to bump into one another."

Angus peered at the dark skies above, wondering how they were supposed to know when the fog had actually arrived.

"According to the forecasting department, the midnight fog will be approaching from the east in approximately fifteen minutes' time. So, if everyone will check that their weather watches are working correctly . . ."

Angus stared at his watch, which already showed the first dense swirls of fog threatening to block out the twinkling stars above.

"And your McFangus guides should now be open at the beginning of chapter twelve."

Angus pulled his fog guide out of his pocket, trying to hide the worst of the sticky tape from Miss DeWinkle.

"According to the McFangus guide, one of the most famous characteristics of midnight fog is—"

Miss DeWinkle stopped abruptly, her gaze traveling upward, and a second later, Angus understood why. Something small, round, and fiery shot across the sky. It fizzled out above their heads with a noise like an exploding firework.

He watched as three more fiery balls followed, and before any of them knew what was happening, the whole sky was alight with bright sparks and streaks of golden light. It was a dazzling display, and the entire roof turned as one to admire it.

"Nobody said anything about a fireworks display, did they?" asked Indigo.

"Those aren't fireworks," said Angus as another batch of bright lights sped across the sky. "They look more like shooting stars to me."

"Shooting stars?" Dougal frowned, his glasses glinting

in the golden bursts of light. "But they can't be. Shooting stars usually burn up when they enter the earth's atmosphere, before they get anywhere near the ground."

Shooting stars or not, however, it seemed they were determined to get as close to the ground as possible. And a moment later, fiery chunks of rock began to rain down on Perilous in large numbers, like burning missiles. They scorched the night air with hot trails of flame, landing with great sizzles in buckets of rainwater, causing clouds of billowing steam to swamp the roof. The admiring *ooohhs* and *aaahhs* from the watching crowd suddenly faltered.

"This has something to do with Dankhart!" said Angus. And he knew that, just like the storm globes, just like the showers of newts, frogs, and snorkel beetles, the shooting stars were no accident. They had been sent straight from Castle Dankhart to cause as much chaos and confusion as possible.

"Dankhart must be planning something," said Angus, pulling Dougal and Indigo to the side as trainees and lightning catchers began to scatter in every direction, running for cover. "He must have found the map! Or guessed where the vaults are!"

"What?" Dougal dropped the remains of a sausage roll he'd been nibbling, in alarm. "How in the name of Perilous did you work that one out?"

"It's the shooting stars, or whatever they really are," said Indigo, understanding immediately. "If Dankhart has decided to go looking for the vaults, then he'd need to arrange a huge distraction, something that would keep everyone really busy putting out fires and give him enough time to open the vaults without being disturbed. And snorkel beetles and frogs just wouldn't be enough."

At that moment, Gudgeon bolted past them; one of his boots had clearly been hit by a burning rock and was leaving a trail of burning rubber behind him. "Well, don't just stand there gawping like idiots, you three," he yelled. "Run for it!"

They didn't need to be told twice. Angus shoved his fog guide hastily into his pocket and dashed quickly toward the trapdoor, dodging to avoid the burning missiles that continued to bombard the roof. He sprinted past Catcher Sparks, who was leaping into a large bucket of rainwater to stop the hem of her coat from going up in flames. He almost collided with Principal Dark-Angel, who was

directing several startled trainees through an obstacle course of smoldering debris.

"Hey!" yelled Dougal from behind, as Angus swerved to avoid the first-aid station, which had quickly gone up in brightly colored flames. "You've dropped your fog guide again, and your letter's fallen out of its envelope. Here—"

Angus spun round to take it from him, only to find that Dougal had stopped in his tracks, his brows knitted together.

"Come on!" Indigo yelled, running back to join them. "We can't stand around here reading letters. We've got to get inside quickly!" She grabbed Dougal by the arm and attempted to drag him toward the safety of the Exploratorium.

Dougal ignored her and remained rooted to the spot. "Why didn't you mention these spelling mistakes in your mum's letter before?" he asked, suddenly sounding agitated.

"Why didn't I . . . what?"

"Didn't you ever consider that your mum might have misspelled all these words on purpose?" said Dougal, gripping the letter tightly.

"Why would she bother doing that?" Angus glanced up at the sky, where several more burning missiles were heading in their direction with alarming speed. "Look, I think Indigo's right. We'd better talk about this inside."

But before they could get anywhere near the safety of the building, shards of burning rock exploded over their heads, showering the roof in flames. They dove for cover behind the weather balloon.

"It all makes perfect sense, when you think about it," Dougal continued, completely ignoring the chaos all around them. "They couldn't just send it to you, or anyone could have seen what it was. . . . they had to hide it, and if I'm right . . ."

Angus and Indigo exchanged puzzled glances. "R-Right about what, exactly?" Indigo asked.

"It's all about this letter." Dougal grinned as if he'd just been given an unexpected birthday present. "This brilliant, amazing, ingenious letter! I would have realized what it really was sooner"—he turned to Angus—"only when you read the letter to me that time, you corrected all your mother's spelling mistakes as you were going along.

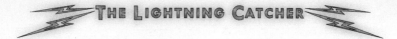

You only read out what you thought she meant to say—not what she'd actually written."

Angus stared at his friend, wondering if he'd been hit on the head by a burning missile and was now hallucinating.

"But . . . that letter's just a load of boring stuff about my relatives," he said.

"Trust me, there's a lot more to it than that." Dougal grinned. "I've read enough Archibald Humble-Pea to recognize a secret coded message when I see one."

"Archibald who?" asked Indigo, confused.

"Humble-Pea. He wrote a book on secret codes and how to crack them. Dougal's dad sent it to him ages ago, and he's been obsessed with it ever since."

"Yeah, and it's a good thing I have been, too." Dougal said. "I'm telling you, this letter is important. Look, I'll show you, it starts off with some waffling old gibberish about your uncle Max, but then we get to this: 'Sorry we've both been so busy lately, but you've been the Koolest about it, as I was telling Taunt Pamela the other day on the phone, which reminds me, Angus, I forgot to mention that she will be visiting us again during the next school holidays, I will have to try Very hard to remember this time that she's allergic to your uncle's snail-and-seaweed pie, Ands that Uncl Lars won't drink anything but that revolting Trim Skim milk.'"

"So? I still don't get it," Angus said, ducking as yet another missile exploded overhead. "How can anything about my uncle Lars be a secret code?"

"It's got nothing to do with either of your uncles, actually," declared Dougal. "It's all about capital letters. According to Archibald Humble-Pea, the presence of a capital letter in the middle of a sentence often denotes the start of a secret message. So in this case, the message starts with the word Koolest, see?" he said, pointing to the word. "Then each word that follows Koolest with a capital letter is also a part of the same message. So that's Koolest, Taunt, Pamela, Angus, Very, Ands, Uncle, Lars, Trim, Skim." Dougal took a pencil out of his pocket and started writing the words down at the bottom of the letter.

"Next we've got to take the last three letters off each word that begins with a capital letter, except for Angus, 'cause that's your name," he explained, half talking to himself as he did just that, "so then we're left with Kool, Ta, Pam, Angus . . . followed by V-A-U-L-T-S."

"Vaults!" Angus gasped, staring at the letters on the page. "The lightning vaults!"

His head was suddenly spinning. This was what Principal Dark-Angel and Scabious Dankhart had both been trying so desperately to find. And he'd had it all along!

"So what's next?" he asked urgently. "How do we finish deciphering the code?"

"According to Humble-Pea, all we've got to do then is reverse the remaining words," said Dougal, his pencil shaking with excitement. "So Kool, Ta, Pam, Angus, V-A-U-L-T-S becomes . . . Look At Map Angus—VAULTS!"

They all stared at the piece of paper, utterly flabbergasted.

"Your mum's not such a terrible speller after all," said Dougal, beaming. "She meant to write every single word exactly as it appears. This letter is a secret message—and it's trying to tell us how to find the lightning vaults."

And despite the fact that they were stranded in the middle of a shower of deadly burning missiles, with nothing to protect them but a weather balloon, Angus couldn't help grinning.

"Dougal—you're amazing!" said Indigo, staring at him

properly for the first time in two weeks. "I never would have worked that out."

"Oh, well, it was just a bit of bedtime reading, really," Dougal said, looking embarrassed and highly flattered all at the same time. "Your mum and dad must have posted this letter to you just before they were kidnapped," he added, turning toward Angus.

"And I've been stuffing it in bags, drawers, and fog guides ever since."

"So all we've got to do now is work out what 'Look At Map' actually means," said Indigo, "and it could lead us straight to the lightning vaults."

Angus stared at the collection of words, commas, and sentences on the page again and felt a sudden sinking in his stomach. The letter looked nothing like a map. There was nothing scribbled on the back, either—no secret symbols, codes, or clues, no set of directions. He had absolutely no idea how on earth it was going to lead them to anything.

"Don't panic." Dougal rolled up his sleeves, looking more determined than ever. "There's loads of ways they could have concealed a secret map in that letter. They could have used invisible ink, for a start; then there's waterproof ink, of course, or stuff that can only be seen by moonlight. . . . If it's in there, I'll find it."

At that moment, there was a loud *CRACK* above their heads. Angus looked up just in time to see a huge chunk of burning rock, five times bigger than all the rest, explode in the night sky, sending hot showers of fire tumbling toward the ground.

"We've got to get inside—now!" Indigo yelled, as the weather balloon they were sheltering behind was struck by a flying missile and began to burn.

They ran toward the Exploratorium, hands over their heads, shoes smoking underfoot. Indigo flung herself toward the open trapdoor that led straight back down to the Octagon and tumbled inside; Dougal followed, falling through the door with a painful-looking belly flop. Angus threw himself toward the safety of the cool stairs as another burning rock exploded overhead, this one much closer than any of the others. He stumbled on the uneven surface, the letter fluttering from his fingers.

"The letter, I've dropped the letter!" he shouted, scrambling around on his hands and knees. He reached out to grab the precious sheet of paper as it floated gracefully toward the ground—but it was too late. The letter had been hit. Stray sparks seared through the paper, and within seconds, hungry yellow flames had consumed it.

"NO!"

Angus watched, horrified, as the letter burned to a crisp, leaving nothing behind but a pile of hot ashes. The only hope he'd had of finding the lightning vaults had just gone up in smoke.

15

THE LIGHTNING VAULTS

"What are we supposed to do now?" Angus said forlornly, kneeling beside the ashes.

"Oh, Angus, I'm so sorry!" Indigo groaned, sinking to her knees next to him. Both she and Dougal had raced back out onto the roof as soon as they'd seen him fall. "We'll just have to find Principal Dark-Angel, tell her everything we know, and hope that she believes us."

Dougal bent down and began raking through the ashes, looking for anything that remained of the letter. There was nothing left except one curled-up corner. He grasped it gently between his fingers and pulled, rescuing a surprisingly large but badly damaged square of paper from beneath the smoldering pile. For some strange reason, he also appeared to be smiling.

"You'd better take a look at this before you go running off to Dark-Angel," he said, handing the wafer-thin square over to Angus.

Singed to a deep tea-leaf brown, it felt crisp and fragile between his fingers. But the heat from the flames had produced a startling effect.

"I don't believe it," Angus gasped. Scorched deep into the paper like a burn was a tiny, perfectly formed map of Perilous, which clearly showed the exact location of—and the hidden entrance to—the lightning vaults.

"But . . . I don't understand. I—I watched the letter burn. There was nothing left."

"Flambeaux!" Dougal said, grinning.

Indigo frowned. "Excuse me?"

"That map's been drawn on flambeaux paper. I remember my dad talking about this stuff ages ago; it's tissue thin and incredibly strong. The lightning catchers sometimes use it in the desert and other hot places where their scientific notes could catch fire and go up in smoke. You can throw it into a fire and it won't even burn. Which

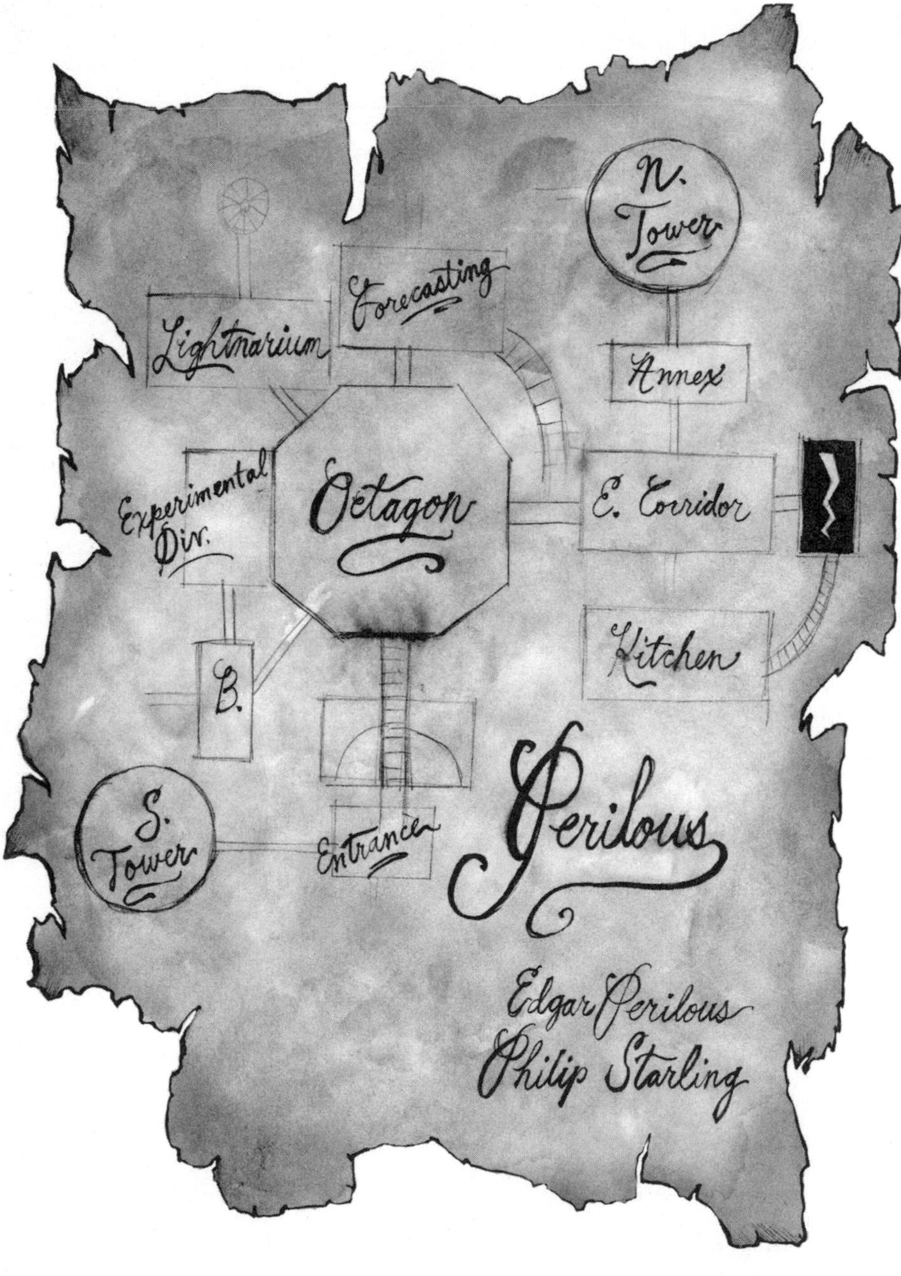

Lightmarium
Forecasting
N. Tower
Annex
Experimental Div.
Octagon
E. Corridor
Kitchen
B.
S. Tower
Entrance
Perilous
Edgar Perilous
Philip Starling

also makes it perfect for hiding important stuff you don't want anyone else to read, of course," he explained eagerly. "Your mum and dad must have sandwiched this piece of flambeaux between two thick sheets of ordinary paper— which obviously went up in flames the instant they got hit, leaving us with the secret map!"

Angus suddenly remembered his own uncle Max and the burning letter that Gudgeon had delivered to the Windmill, on the very night that his world had changed forever.

"Let's get inside before anything else happens to it; we can't look at it properly out here," he said, ducking as more burning chunks of rock soared through the night sky.

Once they were inside, however, they discovered that the Octagon was jam-packed with lightning cubs, all showing off their singed coats and melted boots and discussing the mystery of the burning missiles in loud, animated voices. Just to add to the confusion, at least fifty lightning catchers, armed with buckets of sand and water, were also trying to push their way through the crowds in the opposite direction. For ten minutes, it was almost impossible to move in any direction.

Eventually, Indigo managed to force her way down the stairs and through a door that led to a small private library full of ancient-looking maps. She dragged Angus and Dougal inside with her. Warm yellow light fissures crackled overhead as Angus laid the scorched paper carefully on a desk, gently smoothing down the curled-up corners.

It was really more of a rough sketch than a map. Scribbled down in jet-black ink, with spidery lines and writings, it showed the approximate location of the Lightnarium, the experimental division, and the forecasting department.

"This is really old," Indigo said, inspecting it closely. "It's been signed by Edgar Perilous and Philip Starling. They must have drawn it when the lightning vaults were first built."

"Yeah, and it looks like the entrance is hidden somewhere on the second floor, down the east corridor," said Angus, running his finger over the spot where the vaults had been clearly marked with an odd, fractured-looking lightning bolt. "Hang on a minute, though . . . that corridor doesn't even exist anymore. If you follow the stairs up from the kitchens, you come to a dead end right outside—"

"The weather tunnel!" Indigo finished.

Dougal gulped. "The weather tunnel must have been built over the top of the vaults. No wonder nobody's found them for all these years. Who'd be crazy enough to go searching in there? They're probably buried under half a ton of snow, or half a ton of fog yeti. So what now?" he asked, looking warily at them both. "Do we take this to Principal Dark-Angel, or what?"

Angus thought hard for a moment, then shook his head. He'd seen Principal Dark-Angel frantically try-ing to organize the lightning catchers and desperately putting out fires. Getting her attention would be almost impossible. But there was also another reason he was reluctant to go to her for help, and it had been nagging at the back of his mind since the moment Dougal had discovered the map.

"My parents sent the map to me," he said, thinking it through carefully. "If they'd wanted Principal Dark-Angel to see it, why didn't they just send it straight to her in the first place? My mum and dad wanted me to help them for some reason, and that's exactly what I'm going to do. There's something down in those vaults that Dankhart wants to get his hands on, and I've got to stop him. . . ."

"*We've* got to stop him, you mean," said Indigo, color rising in her cheeks.

"No way." Angus shook his head. "I can't ask you to help me. It's far too dangerous."

"Dangerous or not, we're coming with you," Indigo insisted. "Besides, how else can I ever convince Dougal that I'm not popping up to Castle Dankhart every five minutes for cups of tea with my dear old uncle Scabby."

Dougal flushed a violent red. "Well, I never actually said . . . that obviously just goes to show . . . I mean, of course we're coming with you! But if there *is* something monstrous lurking in those vaults, and if it decides I'm on the dinner menu . . ."

Angus grinned, feeling immensely grateful to them both.

"It looks like the entrance is buried in the blizzard section," he said, turning back to the map and studying it carefully. "If we take a shortcut through the kitchens, we'll only have to poke our heads through the door and we'll probably be able to see it."

They left the room, sneaking past Catcher Mint, who was now ordering all lightning cubs back to their rooms, and then sprinted as fast as their legs would allow through the Exploratorium.

But as soon as they reached the kitchens, it was clear that several shooting stars had come crashing through the ceiling, filling the room with smoking rubble and debris.

"No, you'll just have to go without supper this evening, I'm afraid." A flustered Miss DeWinkle stopped them at the door, refusing to let them go any farther. "We'll all be eating yesterday's leftovers for breakfast as it is."

They turned and retraced their steps, deciding their only choice now was to enter the tunnel from the other end. Angus could vividly recall struggling through the tropical rainstorms, thick fogs, and deep snowdrifts of the treacherous weather tunnel on his very first day at Perilous, and he wasn't looking forward to doing it again. But if it was the only way they could reach the lightning vaults . . .

He skidded to a halt before the circular door set in the middle of the wall, Dougal and Indigo close behind him. "Whatever happens inside this tunnel, we've all got to stick together, agreed?" he said.

Dougal and Indigo nodded solemnly. But it appeared that they would be spared the effort of battling against gale-force winds at the very least, as the first section of the tunnel was surprisingly still and silent, and they ran through it quickly before it could change its mind and send a hurricane chasing after them.

It was only after they had passed through the weather lock and entered the next section of the tunnel that their troubles truly began.

"WOW!" gasped Angus as he tugged the door open and was hit by a sudden blast of intense heat.

The tropical palm trees of the rain forest were gone. In their place was a mini desert, complete with large sand dunes and what looked like an oasis in the distance. A dazzling fake sun was shining overhead, and more worrying still, a nasty sandstorm was gathering strength on the horizon, whirling around in tight, frantic circles.

"Principal Dark-Angel must be planning an expedition to the desert," said Indigo, sounding impressed.

"Either that, or a giant sandcastle-building competition," said Dougal, wiping his clammy forehead with a handkerchief.

"According to my weather watch, those sand dunes have been shipped straight in from the Sahara," Angus informed them. "It says there's a ninety percent chance that we'll start seeing mirages if we cross it, and there's also a severe risk of sunstroke. It's a hundred and four degrees Fahrenheit in there."

Dougal gulped. "So what you're saying is, if we set one foot inside that tunnel we'll be baked alive!"

Indigo, however, was already rolling up her coat sleeves, a determined look on her face. "But if it's the only way we can get to the lightning vaults . . ."

It was like stepping into an overheated oven. The sand scorched the soles of their feet, even through the bottom of their boots, and the air was chokingly dry. The dunes were also extremely difficult to walk across, and their feet sank deeply into the sand, sliding backward with every step they took. After five minutes, they were still battling their way up the steep, shifting slopes of the first dune.

"Inflatable snowshoes!" said Angus, struck by a sudden idea as he stopped to catch his breath. "Remember Catcher Mint told us they stop you from sinking into the snow? Well, I bet they work just as well on sand."

The snowshoes performed brilliantly, inflating automatically and making it much easier to scale the sand dune.

When they finally reached the top, however, they were engulfed by the raging sandstorm, which was now much bigger and more violent. They kept walking, blinded by the storm. Angus covered his face with his hands, but the flying grains of sand whipped at his ears and nose, and he was soon spluttering and stumbling in all directions. Finally, after circling the oasis three or four times, they reached the far side of the tunnel, only to find their exit blocked by a huge sand-colored boulder.

Angus leaned his shoulder against it, pushing with all his might. But the rock was firmly embedded in the sand and refused to budge. He tried again, putting all his weight behind it this time. As he did so, the rock gave a loud warning hiss and turned to glare at him through long, curly eyelashes.

"That's not a rock." Dougal staggered backward in surprise. "That's a camel!"

The camel had been seeking shelter from the storm, hump resting up against the exit. And it was now looking rather grumpy.

"The weather tunnelers must have hauled it in from the Sahara, too," said Dougal, sounding deeply impressed.

Angus frowned. "Yeah, but how are we supposed to get past it?"

"Maybe one of us could . . . could get on it and steer it out of the way," suggested Indigo.

"Yeah, it might just work!" Angus agreed, desperate for any idea. "Dougal's the smallest, so he can do the steering."

Dougal choked, swallowing a mouthful of sand. "I'm not steering that thing anywhere!"

"I'm sure the camel's not exactly thrilled about the idea either, but unless you've got any better suggestions . . ." Angus shrugged.

And before Dougal could start arguing again, Angus was giving him a leg up onto the camel's back. The creature took an instant dislike to Dougal, however, who accidentally kicked it under the chin as he climbed on top of its hump, and it stood up suddenly, shaking him off like an unwanted flea. It then sneezed in a spectacular fashion, showering Dougal in warm, dribbling saliva.

"Urgh!" Dougal groaned, wiping his face with the back of his hand. "I've just swallowed camel spit!"

But the camel had had enough, and it walked away

moodily. Angus pulled the door open and pushed his friends into the small chamber beyond, before it could return.

The next section of the tunnel, which had previously contained the damp, boggy moor, complete with swirling fog and spine-chilling growls, had been packed up completely and was now standing unused and empty.

Thankfully, the only signs that a fog yeti had ever been anywhere near the weather tunnel were a large bed, made from woven twigs and moss and covered with hairy-looking blankets, and a pile of bones that had obviously been gnawed on—recently.

"You don't think those are human bones, do you?" asked Dougal, gulping.

There was no time to investigate, and they crept quietly across the empty space as quickly as they could.

The last section of the tunnel still contained a frozen wasteland filled with deep snowdrifts and icicles; it was also in the grip of a raging blizzard. A fierce wind whipped the flakes into a frenzy, making it difficult to see more than a few feet ahead. After the hot stickiness of the desert, the freezing air chilled them to their bones, and they made very slow progress, slipping and bruising elbows and knees on the hard, icy surface. They quickly reinflated their emergency snowshoes.

Angus plowed on through the deep drifts, hoping that they weren't already too late, that Dankhart hadn't somehow found the lightning vaults before them.

He was just wondering if he should consult the map again, for any clues he might have missed, when his foot slipped and he stopped abruptly. Stretching across the entire width of the tunnel in front of them was a large semifrozen lake. It definitely hadn't been there the last time they'd been through the blizzard section. Several icebergs drifted across its surface like vast, ice-laden ships.

"Well, we c-c-can't cross that." Dougal shivered, his face shimmering with tiny ice crystals. "The ice wouldn't hold our weight for a s-s-second; we'd be up to our necks in freezing water before you could say h-h-hypothermia."

"Then we've got to find a boat or a raft," said Angus, scanning the barren tunnel around them. "There must be an old dog sled or something in here we can use. . . ."

"Oh, but there is!" Indigo's face suddenly brightened.

"And I bet it's easily big enough to hold all three of us. Come with me!"

"But we're heading in the wrong direction," Angus pointed out as Indigo led them back the way they'd just come, through the weather seal and into the empty section of the weather tunnel once again.

Dougal frowned. "What have you brought us in here for?"

"Because we can cross the lake in that!" Indigo pointed toward the large bed that they'd crept past earlier.

Angus swallowed hard. There was just one tiny flaw in Indigo's plan. While they had been battling their way through the snow and ice, the fog yeti had returned from its wanderings, and was now fast asleep in its bed, snoring its head off.

"Y-y-y-yeti!" Dougal gasped in a terrified whisper.

It was the first time any of them had seen it properly. Angus stared at the massive creature, with its great shaggy pelt, feet the size of garbage-can lids, and long, deadly claws.

"If you think I'm riding that thing, you've got another think coming," said Dougal urgently.

But Indigo had another suggestion this time. "Why doesn't one of us distract it instead, while the other two grab the bed and make a run for it?"

"How are we supposed to distract a thing like that?" asked Dougal.

Indigo gulped. "W-we could try throwing it a bone."

Angus stared at the snoring creature, feeling it would be safer to kick a large wasp nest.

"I'll do the distracting," he offered. "Just do me a favor, okay? When you two have grabbed the bed—don't forget to come back and grab me. That thing looks like it could take a polar bear down with one swipe!"

He tiptoed toward the monstrous creature, wondering if he had ever had a less brilliant idea in his life.

It wasn't until they'd almost reached the bed that the yeti woke up, with one loud grunt, and made eye contact with Angus.

"Just get ready to run, okay?" he said, feeling around his feet for a bone.

The yeti growled dangerously, its black eyes boring into Angus.

"Er . . . I don't want to worry anyone," said Dougal,

starting to back away, "but I think that yeti thinks you're trying to steal its dinner."

The creature was on its feet in one swift movement, ready to pounce.

"RUN!" Dougal yelled.

Angus turned and sprinted, the yeti thundering after him with great lolloping strides. Angus swerved quickly to the left, and then to the right, desperately trying to shake it off, but the yeti was surprisingly agile for its size. Angus could feel its hot, sticky breath warming the back of his neck. He could also feel his own legs beginning to buckle beneath him.

His whole life at Perilous suddenly flashed before his eyes. He couldn't believe it was about to be over, before it had ever really begun. He would never learn what was lurking behind the door to the Inner Sanctum of Secrets; he would never experience an invisible fog or have the great pleasure of hiding a storm globe in Percival Vellum's bed. . . .

He urged his exhausted legs onward, his muscles screaming, lungs bursting, desperately hoping that the yeti might turn out to be a vegetarian after all. And he was just about to shut his eyes and wait for the end to come, when suddenly—

CLANG!

A heavy door was thrust open, and he was being lifted off his feet and dragged hastily into the wintry end of the weather tunnel. The door slammed shut again, then—

"Try throwing it a bone!" yelled Dougal, furious with Indigo. "Have you gone completely mental? Angus almost ended up as yeti food, thanks to you!"

"I'm sorry! But what else were we supposed to do?"

Angus lay panting on the floor, clutching his ribs. He'd never been so happy to hear two people arguing in his life. He couldn't help grinning.

Ten minutes later, all three of them were back at the frozen lake. It was an extremely tricky business paddling across the icy water in a large yeti bed, especially as they had to use the gnawed bones as paddles, and they almost capsized twice. Finally, however, after a very close encounter with a hidden iceberg, they made it to the far shore.

"The lightning vaults have to be around here

somewhere," said Angus as soon as their feet touched solid snow again.

He took the map out of his pocket and studied it once more, still feeling mildly euphoric that he'd just escaped the fog yeti. He could almost feel the lightning vaults now, just waiting to be discovered somewhere in the snow and ice. . . .

"Over there!" he said, pointing to a small igloo up ahead of them. "The vaults have to be somewhere near that igloo. There's nothing beyond that except the door that leads back down to the kitchens. Look for anything that's been marked with a fractured lightning bolt."

He began to run toward the igloo, plowing through the deep, soft snow. Here and there the snow had begun to melt, revealing what looked like a gray stone floor beneath it. They crawled around in the slush, their hands and knees getting colder and wetter as they searched. Angus was just beginning to wonder if they were going to have to dig their way through some of the larger drifts when he spotted a familiar symbol etched into the corner of a cracked slab.

The symbol had obviously faded over the years so that

the bottom half had worn away completely, but there was no mistaking what it had once been, and Angus felt his heart skip several beats as he stared at the outline of a fractured lightning bolt.

"I've found it!" he gasped. "I've found the lightning vaults!"

He pushed the snow aside. It was clear that the entrance was still intact, that no one else had reached it before them. There was a jagged crack running the full length of the slab, however, as if somebody at some time might have tried to break it open. Angus ran his hand over the stone and felt a cool breeze coming up through his fingers. He was certain that there was something deep, dark, and hollow beneath. He pressed his ear to the stone, half expecting to hear the muffled roar of some ferocious creature that had been trapped for hundreds of years. But everything was quiet.

He sat back on his heels and was just wondering how they were going to get into the actual vaults when the stone slab wobbled, with a sudden, eerie groan, as if it were waking from a very long sleep.

"Angus—get back!" Indigo screamed.

Angus scrambled to his feet as a terrible *CRACK* split the air, but it was already too late. The gray slab crumbled to dust beneath him, and he was suddenly plummeting headlong down a long stone shaft into cold, rushing darkness.

16

THE NEVER-ENDING STORM

THUD! He'd landed on something thick and soft. All the wind had been knocked out of his lungs, but with a flood of relief he realized he definitely wasn't dead.

"Angus!" Indigo called frantically from a long way above him, her head appearing over the edge of the doorway he'd just fallen through. "Angus! Oh, thank goodness . . . are you all right?"

"I'm fine!" he yelled back, his voice cracking with relief. "I landed on some furs or something. Don't jump down, though," he warned. "Go and get some rope or a ladder!"

He was sure he wouldn't be able to climb back up into the weather tunnel by himself, and whatever he found in the lightning vaults . . . he was certain he would need help with that too. Deep, dark holes had never been a part of his plan.

"Just stay where you are until we get back!" yelled Dougal, peering down at him.

"Well, I can't exactly go anywhere else, can I?"

He heard the sound of their urgent mumblings for a few seconds longer. Then they disappeared, and everything went quiet.

Angus sat on the floor, allowing his eyes to grow used to the dark, although he couldn't see much more when they had. He had fallen into a deep pit; that much was obvious. Judging by the dank smell that was now filling his nostrils, nobody had been down here for a very long time.

He got carefully to his feet. Up ahead, he could just make out what appeared to be a narrow passageway leading down into the cold, dark rock. There were no signs of any fulgurites or experimentation. And Angus was certain that he hadn't fallen into the inner core of the vaults.

He glanced up at the small square of light above his head, hoping he could find his way back to it again, and then began to inch along the slimy walls of the passageway, thick, black nothingness pressing in on him from all sides. Every tiny noise, every rasp of his own breath sounded monstrously loud in the silent tunnel, and he almost yelled out loud when a spider landed on his shoulder. But finally, after what felt like hours, his fingers touched another wall directly in front of him. He stopped dead, his heart beating loudly. Had he found the fabled lightning vaults at last?

He checked swiftly over his shoulder, making sure nothing was creeping up on him in the dark, and was stunned to realize that he was no longer alone. A small light was bobbing down the passageway behind him, getting closer by the second. It couldn't be his friends already, could it? Had somebody followed him down the hole? He almost choked when he saw who it was.

"Mr. Knurling?" he said in a hoarse voice as the librarian emerged from the shadows, dressed in a long, warm coat, carrying an oil lamp. "But . . . what are you doing down here, sir?" The librarian was slightly out of breath, as if he'd been running. He was the last person Angus had ever expected to find in a secret passageway.

"Listen, sir," he continued in a hurry, glad that he was no longer alone in the darkness. "I think Scabious

Dankhart is coming to find the lightning vaults. We have to get some help, now!"

Mr. Knurling shook his head. "Impossible. Principal Dark-Angel is extremely busy putting out fires."

"Well, Rogwood then, or Gudgeon, it doesn't matter who. We've just got to get help before Dankhart gets here."

"Oh, I'm afraid it's far too late for that," said the librarian, a strange smirk on his face.

"W-what?" Angus glanced swiftly over Mr. Knurling's shoulder, wondering if he'd missed somebody else concealed deep within the shadows of the pitch-black passageway. There was also something very odd about the way the librarian was looking at him. Something odd about the way he was standing so calmly at the entrance to the lightning vaults when, at any second, Scabious Dankhart could sneak up behind them. Was Mr. Knurling still suffering from his hailstone concussion?

"Sir, look, I don't think you understand—" he began again urgently.

"On the contrary, Angus McFangus," the librarian interrupted. "I understand everything perfectly. It is *you* who is in the dark."

And with one swift movement, he removed the greasy monocle from his right eye, scooped out his own eyeball with a stomach-churning squelch, and replaced it with something from his pocket. Even in the darkness, Angus could tell that it was a large, black, glittering diamond.

"Dankhart!" Angus tried to take a step back and found himself already pressed hard against the cold wall.

He watched in disbelief as Dankhart calmly removed his stiff blond wig. Underneath it was a mass of tangled black hair that fell to his shoulders in knots. His neat white teeth, too, were nothing more than a sham, a false set to disguise his own shriveled stumps. Angus flinched as Dankhart spat them out, then peeled a tight layer of rubbery skin off his face to reveal deep pocks and scars beneath. The hideous transformation was complete. And Angus suddenly realized, with a sick feeling, that Dougal had been right. Despite all of her protestations, there was a strange and terrible family resemblance between Indigo and her villainous uncle, in the length of their necks and the hollows of their cheeks. But where Indigo's face was kind and friendly, Dankhart's was full of malevolent triumph, of dangerous, diamond-clad menace.

"We meet at last, Angus McFangus," said Dankhart. "What an honor this must be for you."

Angus felt a deep revulsion in his stomach. "You kidnapped my parents!" he yelled, anger bursting through a wall in his chest. "What have you done with them?"

"Tut tut, Angus, where are your manners? A man of my greatness deserves a little more respect."

"I don't see what's so great about locking people up in dungeons!"

Dankhart smiled, his diamond eye sparkling.

"You are too young perhaps, to appreciate the full brilliance of my plan. But you must agree that to walk among the lightning catchers for a full term, without a single one of them recognizing me, is a very great achievement indeed. Even the Dark-Angel failed to notice she had an impostor in her midst. How I would love to see the look on her smug face when she learns of the deception. But I am getting carried away with my own brilliance, Angus. There is work to be done in the lightning vaults, and you shall have the great honor of accompanying me." He took a length of cord from his coat pocket and grabbed Angus.

"Geroff me!" Angus fought hard against the iron grip,

desperately trying to free himself, but Dankhart was too strong. He bound Angus's hands tightly behind his back, then pushed him roughly to one side of the tunnel.

Dankhart found a hidden lever near his feet, and with a slow grinding of gears he began to activate the solid stone doors. Angus stared around, desperately searching for a way out. Even if he managed to escape down the stone passageway without being caught, how could he climb out of the hole? He struggled violently against his bonds. He had to free his hands, he had to make a run for it. . . . But the rope held fast, tearing into his skin, and he slumped against the wall.

He watched the great stone doors inch their way apart. Dankhart's smile widened to a repulsive, stumpy sneer. Angus held his breath, waiting, as the vaults were finally revealed.

They were even more magnificent than he'd dared imagine. Dozens of dome-shaped caverns were spread out before them, locked together like a honeycomb. The walls were covered with deep scars, and hundreds upon hundreds of long, frozen lightning bolts were hanging from the ceiling like a colony of misshapen bats.

"Welcome, Angus, to the lightning vaults!" said Dankhart, pushing him inside.

Angus stared down at his feet; he was standing on a rolling sea of solid emerald glass, just as Oswald Blott had described in the holographic history. It gave everything an eerie underwater glow. And despite the fact that he was in the company of a lunatic who was probably going to kill him as soon as he got the chance, Angus was awestruck.

"None who are now living have ever seen this wondrous sight." Dankhart lit several dusty candles in a bracket on the wall with the flame from his oil lamp. "You should thank me for the great opportunity I have given you."

Angus wasn't about to thank Dankhart for anything. He glared at the foul, gloating villain who was now parading up and down on the glass floor as if he had built the vaults himself.

"I have waited a very long time for this glorious moment," said Dankhart. "For years I have been searching endlessly for the lightning vaults. I have stolen every map I could lay my hands on and pored over them, searching for any tiny hidden clue, any hint of their secret whereabouts, but all to no avail. Indeed, I had almost given up all hope of ever finding the vaults when I discovered that the Dark-Angel had instructed two of her most trusted lightning catchers, Alabone and Evangeline McFangus, to search for them. And I knew all I had to do was be patient, and I would be rewarded.

"Eventually, they found the location of the vaults, and before they could inform the Dark-Angel of their discovery, I had them kidnapped."

"I bet they didn't tell you anything," Angus shot back angrily, struggling against the rope binding his hands. "They'd never let someone like you know where the vaults were."

Dankhart's diamond eye glittered malevolently in the candlelight. He swept toward Angus and struck him hard across the face with the back of his hand. A sharp pain shot through Angus's cheekbone, making his eyes stream with water.

"Your parents proved to be far more stubborn than I had anticipated, yes." Dankhart kept talking, as if nothing had happened. "They would not part with the information I needed, even with a little gentle . . . persuasion." He grinned nastily, and Angus tried not to imagine what he meant.

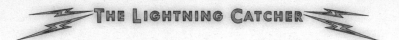

"Luck was on my side, however. I discovered, from a very reliable source, that the Dark-Angel had also sent for their one and only son. I knew at once that there could be only one reason for her to do so. She suspected that somehow your parents had sent the map to you. And I instantly dispatched my most capable servants to intercept you, before you could enter the vile walls of this Exploratorium. But that fool Felix Gudgeon set off a storm globe, and they were forced to flee."

"They didn't try very hard, then, if one tiny storm globe made them run for it," said Angus, suddenly wanting to make Dankhart angry. "None of the lightning catchers would have been that cowardly—ever!"

"You have a very good opinion of your fellow lightning fools. I wonder if you would still think so highly of them if you knew their true history. Do you know what secret lies within these vaults, Angus McFangus?" asked Dankhart, a lopsided smirk revealing his hideous, pockmarked gums.

Angus didn't answer. Not even Dougal had known what monstrous secret might be lurking in the very depths of the vaults.

"Come then, Angus." Dankhart grabbed his shoulder and shoved him toward one of the largest caverns at the back of the vaults. "Let me show you what your lightning-catcher heroes have created in their greed for knowledge and greatness."

Angus stumbled, staggering sideways into walls and pillars, until at last they stopped in front of a solitary storm globe that had been placed carefully on a marble pedestal. Five times the size of any normal globe, it was extremely old and angry looking and covered in a fine layer of dust. There were several small cracks running across its surface, and a violent storm was raging inside it, charging the air around it with dangerous electricity. Angus could feel the power of the storm crawling over his skin, and he shuddered.

"Almost three hundred and fifty years ago now, the lightning catchers created a never-ending storm," said Dankhart, pacing around the pedestal. "You see it before you now, Angus, a triumph over nature itself, a glorious, wondrous achievement never before seen in this world. Its sole purpose was to produce a constant supply of light-ning here, within the safety of the vaults, lightning that could be ripped apart and studied for the greater good of man." Dankhart sneered. "But once again the lightning catchers underestimated the glorious power of this magnificent force of nature. The storm got loose during one of their more ambitious experiments, causing chaos and destruction. The lightning vaults were evacuated immediately. But unbeknownst to those who fled, two young trainees, desperate to see the never-ending storm for themselves, had crept into the vaults and hidden, and they were left behind. The storm struck with its full force . . . and both were killed."

Angus shuddered, picturing every detail of the tragic scene.

"Their names," Dankhart continued, "were Jacob Starling and Fabian Perilous."

Angus understood instantly and felt a sudden wave of nausea. The awful double calamity had robbed both Philip Starling and Edgar Perilous of their own young sons.

"Ashamed of the terrible accident they had caused, vowing that no such catastrophe would ever occur again, the lightning catchers sealed these vaults forever," continued Dankhart. "They entombed the storm in a glass sphere, hoping to contain it and the dark stain on their history for all eternity. I, however, have a much better use for it."

"What are you going to do with it?" asked Angus, keeping his eyes firmly fixed on Dankhart and the globe.

"Why, I intend to release it, of course. This storm has the power to destroy entire islands, whole cities if I allow it; to wreak havoc and cause delicious mayhem. The era of the dreary lightning catchers is over," Dankhart crowed with triumph, and his voice echoed horribly through the vaults. "It is time that I, Scabious Dankhart, take my place as the true lord and master of the weather! And who better to test the power of the storm than you?" He ripped the coat from around his shoulders, revealing a thick lightning deflector suit beneath. Around his neck was a shiny brass instrument. Angus recognized it immediately. It was a storm snare.

He froze under Dankhart's black diamond glare, finally understanding the villain's plan. Dankhart was going to watch him fight for his life, while he himself stood safe and protected from the vicious power of the never-ending storm. And when it was over . . . Dankhart would capture the storm inside the snare and sneak it out of Perilous.

Somehow he had to stall Dankhart. He needed time to think, to plan his next move. Nobody was coming to help him now, Angus realized with a sinking feeling in his stomach. Dougal and Indigo had obviously run into trouble on their way to fetch help, and none of the lightning catchers were even aware that he was in danger.

It was all happening just as Dankhart had planned. All except for one tiny, hope-filled fact—Angus was a storm prophet. For the first time ever, he knew it was true, and he felt a thrill of excitement. It was the only chance he had of escaping the vaults alive.

"Wait!" he yelled as Dankhart reached for the globe. "I don't understand. W-why have you been pretending to be a librarian all this time?"

Dankhart hesitated, his hand hovering. "And why would a boy who is about to die wish to know that?"

"To understand," Angus said, thinking quickly, "to understand the brilliance of your plan."

Dankhart studied him shrewdly for a moment.

"Very well. It is perhaps only fitting that you learn of my true greatness before you perish," he said with an air of supreme arrogance. "When my servants failed me so badly at the pier, I was forced to act swiftly. I could not risk the map falling into the Dark-Angel's hands, never to be seen again. I saw only one way forward—to continue the search myself. And once again, fortune gave me the ideal opportunity," Dankhart said. "I already knew that the old librarian had been trusted to hire his own replacement, and that he had chosen a man named Knurling. I also knew that nobody else would meet this replacement until the day he arrived at Perilous. My plan was brilliantly simple. I persuaded Mr. Knurling that I should take up his position instead. Once inside these walls, I was beyond suspicion. I continued my search unhindered.

"Unfortunately, the Dark-Angel had seen to it that others were also joining Perilous at the same time, including my own very disappointing niece. A poor addition to the Dankhart family, just like her weak and feeble mother. But Indigo Midnight will be dealt with, when the time is right." Dankhart spat on the floor, and Angus felt a violent chill shivering through his body.

"I had to pick you out from the other forgettable trainees, a task that proved far trickier than I had imagined. I therefore arranged to have some interesting amphibious showers sent over to serve as a distraction while I searched for more information."

Angus thought of the frogs falling over Buckingham Palace but said nothing. He glanced swiftly around the lightning vaults, looking desperately for a way out. But the tight honeycomb structure appeared to be sealed in all directions; there were no other doors or exits except the one he had just come through.

"I began to search every room I could think of in an attempt to discover your identity. But all to no avail. In my frustration, I even searched the library for any rare books that may have contained another, forgotten copy of the map itself. But I had miscalculated where the storm globes would fall, and my task was cut short by the hailstones."

"You were knocked unconscious, you mean," Angus said, trying anything to keep Dankhart's attention away from the globe. "One tiny lump of ice, and you were out cold for hours."

"It was a minor setback." Dankhart felt for the bump on his forehead. "But nothing more. And then finally, after all my efforts, it was by chance that I discovered you. It was the doctor who gave you away."

"Doctor Fleagal?"

"The fool Fleagal spoke of your mother, Evangeline, and her adventures in the fog tunnels. And I knew at last who you were. Then all I had to do was arrange one last fiery shower to keep the lightning catchers occupied. I planned to search your room for the map. But then I watched as you and your friends broke away from the rest of the lightning cubs in the Octagon . . . and I followed. I kept my distance, watching you stumble through desert sands, the ice and snow. I even feared I'd have to save you from the fog yeti myself. Finally, though, you brought me straight to the door of the lightning vaults," Dankhart concluded with a twisted smile. "Both you and your parents have been invaluable. I am loath to admit it, Angus, but I could not have done it without you."

Angus forgot all about the storm globe for a moment. He wanted nothing more than to break free of his bonds and smash Dankhart's smirking face with his bare hands.

"You've found the lightning vaults," he said, "so let my parents go!"

"Why, I have no intention of ever letting your parents go, you foolish boy," Dankhart sneered. "They know far too much about the other dark and delicious secrets hidden within the walls of this Exploratorium. The lightning vaults are but the tip of a very muddy iceberg. And now, on to what I came for!" He finally turned his attention back to the globe, and Angus knew that his time had run out.

Dankhart snatched the ancient sphere greedily from its pedestal, caressing it between both hands as if it were a priceless jewel. Then he raised his arms high above his head and smashed it to the floor—shattering the glass into a thousand tiny pieces.

Angus watched, frozen with fear, as the storm rose above their heads, already rumbling with dark fury and menace, promising to unleash a weather rage so violent it would destroy the lightning vaults completely.

"Come, Angus! Face your doom like a true lightning catcher!" Dankhart made a sudden grab for him, but Angus dodged quickly out of his reach and darted behind a large stone pillar. There was a violent flash of white light. The sheet of emerald glass cracked beneath his feet.

"There's nowhere to run, Angus!" yelled Dankhart above the deafening rumble of thunder that followed.

"You will be struck by billions of volts of lightning before you even reach the door. The end will be quick . . . if you are lucky."

Angus struggled against the rope. He had to free himself now. He flung himself down onto the cracked floor, found a jagged edge of glass, and quickly began to saw at the rope that bound his wrists. He could feel the electricity in the air, gathering force. Great webs of lightning tarantulatis spun across the ceiling, filling the vaults with an unearthly, chilling glow.

"Look how the lightning seeks you out!" Dankhart cried. And Angus was forced to dive again, his body smashing into the hard glass floor as a jagged fork of blinding light struck out. It missed him this time by a mere hairsbreadth.

He scrambled to his feet, and with one last tug his hands were finally free. He darted behind another pillar, his heart racing. Dankhart was going to make him scurry around the vaults like a frightened rabbit before allowing a lethal shock of lightning to stop his heart dead.

Another burst of light, and he was thrown off his feet, his head slamming against the wall of the vaults behind him. He closed his eyes tightly, his ribs aching. He had to

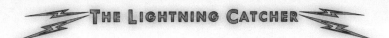

figure out where the lightning was going to strike next. He had to stop Dankhart from stealing the storm and unleashing it on the island and the world beyond. He had to see the fire dragon now, in all its shimmering fire and heat, if he was ever going to escape the vaults alive.

He willed the creature to appear and help him, just as it had done in the Lightnarium when Indigo had been in mortal danger; and even on the fog field trip when it had helped him rescue Percival Vellum from a fognado. He waited, hoping desperately, but his brain was a twitching jumble of fears, and the insides of his eyelids remained a cold and lonely black.

"The time has come, Angus."

A clammy hand closed around his wrist. He struggled with all his might as Dankhart dragged him out from the shadows and into the very center of the vaults before flinging him to his knees.

"I won't forget to tell your precious parents how you suffered," Dankhart said, circling him now like a hungry wolf. "I will describe for them in agonizing detail how you scurried around the vaults, trying desperately to cling to your feeble, insignificant life."

Above them, lightning sparked and flickered restlessly, preparing for another strike. This time the strike would be fatal. Angus looked around the vaults frantically, but the door was thirty feet away. He'd never make it in time. The storm was going to kill him as he crouched on the floor. . . .

"Are there any last words, Angus McFangus?" Dankhart taunted him. "Are there any touching messages you would like me to pass on to your loved ones, so I may enjoy their misery too?"

"Yeah, I've got a message." Angus clenched his fists tightly. "You can tell them this!" He launched himself at Dankhart, knocking him over sideways.

Angus scrambled to his feet again, ready to make one last desperate dash for freedom. Then the fire dragon finally appeared. Angus staggered backward as it burst into the vaults with a roar. Magnificent, terrifying, with molten fire dripping from its outstretched wings, it hovered above him.

"A fire dragon?" Dankhart's voice rose in sudden alarm. "What are you doing, you foolish boy?"

But for once Angus knew exactly what he was doing.

His thoughts flickered briefly to his mum and dad, to Uncle Max, Dougal, and Indigo. Then he stared deep into the creature's eyes as he somehow knew he must.

For one electrifying moment, he felt the full force of the never-ending storm shudder violently through every atom in his body, as the storm and the dragon merged into one, twisting and tangling together, then—

BOOOOM!

A huge explosion shook the vaults. Light burst from every direction; Angus caught a glimpse of the dragon as it descended upon a startled-looking Dankhart in a ball of flame. Then his head hit the floor with a sickening crunch, and he knew that it was over . . . everything was over. . . .

17

THE LAST SURPRISE

Angus opened one eye carefully. He appeared to be lying flat on his back on a cold stone floor in the middle of a dark passageway. There was a dull throbbing in his ears. Someone had put something soft under his head, and several blurry figures were swimming before him, like the fragments of a broken dream. The fragments finally came into focus and he realized, with a start, that they were Aramanthus Rogwood and Felix Gudgeon.

"Just lie still for a few minutes, Angus," Gudgeon said, peering down at him. "You've had a nasty shock to the system."

A shock to the system . . .

Angus sat bolt upright, remembering everything in a terrible rush, amazed, for the second time that day, to find himself still alive.

"Dankhart!" he burst out in a panic. "He's released the never-ending storm. He's going to use it against the lightning catchers and everyone on Imbur. And he's been disguising himself as Mr. Knurling all term."

"Calm down," said Gudgeon, forcing him to lie back again. "Dankhart's gone."

"G-gone? But where? I . . . I don't understand."

"It seems you're not the only one," said Gudgeon. "None of us had a clue what was going on until I was cornered by two very agitated friends of yours, who seemed to think you were in trouble. Then we found you down here, about to be vaporized by that ancient storm. We also found these." He held up a stiff blond wig and a greasy-looking monocle. "Reckon we should have guessed it was Dankhart hiding under this all along. False teeth and wigs can't do anything to hide that stench of his. But he'd already made himself scarce by the time we got down here. Probably scuttled his way through a crack in the walls before some lightning tarantulatis improved his ugly face."

"But the never-ending storm . . . ," Angus persisted.

"The storm is being encased in a brand-new globe by Principal Dark-Angel as we speak," Rogwood explained, his amber eyes fixed on Angus with concern. "It will be sealed once again inside the lightning vaults, where nobody else can get to it, and the map will be destroyed. Dankhart will not be unleashing it on anyone."

"The maniac's plans all came to nothing in the end, thanks to you and your friends," Gudgeon added with satisfaction.

Angus sank back, his head buzzing. It was over. Dankhart had fled from Perilous and the storm was contained once more. And yet there was something else still nagging at the back of his mind, something important, something—

"But he's still got my mum and dad!" he yelled suddenly, trying to sit up again. "They're trapped in one of his dungeons."

"Your parents are made of strong stuff," Gudgeon said, and his eyes were fiercely bright. "It'll take more than one lumpy-faced lunatic with delusions to make them crack. They'd be proud of you, for finding your own way down into the vaults and taking on Dankhart all by yourself. And you can bet your last silver starling we haven't seen the last of him yet. He'll be back, with more of his crackpot schemes, and next time we'll be ready for him."

And then Gudgeon did something very unexpected. He smiled broadly at Angus.

"You're to go with Rogwood now, there's something we think you ought to see. Principal Dark-Angel wouldn't like it if she knew what we were up to, but we reckon you've earned it after the lightning vaults."

It took some time to clamber back up into the weather tunnel, especially since they had to climb a long rope ladder—which Angus found especially difficult as neither his arms nor his legs were working very well. Rogwood led him quickly through the blizzard section, which now appeared to be melting, and down to the deserted kitchens.

"Where are we going?" asked Angus.

He found out ten minutes later when they entered a part of Perilous he had never been allowed anywhere near before: the lightning catchers' living quarters. Rogwood stopped outside one of the doors, pulled out a large bunch of keys, and opened it. He ushered Angus inside. Angus didn't have to ask who the room belonged to. It was filled with a whole host of photographs that he instantly recognized: there was one of his mum and dad on vacation in Canada; another of them in the garden at the Windmill; one with Angus in it from the previous Christmas, just before Uncle Max had set fire to the plum pudding and half the decorations.

His mum's slippers were tucked neatly under the bed. His dad's reading glasses had been left carelessly balanced on top of a pile of books, almost as if he would be coming back at any minute to retrieve them. Angus looked around the cozy, comforting room and swallowed a large lump in his throat.

"Your mother and father always did intend to tell you about Perilous when the time was right," said Rogwood, watching him kindly. "They already had you enrolled as a lightning cub, and I believe they were intending to give you this when you arrived." He picked up a small gift-wrapped box and handed it to Angus. "I'm sure they would not mind if you opened it now."

Angus tore off the paper carefully. Inside was a small wooden box. He opened the lid to find a silver belt buckle, shaped like a bolt of lightning tarantulatis. He blinked, holding back the tears that suddenly threatened to overwhelm him, wishing that his parents were both standing here with him now.

"Dankhart's never going to let them out, is he?" he said, staring at the buckle thoughtfully. "He said something in the vaults about the lightning catchers having all sorts of secrets, and my mum and dad knowing what they were."

"If your mother and father know anything, Angus, it is how to look after themselves. They have been thoroughly trained in the weather tunnel, they've been stranded in the middle of drought-ridden deserts, they have parachuted onto the frozen poles with nothing but their wits and their weather watches to guide them, and they have always come out smiling. Dankhart's dungeons will be nothing more than an inconvenience to them. We will find a way to bring them back to Perilous where they belong. I can assure you, they have not been forgotten."

Angus nodded, then thought for a second before asking a question that had been bothering him, ever since he'd first seen the never-ending storm.

"Sir, there's something I don't understand. Why were

my parents trying to find the map of the vaults in the first place? Why not just leave them sealed up?"

Rogwood sighed. "The glass sphere that the storm was contained in was coming to the end of its life. Several of the senior lightning catchers, including me, had calculated long ago that it could not withstand such a constant battering for very much longer. Principal Dark-Angel sent your parents to find the map and the vaults so the storm could be rehoused in a much stronger globe, before it could break free and destroy us all. This is an immensely tricky and complicated task, which the principal is tackling even as we speak. After she has managed to secure the storm, the vaults will be resealed, and no one will be entering them again for a very long time to come. We are not proud of the storm, Angus," Rogwood added, with a somber shake of his toffee-colored beard. "It was a foolish enterprise to undertake, an arrogant one. How did we ever think that we could contain such an angry storm for any length of time and bend it to our will? It's a delusion that Scabious Dankhart still maintains. But we must take responsibility for our mistakes, even those made hundreds of years ago."

Angus knew Rogwood was speaking of the terrible

accident that had killed the sons of both Philip Starling and Edgar Perilous.

"The matter has been dealt with—for the time being, at least. And now I have a question of my own," he said, amber eyes shining. "I would very much like to know, if you will tell me, how you and your friends found the map."

Angus took a deep breath and told Rogwood about the letter from his mum and how Dougal had uncovered the secrets that it contained.

"Most impressive indeed." Rogwood smiled, his eyebrows raised. "I must remember Mr. Dewsnap's talents for code breaking. They may come in very handy someday. And am I also right in thinking that you found some use for your own talents as a storm prophet in the lightning vaults?"

Angus thought of the dragon and how it had finally appeared, in his moment of darkest need, almost as if it had heard his plea for help. He tried to remember exactly what had happened next, how the dragon had triggered some deeply hidden instinct inside him, and how he'd suddenly known exactly what to do. The precise details, however, seemed strangely dim and murky now, like a memory that had already faded. The fire he'd felt coursing through his body in the vaults had also gone, and he wondered if the fury of the never-ending storm had affected his brain cells.

One thing Angus was utterly convinced about— Dankhart had seen the terrible creature too. He would never forget the look of terror on his face as the dragon and the storm had merged, and then descended upon Dankhart in a ball of raging fire.

"Sir, Dankhart saw the dragon, too, but how?" he asked Rogwood, frowning. "I thought you said it was just a vision, a warning of danger?"

"I am afraid that question requires a long and very complicated answer." Rogwood sighed. "And I fear that now is not the right time for such important discussions to take place. Forgive me, Angus, I hope you will trust that I have your best interests at heart. I can only assure you that all will be revealed in the fullness of time."

Angus pondered this mysterious answer for a moment.

"Sir," he said again, "would it be okay if we didn't tell Principal Dark-Angel about me seeing another fire

dragon? She'll only want Catcher Vellum to test my brain again, and I think I've seen enough lightning bolts for one day."

Rogwood smiled kindly. "My lips are sealed, Angus. We shall keep that information just between ourselves . . . for as long as possible."

Angus was allowed back to his room later that night only after he had been thoroughly checked over by Doctor Fleagal. Thankfully, he had escaped his electrifying encounter with only a few minor cuts and bruises.

As he made his way wearily down to his room, he was glad to find Indigo and Dougal waiting for him outside his door. His friends looked extremely relieved to see that he was still alive.

"What happened? Did you stop Dankhart?"

"Did Gudgeon get to you in time?" Dougal rushed toward him, his hair rumpled, his glasses still smudged with camel spit and sand. "You should have seen him when we told him you were in trouble."

They went into Angus's room, where he filled them in on everything that had happened since he'd fallen into the dark passageway under the weather tunnel. It took quite some time to convince them that the librarian had really been Dankhart in disguise.

"You mean we saved my own uncle after the storm globes, and I didn't even realize it?" Indigo gasped, horrified.

When he described how Dankhart had popped a sinister black diamond into his empty eye socket, Dougal turned green and had to sit with his head between his knees, recovering.

"Mind you, I always thought there was something fishy about a librarian who didn't want anyone setting foot in his library," said Dougal, as soon as his face had returned to its normal color.

When Angus got to the part about the lightning vaults themselves, both Dougal and Indigo listened in silence, only stopping him when he described the never-ending storm.

"I can't believe the lightning catchers made something so dangerous," said Indigo. "Just imagine if it had gotten loose all by itself and gone raging about the island."

Dougal nodded. "Just imagine if Dankhart had gotten

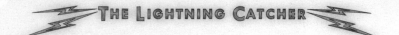

his grubby hands on it! We'd all be dodging lightning bolts for the rest of our lives."

They sat for several hours more, discussing the dramatic events of the evening, with Angus listening to Dougal and Indigo discuss what the lightning catchers should do if anyone else ever tried to break into the vaults again.

Now that Dankhart was gone, Angus felt enormously tired and wrung out like a sponge, every fiber in his body aching. And his mind kept drifting back—not to Dankhart, but to his parents' room in the lightning catchers' living quarters. He kept a tight grip on the belt buckle in his pocket, and he knew that, despite what Rogwood had said, his parents were no closer to coming home than they had been when he'd first arrived on Imbur. He also knew that as long as they were trapped in one of Dankhart's dungeons, he would never be able to rest easy; he would never be able to gaze out across the town of Little Frog's Bottom and beyond without wondering if he would ever see them again.

Angus was shocked to discover the following morning that none of the other trainees seemed to know anything about the events in the lightning vaults. They were still discussing the shooting stars, one of which had burned a hole right through the ceiling of the experimental division, causing the storm vacuum to explode in a magnificent shower of hot dust and flames.

"Principal Dark-Angel must have hushed the whole thing up, for the time being at least," Dougal said, helping himself to a hearty breakfast of double sausage, eggs, and bacon as they sat in the damaged kitchens. "Probably didn't want everyone thundering through the weather tunnel looking for the entrance. I hope Catcher Sparks doesn't expect us to glue the storm vacuum back together again," he added, frowning.

Angus was also surprised to hear that Miss DeWinkle had organized another midnight fog viewing, and that the damage done to the roof by the burning chunks of rock wasn't half as bad as everyone had first feared. Angus himself, however, was forbidden from taking part by a concerned Doctor Fleagal, who ordered that he get as much rest as possible, and he was forced to stay behind in his room.

"It was absolute chaos!" Dougal informed him afterward, peeling off his gloves and scarf. Indigo also crept

into Angus's room, pink cheeked and tired, to tell him about the events of the night.

"Violet Quinn and Jonathon Hake had to be taken up to the sanatorium with fog exhaustion," she said.

Dougal grinned. "And Percival Vellum accidentally tripped over the end of the weather cannon and landed headfirst in a bucket full of dead tadpoles. Couldn't have happened to a nicer lightning cub," he added gleefully, making Angus laugh hard.

"Clifford Fugg got a bad case of fog disorientation," said Indigo as soon as he'd regained control of himself.

"But Indigo saved him from falling off the roof," Dougal explained, "and now Miss DeWinkle's going around telling everyone how brave she is."

Indigo blushed furiously at this and announced that she was going to bed before she got caught loitering in the boys' corridor.

"I think we might have seriously underestimated that girl, you know," said Dougal as she snapped the door shut behind her.

"*We've* underestimated her?" Angus said, with eyebrows raised.

Dougal smiled sheepishly. "Yeah, well, I might have been wrong about her," he admitted. "She couldn't have had anything to do with her uncle, could she, not after everything that's happened. I mean, we never would have made it through the weather tunnel if it hadn't been for Indigo, even if she did make us paddle across a frozen lake in a giant yeti bed."

Angus laughed. Now that the ordeal in the weather tunnel was behind them, Dougal was eager to send some treats up to the fog yeti, to make up for the fact that they had stolen its bed.

"Do you get the feeling that being friends with Indigo could get us into trouble, though?" Dougal added, sounding slightly anxious.

"Yeah," Angus said, "and loads of it."

He had decided not to mention Indigo's startling resemblance to her uncle, not even to Indigo, since it would only upset her. Nor had he mentioned Dankhart's chilling threat that he would deal with her when the time was right. Being friends with Indigo could easily get them into serious trouble—the kind of trouble they would never let her face alone.

▲ ▲ ▲

Two days later, it was Angus who found himself in hot water when he was called up to Principal Dark-Angel's office by a very stern note, which was addressed for the first time to "Angus McFangus."

The effort of squeezing the never-ending storm into its new globe had left the principal looking tired and worn.

"I am sending you back home to the Windmill for a few weeks' rest and recuperation," the principal began in a somewhat frosty manner, without looking up at him. "You will be taking this evening's ferry back to the mainland."

Angus stared at her, thunderstruck. Whatever he'd been expecting—a detention, a telling-off, or maybe even praise for his efforts—it had not been this.

"But, Principal, I—"

"Gudgeon will accompany you on your journey, of course. You will stay in Devon with your uncle Max until we decide what is to be done with you, McFangus."

"Done with me? But Principal Dark-Angel," Angus protested, "I can't leave now, we're supposed to be scraping rust off the cloud-busting rocket launcher next week. Catcher Sparks has already given us our own rust buckets and everything. And . . . well, all my friends are here."

"Perhaps you should have thought of that before you decided to go charging off through the weather tunnel in search of the lightning vaults," said the principal, her thin lips pressed together tightly. "You put yourself and others at very great risk, and I cannot condone such rash behavior."

Angus stared at the principal in disbelief.

"I am aware, McFangus, that you have been extremely concerned about your parents, and that must have played some part in your actions," she continued, without any hint that she understood his actions at all. "Perhaps I should have been more forthright with you about their predicament from the start, but that does not excuse you. When you discovered that your parents had sent you a map of the lightning vaults, you should have brought it directly to me!"

Her last few words sounded slightly hysterical, and Angus stared at her almost as if he was seeing her for the very first time. Her face looked haunted, gaunt even. And Angus wondered again why his parents hadn't sent the map directly to Principal Dark-Angel. What possible

reason could they have had for posting it to their eleven-year-old son instead?

"That will be all, McFangus. You may go." She glared at him. "You will be hearing from me when a decision about your future here at Perilous has been made."

An hour later, Angus was drying his boots and squashing them into his bulging bag, feeling slightly dazed by the rapid turn of events. Indigo and Dougal sat on the edge of his bed, watching helplessly.

"I can't believe the miserable old bag's sending you home!" Dougal burst out angrily.

"We're the ones who stopped Dankhart—or hadn't she noticed?" Indigo added, folding her arms.

"Yeah." Dougal nodded. "He would have been halfway across Imbur with the storm globe stuffed under his coat if we hadn't gotten there first."

"Look, she hasn't said I can't ever come back," said Angus. "She probably just wants to get me out of the way for a while, till they work out what Dankhart's going to do next. Anyway, it'll be Christmas soon, and she's bound to let me come back in the new year, isn't she?"

There was a definite feeling of sadness in the air, however, as Dougal and Indigo accompanied Angus down to the courtyard, where he was to wait for Gudgeon in the gravity railway carriage. Angus was looking forward to seeing Uncle Max again, and finding out which new inventions he'd been working on, but he would be extremely sad to leave Perilous behind.

Without even realizing it, he'd already come to think of it as his second home. He would miss spending his days in the highly unpredictable and flammable experimental division. He would miss listening to the lightning catchers at mealtimes, arguing over the best way to escape a sudden icicle storm. He would even miss the nervous excitements of the fog field trips, although quite a large part of him was glad he wouldn't be blundering his way through any tropical fog for some time. But more than anything else, Angus knew he would miss his two best friends.

"I can't believe you're leaving before the highlight of the whole fog season," Indigo said, giving him a very watery-looking smile as the doors to the carriage opened and he stepped reluctantly inside. Miss DeWinkle would be taking all of the first years on an extended fog field trip the

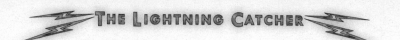
following week. They would be camping out in Imbur's boggiest marshes for six whole days, to tackle any lingering vapor sickness and keep personal fog diaries.

"Can you imagine it?" Dougal smirked. "Pixie Vellum, stuck in a bog."

Angus grinned. "Look, here's my uncle's address," he said, handing small slips of paper to them both. "Let me know what happens. And if Pixie Vellum does get stuck in a bog . . . I want photographs and detailed descriptions."

Then it was time to go. Gudgeon emerged from the entrance hall and joined Angus inside the carriage.

"You'll be back," Dougal shouted confidently as the doors began to close. "Principal Dark-Angel can't keep you away forever."

Indigo waved, wiping a tear quickly from her cheek.

"Just try not to annoy any more camels while I'm gone, okay?" Angus shouted as the carriage finally began to plummet toward the ground.

And he knew, as he watched Perilous growing smaller and smaller above him, that Dougal was right. One way or another, he'd be back.